GOING WILD

LISA McMANN

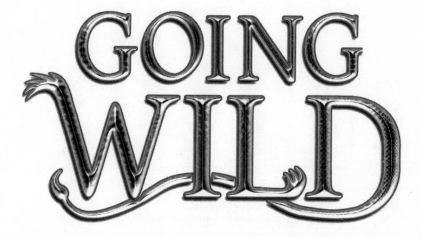

GOING WILD

HARPER

An Imprint of HarperCollins*Publishers*

Library of Congress Control Number: 2016936328

ISBN 978-0-06-233714-6 (trade bdg.)

Typography by Sarah Creech

16 17 18 19 20   CG/RRDH   10 9 8 7 6 5 4 3 2 1

❖

First Edition

To the real Maria Torres . . .

and secret superheroes everywhere

CHAPTER 1

Breaking and Entering

It was a moonless winter night when a stealthy man in a long black trench coat inched through the aisles of a dark laboratory. He didn't need much light since he knew the place well—he'd be able to tell by feel when he found what he was looking for.

When he came upon a glass case, he thrust a metal pick into the lock and turned it. The lock clicked, and the man slid the door aside.

A shrill alarm pierced the air, and the man cursed under his breath. He lunged for the contents, blindly grabbing what he could from inside and dashing for the door. He ran through the hallway and flew down the stairs, coattails flapping, all the way to the ground floor and into the night.

The alarm was just as loud outside. The man heard sirens in the distance and fled down the sidewalk into the darkness.

As he rounded the corner and ran under a streetlight, he glanced at the items he clutched. He grimaced, frustrated that he'd only managed to grab two of the devices he'd wanted: his own and one other. But the alarm on the glass case had been unexpected. There hadn't been one in the past. *Dr. Gray must be growing paranoid*, he thought.

He heard footsteps behind him, and his heart jumped into his throat. A figure in a sleek bodysuit came speeding toward him and lunged for his feet, managing to shred his pant leg with razor-sharp fingernails. The man tripped but kept going as a second figure appeared in front of him. It screeched and jumped up in the air like an acrobat, pushed off against a building, and landed on him.

"Oof!" cried the man as he went down. He slammed his hand into the attacker's face, then scrambled to his feet and stumbled onward, still clutching the precious items.

With lungs burning, the man glanced over his shoulder as the sirens grew louder. The two figures gave chase again. The man ran full throttle through the shadows of the inner city and ducked down an alley. He ran toward a grouping of trash cans, breathing hard and trying not to make any noise.

A woman stepped out of the shadows. The man slowed. He couldn't speak.

"I suppose you did that," she muttered, indicating the sirens.

The man nodded. "Sorry," he gasped. He handed her one of the items and kept his own, and dashed away, not waiting to hear her reply. When he looked over his shoulder, he saw her climbing up a fire escape and disappearing over the edge of a roof. He could hear the footsteps of the two attackers in the distance.

Soon the man came upon a lone vehicle parked alongside the curb. He wrenched the door open and got in, and sped off into the

• • •

Thirty minutes later, the man pulled into a parking spot on the top level of the airport parking garage. He looked all around and expelled a relieved breath, then dabbed the sweat from his forehead and smoothed his hair. He checked the rips in his pant leg for blood and wiped his ankle clean. Satisfied, the man reached for his passport and overnight bag, and opened the car door.

Tires squealed. An SUV skidded wildly into view. Three figures in full bodysuits, like the ones the man had escaped from earlier, burst out and rushed at him. Before he could yell for help or lock himself inside the car, the figures grabbed him and ripped the device from his hands. Then they bound his wrists, shoved a cloth in his mouth, and tossed him into the back of their SUV. A moment later, they were off.

CHAPTER 2

The Package

Charlie Wilde let the front door slam behind her and shuffled listlessly to the living room for the last box. She gave a fleeting look around the empty house and sighed. The Wildes' cats, Big Kitty and Fat Princess, warily circled and sniffed at two pet carriers on the floor. Their dog, Jessie, whined and paced anxiously at the window. "I feel you," said Charlie. "Believe me."

Charlie's younger brother, Andy, followed her in, carelessly dragging snow across the carpet. Without a word the kids lifted the box and carried it out of the house together. The door slammed again, and the children waited at the back of the moving truck for their mom to grab the box from them.

All around, the noises of the city went on as if everything was normal: honking horns, waves of music from passing cars, and the occasional siren. But things were far from normal for Charlie. When her cell phone vibrated in her pocket, she balanced her end of the box with one hand and reached for it.

It was a text message from Charlie's best friend, Amari, consisting of two emojis: a sad face with a teardrop and a green moving truck.

Charlie used her thumb to reply with a row of sobbing girl faces.

Andy, who was ten, grew bored waiting for their mother and started smacking the heel of his boot into the ice on the driveway to see if he could make a hole. After one particularly hard kick, he accidentally dropped his end of the box. The lid slipped off, and a couple of coffee mugs spilled out onto the ice.

Charlie sighed and lowered her end of the box to the ground. It had been a long, cold morning. Now that the house was empty and she'd said good-bye to her friends, she just wanted to get moving.

A blue car slowly passed by, the driver peering out the window like she was searching for an address. The car kept going, and Charlie turned back to Andy, who was just standing there. "What are you waiting for? Pick up that stuff," she said. "And quit messing around."

"You quit," muttered Andy. He dropped to his haunches and pulled off his gloves.

Charlie's mom poked her head out from the moving truck. "Any more boxes?"

Charlie frowned and stared stonily at the driveway.

"This is the last one," Andy said. He chucked the coffee mugs into the box and smashed down the lid.

"Impressive," Charlie said sarcastically. She helped him lift the box up to their mom, who put it on top of a stack and shoved a sleeping bag next to it to keep it in place. They could hear their dad grunting from inside the truck as he tightened the straps that would hold the fragile stuff in place for the seventeen-hundred-mile journey, taking them from the awesome city limits of Chicago to what Charlie called Absolutely Nowhere, Arizona.

"Almost done," their father called out. "Load up the warm bodies and we're out of here."

"Okay, kids," their mother said, "crate the cats and grab Jessie. We'll put them in the car with me. You two ride in the moving truck with Dad." She jumped out onto the driveway. "We'll know soon enough how well this'll work—I'll spare you the meowing and the puking for the first few hours, at least," she said with a wry smile. All three pets had been rescues with unknown pasts, but the animals had one thing in common: they hated riding in the car. Jessie got carsick if she moved around too much, and Big Kitty was especially skittish and had an earsplitting, banshee-like *meowl* whenever she wasn't enjoying herself. Fat Princess chewed on things when she was anxious.

Andy darted inside, and Mom gave Charlie's shoulder a squeeze as she passed. Charlie pulled away. She could hardly believe this was it—their last moments in their beloved house.

As Charlie lagged after them, she saw the blue car coming back this way just as slowly as before. She hesitated at the door to watch it. But a second later Andy began hollering from inside. The cats were clearly not cooperating. Charlie went to help.

Ten minutes and several scratches later, the cats were

successfully enclosed in their crates. Charlie and Andy each carried one out to the Subaru. While Charlie carefully loaded them into the backseat and secured them with seat belts, Andy opened the hatch for the dog. He unfolded the waterproof sheet they kept back there and spread it out in case of an unfortunate barfing incident.

"I'll get Jessie," Charlie told him once the cats were loaded. As she jogged back to the house, she saw a small package propped up next to the door. "Where did this come from?" she murmured. She picked it up and looked around, but saw no one.

"Is this yours?" Charlie called to her dad, holding it up.

Her father appeared at the back of the moving truck and started lowering the roll-up door. "I don't know," he said, hopping out and continuing to pull it downward, "but anything that doesn't make it in here in the next two seconds has to ride on your lap for three days."

"Eep!" Charlie tossed the package into the back of the truck, just making it.

"First goal of the spring season," her dad remarked as he slammed the door closed and latched it. "Nice shot."

"Yeah," Charlie said, but it came out halfhearted. Her stomach hitched as everything about moving away suddenly became so immediate. The truck was loaded, the house empty. She'd never play soccer with Amari or her other friends again.

At least I'll be able to play soon, Charlie thought. If there was one nice thing about having to move so far away, it was that her new school in Navarro Junction had a sixth-grade girls' spring soccer team, and tryouts were next Thursday. But Charlie would give that up in a heartbeat if she could just stay in Chicago. She closed her eyes and swallowed hard.

"Have you got Jessie?" her dad asked, and started toward the driver's door.

"I'm getting her," Charlie said, her eyes flying open again. She darted into the house, past her mother, who was grabbing snack bags from the kitchen counter. Charlie took Jessie by the leash and rested her hand on the dog's head, trying to calm her. She looked around one last time, letting another sigh escape.

"Charlie," her mom called, the click of her boots echoing in the hallway as she walked toward the door. "We're ready! Time to go."

Charlie felt a wave of anxiety, and tears sprang to her eyes. "Just give me a second to say good-bye to my house!" she yelled back with more attitude than she probably should have had. But she couldn't help it. Didn't her mother understand what she was doing to her? Charlie had lived in this house since the day her parents brought her home from the hospital. Her whole life was here. And now everything was falling apart.

CHAPTER 3

Starting Over

The Wildes rolled into Navarro Junction on Friday afternoon, just in time to get a quick tour of Andy's and Charlie's schools. When they moved into their new house on Saturday, they got everything unloaded into the garage and their beds and desks set up, and that was about all they could manage before they collapsed.

On Sunday Charlie stood in the garage and stared at the stacks and stacks of boxes that still needed unpacking. She wondered idly where her soccer stuff was, but looking for it seemed like an overwhelming task. Besides, her thoughts were consumed with having to start school in this strange place. It made her stomach hurt to think about it.

She turned away from the mess and instead took in the neighborhood. All the homes had stucco siding and ceramic-tiled roofs, which reminded her of gingerbread houses.

The street was quiet, and there was no one outside that she could see. She went to the screen door and called inside, "I'm going for a walk!"

"That's great, honey!" came her mother's overly cheerful reply.

Charlie frowned at her mom's enthusiasm—after all, it was her fault they had to move—and ventured down the driveway to the sidewalk. It was weird taking a stroll in such an unfamiliar place and thinking at the same time, *This is where I live now.* She slipped her hands into her hoodie's pouch pocket and clutched her cell phone. It made her feel better, somehow, to know that Amari was just a text message away. Charlie took a photo of her house and sent it to her, then kept walking.

It was quiet compared to her old neighborhood. There were no skyscrapers here, no honking horns or random sirens at all hours of the day and night. No businesspeople rushing down the sidewalk to work or to get in line at the coffee shop, or to catch the train like Charlie often did. That had been an adventure every day. Life was happening everywhere all the time at a breakneck pace, and a kid had to be quick to keep up. Of course Charlie had to be cautious when she was out alone in the city, but her parents had made her and Andy take self-defense and safety courses at the Y since they were little. And because her mom was an ER doctor, Charlie even knew CPR—you never knew when that could come in handy. By the age of twelve she'd been able to handle just about anything, but if she'd ever needed help, her stay-at-home dad had always been available by phone.

Now, walking through her new neighborhood with its strange stone-covered yards, cacti, and flowers blooming in February, Charlie felt uneasy and unsure about what to do with herself. It was too calm here. If she were back home, she could meet up with her friends or take the "L" train somewhere exciting. But here there wasn't much of anything going on—not that she knew of, anyway. Her mind returned to school and the quick tour they'd taken in and out of a jumble of small buildings. She began to worry about getting lost or finding a place to sit at lunch tomorrow.

Charlie picked up her pace, always expecting to see tall buildings around the next curve in the road but never finding them. Navarro Junction was an hour's drive from Phoenix, plopped down in a valley in the Sonoran Desert. There weren't many trees, but mountains surrounded them. When their Realtor had handed Charlie's parents the keys to their new house, he'd joked that the schoolkids always knew which way was home based on which mountain range they were looking at.

Charlie hadn't understood why it was funny. Didn't kids here memorize street names? In Chicago, the president streets went east-west. If you got lost, you just walked until you hit one and figured out your way home from there.

Charlie squinted against a sudden squall so she wouldn't get dirt in her eyes and flipped her hood over her head. She jogged across the street and saw a tiny children's play area between two houses, surrounded by stones. A couple of giant saguaro cacti stood in one corner. Charlie knew what kind they were because, on the long drive, their father, a biologist, had talked about how different the plant and animal life would be in their new home. The saguaros were the tall ones often pictured in postcards of sunsets and cowboys and ghost towns, their prickly arms pointing out and up to the sky. Charlie looked at them, puzzled. Who would put something so prickly near a kids' play area? It didn't make sense.

Charlie's phone vibrated in her pocket. She stopped walking and pulled it out, smiling when she saw that Amari had sent a photo in return. Charlie looked closely and realized it was a photo of Charlie's old house, with snow falling all around. "Bet you're a lot warmer over there!"

Charlie's eyes teared up. Amari had gone out in the cold and snow to do that for her. She longed for her friend.

"I miss you," Charlie replied. "And snow."

"Seriously, don't miss snow," wrote Amari. "Totally overrated."

"Haha," wrote Charlie, though she was far from laughing. There was so much she wanted to say to Amari about how different it was and how sad she felt, but trying to find the words was too painful.

Instead she typed, "I should have given you my new snow boots." There was definitely no need for the new boots Charlie had gotten for her birthday last fall. That was before Mom dropped the bomb about moving.

"You'll need them when you visit," replied Amari. "Or when you go skiing in the mountains! Lucky."

"I suppose," Charlie wrote.

"Are you moved in?"

"Not really. Everything's a mess. Big Kitty freaked out and hid behind the stove. She hasn't come out yet."

"Oh no! She'll feel better soon," wrote Amari. "And she'll come out when she gets hungry enough."

"Yeah, I hope so. Thanks."

There was a pause, and then Amari replied, "Hang in there!" with a brightly smiling emoji.

Charlie's eyes lingered on the screen, but she couldn't think of anything to say to that. She tried to swallow the lump in her throat, and then she shoved the phone back into her pocket and continued walking, making a loop that she hoped would bring her back to her house.

She passed a large grassy area, noting it would be a good place to kick a soccer ball around, and turned down her street. Charlie scanned the driveways looking for their Subaru, but she didn't see it, and for a frantic moment Charlie couldn't remember which house was hers. Why would anybody want houses to all look the same?

Finally Charlie spotted the right house number. She headed up the driveway just as her dad pulled in and parked.

"Help me with the groceries?" he asked, getting out.

Charlie shrugged. "Sure."

Charlie's father, Charles Wilde, was tall and lean and wore glasses, and she was named after him. Amari had once told him that he looked exactly like a scientist was supposed to look, which had made him laugh, though to Charlie he just looked like a dad. Technically he was a doctor, like Charlie's mom, but he often joked that he was only the PhD kind, which didn't count for squat most of the time. And he hadn't actually worked as a scientist in years, so it was a little weird for Charlie to think of him as one. That was about to change, too.

They brought everything inside and began putting things away in the empty refrigerator and pantry. Charlie's mother flew past them, car keys jangling. "I'm running into work for a couple of hours," she said, her face lit up. "They've got paperwork for me, and one of the doctors called in sick, so I guess I'm jumping right into the fray." She grinned. "I don't know when I'll be home—don't hold dinner."

"Good luck!" said Charlie's dad, swooping in to give her a kiss before she rushed off.

Charlie didn't say anything. Soon they heard the car pulling out of the driveway.

"I thought she wasn't starting until tomorrow," said Charlie.

"Yeah, me too," said her father. "But we knew it would be a little hectic once we got here."

Charlie looked around for a bowl to put some fresh lemons and limes in, but there wasn't one. She lined them up in a row on the counter instead.

"So," Charlie's dad said, putting milk in the refrigerator, "did you take a walk around the neighborhood?"

"Yep," said Charlie.

"What did you think?"

Charlie rolled her eyes at the pantry shelves. "Boring."

Charlie's dad stopped what he was doing and came over to the pantry doorway. He studied his daughter. "Do you want to talk about it?"

"Talk about how boring it is?" Charlie said with an edge to her voice. "No thanks."

Her father pressed his lips together, and Charlie knew she'd gone too far, but she couldn't help it. She didn't want to be here. Final answer.

"Look," said Dad, "I know this is hard on you. But Mom had a great opportunity, and we just couldn't—"

"Just couldn't pass it up," said Charlie. "I know." She'd heard that line a thousand times. "But that doesn't make me happy about it." She brought some items to the pantry and pushed them around on the shelves, trying to make it look like what they'd had back home in Chicago. Her eyes stung.

"Aw, kiddo." He put his hand on Charlie's shoulder. "It'll get better. I promise."

Charlie doubted it. "Maybe for you and Mom. But not for me." She pushed past her father and blindly unloaded the rest of the groceries onto the counter, opening cupboard doors and closing them again, feeling completely lost as to where to put things. Then she gathered up the empty bags, trying to figure out how to recycle them when they didn't even have a recycling bin yet. She smashed them together into a big ball. "This house is so stupid," she said bitterly.

Dad glanced sharply at Charlie, then his face grew sympathetic. But it was clear Charlie needed to blow off steam. "Just put all the cupboard food in the pantry for now and the refrigerator stuff in the refrigerator. We'll sort it out later."

"Fine," said Charlie.

Charlie's father eased his way out of the kitchen so Charlie could bang around undisturbed. "I'll be in my study getting ready for tomorrow," he said.

When the groceries were all put away, Charlie fled to her room.

As she lay on her bed, Charlie fumed. She was furious at her mother for making them move here. Dr. Diana Wilde had been offered an amazing job as head of the emergency room at the hospital in Navarro Junction. It was an opportunity she would've never had in Chicago—or so she repeated about fifty times a day to all their friends, neighbors, and relatives back home. The ER here was understaffed, and she'd be working a really crazy schedule, but the commute was only ten minutes—and she could even take the bus so they wouldn't need to buy a second car. She was so pumped up about it that Charlie didn't think she'd even noticed how unexcited her own daughter was about this "great" opportunity.

And her father was messing things up, too. He accepted a position teaching biology at the nearby community college, filling in the rest of the school year for a professor who was taking a leave of absence. So he was excited to work outside the home again for the first time in a long time. Charlie felt like all her lifelines were being taken away at once.

After a while of moping, Charlie heard Andy and her father talking, but she couldn't make out the words. When curiosity got the best of her, she slid off the bed and found them in her father's study. Dad was on the floor under his mahogany desk, setting up his computer. Andy was sitting on the desktop, plugging in the speakers.

"If you're teaching tomorrow," Andy was saying, "who's bringing us to school?"

Charlie leaned against the doorframe, wondering the same thing.

"My first class starts at nine. I'll drop you off on my way. I've got time to go inside at both schools, so don't sweat it."

"That's okay," said Charlie coolly. "I'm good."

Dr. Wilde looked up from under the desk. His hair had fallen forward. "All right, suit yourself."

"You're going in with me," said Andy. "I don't know how to get anywhere."

"We took a tour," said Charlie disdainfully. "How can you not remember?"

"I wasn't really paying attention. I was looking at the kids."

On Charlie's tour she'd tried not to make eye contact with anybody—but they were all staring at her. "Well, no wonder, you goof." But Charlie's confidence faltered as she tried to remember exactly how her campus was laid out. Everything was muddled.

Andy turned back to his dad. "Are you going to be home after school like always?"

"These first few days I will—I'll pick you both up from school until we get the hang of things. After that you'll ride the bus home sometimes, and Charlie will be able to walk," said Dr. Wilde. He disappeared under the desk again. "I'm teaching evening classes twice a week, so some days you might come home from school and be alone for a few hours, unless Mom is home. But you two are old enough to handle it."

"Home alone," said Andy, nodding. "I like it."

Charlie crossed her arms in front of her, a look of consternation on her face. It felt wrong, her father going to work, especially when everything else was so unsettled. Who was going to be home to cook and keep their schedules organized . . . and go to their after-school events? "So I'm stuck babysitting?" she asked.

"I don't need a babysitter," Andy said. "Besides, you might not be here much either if you make the soccer team. I'll take care of myself just fine." He seemed very eager to do so.

"It won't be every day," said their father. "And it's only for three months. If I like teaching and it's working for our family, I can try to stay on. And if I don't, I can quit."

"Great," Charlie said icily. "Can I say the same thing about living here?"

Andy scowled at her. "Why are you being so annoying?"

Charlie shrugged. "Clearly you wouldn't understand what it's like to have friends and a life back home."

"I already have one friend here," Andy said smugly. "Met him this morning while you were still sleeping. He lives down the street and is letting me use his old longboard until we can unpack mine." Andy turned back to his dad. "Your job sounds cool, Dad. I've always wanted to have the whole house to myself. Does my school end before Charlie's? I hope so. Hey . . . what exactly is biology again?"

Charlie sighed and went to her room.

CHAPTER 4

First Impressions

Charlie's school was in walking distance, but she wasn't sure how to get there yet, so she definitely didn't mind having her dad drive her, especially the first day. She was so nervous she hadn't slept well or eaten much breakfast. As they rode along, she stared out the window, ignoring Andy, who chattered like a chipmunk in the backseat.

Her dad stopped at her school first. When they pulled up to the drop-off spot by the big Summit Junior High School sign, Charlie's hands began sweating. She wiped them on her jeans and picked up her backpack.

Dr. Wilde leaned sideways so he could kiss her on the head like he'd done every day of her entire school career. Charlie stiffened and pretended not to see. She opened the door and put one foot onto the curb. "Bye."

Her dad blinked, then sat up straight, trying to hide the hurt look on his face. "Are you sure you don't want me to go in with you?"

"Yeah," Charlie lied. She looked back at Andy. "Good luck, squirt face," she said. "Don't get in trouble on your first day."

Andy grinned and slapped the back of her seat. "Don't be annoying on *your* first day."

Charlie managed a weak smile for his sake. He had to be at least a little nervous too. She got out of the car, then walked slowly to her doom.

When she reached the school steps, she stopped and glanced over her shoulder. Her dad was still sitting there, waiting until she went inside. Charlie felt very alone.

It's not like she *had* to go in without him—but things were different now. She was twelve, not a baby, and this was junior high. Charlie had seen the campus, and she tried telling herself it was no big deal—her sixth-grade class in Chicago was bigger than this entire school. But now she wavered. This was harder than she'd expected it would be. Everybody else knew each other, and she was alone. Kids were looking at her.

She expelled a heavy breath that sent her bangs fluttering in the cool air and tried to focus on something positive, like the upcoming tryouts for the soccer team. Amari, for one, was jealous that Navarro Junction had a spring team. Or at least she pretended to be, which was nice.

But this place felt foreign. Half the kids were wearing shorts—in winter. And the layout of the school was really different from the four-story mammoth brick building on the corner of two busy streets back in Chicago. This campus was central to several quiet neighborhoods, and each of the small, separate school buildings housed a different subject of learning. So there was a building for math, science, language arts, and so on, as well as an auditorium and a library. And while there were outdoor walkways between, there were no huge maple or oak trees standing tall and uprooting the sidewalk like back home. The few trees lining the property here were scraggly and sparse and looked like they were trying to figure out how to grow leaves.

Charlie held her head high, climbed the steps, and marched inside, wearing the fake face of confidence she'd often put on when dealing with something scary back in the city. "Let's get this over with," she said under her breath, and forged through the crowded hallway toward the office.

The school looked new inside, and the walls were free of lockers. On their tour, Charlie had seen clusters of them outside, of all places, between buildings. Clearly students really didn't have to worry about the weather here. When Charlie reached the office, she paused for a moment, then squared her shoulders and opened the door.

A man sat behind a counter studying papers and scribbling on them with a green pen that had a fake sunflower attached to it. He wore a bright yellow button-down shirt, with a silver-and-leather bolo tie around his neck. He looked like he could be in a Western movie. Charlie slid her backpack off her shoulders. It thumped to the floor.

"Good morning," the man drawled in a deep voice. He looked

up from the paper he was writing on.

"Um, hi." Charlie wasn't sure what say.

"What can I do for you, young lady?"

"I'm— Hi," she said again, flustered. "It's my first day." She shifted her feet. "I'm new," she added, though she thought that was becoming pretty obvious by now.

"Oh!" he exclaimed. "Of course. One second . . ." The man took off his glasses and put one of the stems between his teeth, then flitted through papers on the desk, looking for something. He dropped the drawl. "Ah yes. Welcome, new student. I am Mr. Anderson. And you are . . . C. It's a C name, right? We're expecting you, of course." He grabbed a folder and looked at the sticker in the corner of it. "Charlotte . . . ? Isn't it?"

"Yes. Charlotte Wilde," she said. "But I go by Charlie."

The eccentric man clasped his hands together. "Of course, Charlie—avoid the spider and pig jokes at all costs, hmm? I don't blame you. We're so glad to have you here at Summit. So you're an actor?"

Charlie blinked. "Um, what?"

"You like to act? Or are you more of a backstage type? I noticed you're enrolled in my theater class sixth period."

"Oh—uh, yes, I guess so." Charlie was confused. The office receptionist was apparently also the theater teacher. She knew this school was a lot smaller than her old one, but this was ridiculous. She started to say that she'd only enrolled in theater class because she thought it would be easy and her mom figured it was a good way to make friends, but then she realized it would be better not to mention it.

"Great!" Mr. Anderson said, energized. "I've already chosen a cast for the current musical—*Bye Bye Birdie*, my *favorite*!—so you'll have to be assigned to stage crew. All right?"

Charlie smiled weakly. "Sure."

"Lots of after-school opportunities as well," he said.

Charlie grew concerned. "But I might have soccer," she said.

"Don't worry, it's optional."

"Oh, okay," said Charlie, relieved.

"One moment," Mr. Anderson went on. "I'm going to track down your guide for the day." He rolled his chair sideways to the next station and grabbed the phone.

Guide? thought Charlie. She didn't know what he was talking about.

When he hung up, he rolled his chair back to his original spot. "Kelly Parker will be right here—you'll love her. She has your identical schedule, so she'll take you around today and have lunch with you and all that jazz."

Charlie let out a breath she didn't realize she'd been holding. "Okay. That's—that's cool." It was a relief to know she'd have someone to help her. Everything was so much easier when you had friends. Maybe Kelly would be one.

While she waited, a couple of kids trickled into the office to drop off notes and pick up papers from Mr. Anderson. He spoke to all of them in his slightly strange manner, but they seemed to like him. He called some of them "minions." Charlie decided it was probably because he couldn't remember their names. Adults did stuff like that a lot.

When they left, Mr. Anderson smiled sympathetically at Charlie and leaned across the desk. "You know," he said in a normal, quieter voice, "there's only one thing worse than moving halfway across the country and starting at a new school, and that's moving halfway across the country and starting at a new school in the middle of the school year."

Charlie dropped her gaze. "Yeah, that pretty much sums it up," she said. She wanted to say it stank, but she didn't think that would be polite.

"Give us a fair shake, though. I think you'll like it here. A new adventure at every turn."

Charlie wasn't sure what that meant, but she nodded anyway. "Yes, sir."

He studied her folder, slid some papers into it, and handed it to her. "Here you go. Inside you'll find your schedule and a map that shows you where your classes are in case you get separated from Kelly. And I've circled the location of your locker, right outside this building in the covered walkway. Did you bring a padlock, or do you need to rent one from the school?"

Charlie took the folder. "I brought a lock. Thanks."

"Excellent," Mr. Anderson said. "I'll see you in class. We'll be doing some set building after school later this week and next week over lunchtime if you'd like to help. Lots of kids chip in. It's not required, but I'm warning you, it's fun." His eyes twinkled.

"I'll ask my parents."

Mr. Anderson's gaze tracked to the door behind Charlie as it opened. "Ah, good," he said. "Here she is."

Charlie turned. In walked a pretty, athletic-looking girl, a little taller than Charlie. Her blond hair was loosely woven into a French braid around her head. It kind of looked like a crown.

"Kelly," Mr. Anderson said, "this is Charlie Wilde. She's going to tag along with you today to get the lay of the land."

Kelly gave Charlie a scrutinizing look. "Hi there," she said. She had a sunny smile on her face, so bright it almost seemed fake. "It's *so* nice to meet you. I'm glad I get to keep an eye on you today."

"Me too," Charlie replied tentatively. "Thanks for showing me around." She wasn't sure what to think about Kelly's odd smile. *Maybe that's just how she looks*, Charlie thought. She cast a fleeting glance at Mr. Anderson, but he'd put on his glasses and dived into his pile of papers again. So she picked up her backpack and offered Kelly a guarded smile. "Lead the way, I guess," she said.

"Sure. Follow me." Kelly pushed the door open with her shoulder and went out into the hallway. "Sooo. Charlie, huh?"

Charlie took long strides behind her to catch up. She wasn't really worried about losing sight of Kelly's crown head in the crowd, but she didn't want to take any chances. "Yeah. It's short for Charlotte. Named after my dad, Charles." It was an automatic answer.

"Named after your *dad*? That's weird. Did your parents want a boy or something?"

Charlie blinked. "Um, yeah," she said, a sinking feeling coming over her. "That's exactly it." It was going to be a very long day.

CHAPTER 5

A Very Long Day

Charlie followed Kelly from building to building making small talk, a smile stuck on her face. She knew it was important to make a good impression with the students and teachers, but inside she was dying a little. She wasn't sure how to act with these kids who all knew each other and had one thing in common: they didn't know her.

Her face hurt from smiling. And from repeating phrases like "Short for Charlotte. Named after my dad, not the spider. No, his name is Charles. Yes, it was a great book. No, I don't mind that Charlotte dies. It's integral to the story." That last line tended to stop the kids' questions about her name, probably because they didn't know what *integral* meant.

Kelly was nice to everyone—to their faces, at least. Between classes Kelly breezed through the hallways and across the courtyard, speaking cheerily to the students who seemed to go out of their way to say hi to her. But in between pleasantries Kelly kept a running commentary in a low voice to Charlie, explaining who people were and what she liked—or didn't like—about them.

"Hey, Kel," said a plain-looking girl in a brown dress.

"Oh, hi, Carmelita," exclaimed Kelly. "Great job finding those stage props."

"Thanks! I got them at a garage sale," said Carmelita, beaming.

Kelly gave her the thumbs-up as she whisked away and muttered, "That's probably where she got her clothes, too."

Charlie frowned. "You never know what you can find," she said lightly.

Kelly turned to her. "Really?" she asked.

"Well, yeah," said Charlie as she followed Kelly into another building and down a hallway to the next classroom. "I mean, I'm guessing that when your family has a garage sale, people think they've come across some pretty nice stuff."

Kelly knit her brow. "My family doesn't do garage sales," she said, like it was beneath her. "We donate."

"Oh," Charlie said. "That's . . . really interesting." She wasn't sure she wanted to keep discussing it. She was relieved when the teacher walked in so she could report to him and get her seat assignment.

At lunch students waved at Kelly from the back table in the cafeteria and moved to make room for her and Charlie. Kelly introduced Charlie all around, and Charlie felt a little uneasy until she discovered that she didn't have to talk so much within this group of chatty students. It gave her a chance to eat her lunch, and she was starving after her light breakfast. Once Kelly got up to leave, with

Charlie following, the commentary returned.

"Did you notice the girl who sat across from me?" Kelly said in a hushed voice on their way to drop off their lunch trays. "Her brother got arrested last year." She whispered the last word. "Shoplifting."

Charlie cringed. She didn't want to know that. But she also didn't want to alienate Kelly by telling her to stop—she was stuck with her for the rest of the day. Charlie had known people like Kelly at her old school, and she'd steered clear. But she couldn't do that now. Kelly was all she had.

With a sinking feeling she started to realize that if Kelly gossiped about other people to her, a complete stranger, she would probably do the same about Charlie. That made Charlie want to be very careful about how she acted. Yet Kelly continued to be outwardly charming to almost everyone, and they all seemed to like her. Maybe they were all too scared to act any other way.

"So who's your best friend?" Charlie asked, thinking the best way to get through the rest of the day was to be the one asking the questions. "Was she there at lunch?"

Kelly's face clouded. "Oh, you know," she said. "I think having a best friend is kind of babyish, really. Don't you?" She waved to a group of boys walking down the hall the other way, and they all waved or lifted their heads or smiled in acknowledgment.

"Hmm." Charlie nodded thoughtfully, but totally disagreed. Having Amari as a best friend was not babyish at all. Maybe Kelly thought that way because she didn't have one.

On their way to sixth period, Kelly kept on with her cheery, outgoing personality, while never failing to follow up with casual, sometimes biting remarks about people once they were out of earshot. Charlie was growing tired of it. She almost stopped Kelly several times, but then remembered that if she did something to make Kelly mad, Kelly might just tell the whole school behind her back—and that was just not something Charlie needed to happen on her first day. Charlie began to dread the time between classes almost as much as she dreaded facing another period where she had no idea what was going on. The entire day was overwhelming.

As Kelly and Charlie walked through the sunny courtyard to the auditorium for sixth-period theater class, a girl with black hair and an athletic build waved. "Three days!" she belted out to Kelly.

"Can't wait," said Kelly, with a genuine smile this time. Charlie looked on curiously.

"Hiya, Charlie," the black-haired girl said. "I'm Maria Torres. I'm in your first and second periods, though I'm sure you wouldn't remember me." She flashed an infectious grin.

Charlie felt herself smiling back. "At this point I can't even remember what my first- and second-period classes are," she said.

"Math and science," Maria said with a laugh, and continued walking. "See you around!" she called, and waved at the girls.

Charlie waited cautiously to see what negative thing Kelly would say about Maria, but the girl was silent.

"What's happening in three days?" Charlie asked.

"Soccer team tryouts," said Kelly.

"Oh, right!" said Charlie, growing excited. "You play soccer? Me too! I'm definitely going to be there."

"Yep," said Kelly, who didn't seem nearly as excited. She pushed through the door and narrowed her eyes at Charlie. "Are you any good?"

Charlie was taken aback, and then she struggled over how to answer. If she said yes, would Kelly think she was bragging? If she said no . . . well, that would be silly. Charlie shrugged and tried to look mysterious.

Kelly put on her plastic smile again as theater students surrounded her with questions and shoved fabric for costumes in her face. Soon she was swept away, leaving Charlie standing alone, trying like mad to figure out what Kelly's deal was. But soon Mr. Anderson and his bright-yellow shirt beckoned her backstage and explained what the class was working on to prepare for the big show. He introduced her to Sara, the stage manager, and then assigned her to work with the student props manager, Carmelita, the girl Kelly had talked to in the hallway earlier. Carmelita kept Charlie on the move fetching things.

At first Charlie didn't know the difference between upstage and downstage, and she had stage right confused with stage left, so she wasn't very useful. But Carmelita and the other crew members helped her out, and by the end of the class period she was feeling more confident. Despite her initial confusion, she really liked the unstructured atmosphere of theater class and the friendly students. The fact that there was no homework wasn't bad either.

Every now and then Charlie glanced at Kelly, who was fully in her element as one of the lead actors in this musical. She rehearsed scenes in the back of the auditorium with fellow actors who often asked her advice on how to deliver their lines. Charlie wondered what sort of mean things Kelly would say after class about them.

When the bell rang, Charlie caught up with Kelly as usual. Walking to their last class, Kelly was preoccupied with texting, even though they weren't supposed to be on their phones during school. They passed two teachers on their trek to the language arts building, but neither of them seemed to care. Maybe Kelly had special powers with teachers, too.

"Is everything okay?" Charlie asked when Kelly stopped outside the classroom door to finish texting.

"Ugh, parents," said Kelly, not looking up.

"Yeah, tell me about it," agreed Charlie. "They're the worst."

"For sure." Kelly put away her phone and stared at Charlie for a long moment, as if she was going to say something more. But then the warning bell rang, and the look on her face went away. The two dashed into the room and separated, Kelly to her desk and Charlie to get her final seat assignment of the day.

The teacher gave her a seat by the window. As Charlie stared outside at the tops of the barren tree branches, her mind wandered.

She was exhausted from the new faces and questions. All day long, students and teachers had wanted to know why Charlie's family had moved in the middle of the semester, and what kind of jobs her parents had, and how she liked it here. And she'd answered them all, over and over again, to be polite. Now the day was almost over, and Charlie couldn't wait to call Amari and tell her about it.

A wave of homesickness swept through her. She wondered how long it would take her to walk back to Chicago.

"Charlie?" the language arts teacher said, interrupting her thoughts. "Something interesting going on out there?"

Charlie whipped her head around to face the front, her cheeks growing warm "Sorry," she said. "Just . . . doing a, um, a math problem in my head that I was stuck on in, um, in math class. Earlier, I mean," she mumbled. She glanced across the room at Kelly for support, but Kelly was whispering something to the boy in front of her. The boy glanced sidelong at Charlie.

Charlie shifted uncomfortably. Was Kelly talking about *her* now? She forced herself to face the whiteboard, where the teacher was pointing to a sentence and talking about direct objects, but her mind swam.

Finally the bell rang at the end of the day, and Charlie couldn't be more ready for it. Flustered and not sure what to say to Kelly, she decided a hasty thank-you would do. She smiled weakly and ran out of the language arts building, reoriented herself to the lockers, and then followed the masses to the pick-up area in the circle drive. She scanned the line of cars, looking for her dad.

When she finally found him, she walked rapidly toward their car and climbed inside.

"Let's go," she said, closing the door.

Her dad pulled away from the curb. "How was it?" he asked, his voice guarded. It was like he already knew.

Charlie clipped her seat belt together, then leaned her head against the headrest, closed her stinging eyes, and sighed, exhausted. "I want to go back to Chicago."

CHAPTER 6

Figuring Things Out

After school Charlie collapsed on her bed and called Amari. She told her about all the things that were strange and different and unsettling about her new school. And how Kelly had talked about her behind her back already.

Amari was sympathetic. "I'm so sorry you got stuck with that gossipy tour guide," she said. "She sounds kinda sneaky. Maybe you can avoid her."

"I'd like to, but she's in all my classes," Charlie said glumly. "And she plays soccer, too."

"It figures," said Amari. "Did anything good happen?"

Charlie tried to pull herself out of her gloomy mood. "I guess theater class was all right."

"That's great! Well, it's a good start, at least. Right?"

There was a tiny edge to Amari's voice that puzzled Charlie at first, but then she realized Amari was probably getting tired of hearing her complain all the time. Charlie didn't blame her. "Yeah, for sure," she said sheepishly.

Soon Amari had to go, and Charlie reluctantly turned to

the piles of homework she had racked up throughout the day. Luckily all but one of her teachers had been lenient on due dates and said she could have extra time if she needed it. That was a relief, but with soccer coming up, Charlie wanted to get as much work out of the way as possible. Besides, what else was she going to do?

Charlie's mom came home from work and popped her head in right as Charlie was climbing into bed. "Hey, kiddo!" she said. She put her hand up to cover her yawn. "How was your first day? Everything go okay?"

"I don't want to talk about it," said Charlie grumpily, ignoring the part of herself that did. She wanted to stay mad at her mom for making them move here.

"Sounds pretty rough. Are you sure you don't want to talk it through?" She entered the room and sat down on the edge of Charlie's bed.

"I already called Amari about everything, and I'm tired. Have you found my soccer stuff?"

"Um . . . when do you need it again?"

"Thursday."

"I'll look for it," promised Charlie's mom. "Want me to tuck you in?"

Charlie frowned. Her parents rarely did that anymore. "No, that's okay."

"Aw, come on," said Mom. "These hands were made for it." She wiggled her fingers.

"I thought they were made for emergency surgery," said Charlie drily.

"That too," agreed Mom. She straightened the comforter and gave Charlie a questioning look.

"Oh, all right," Charlie said reluctantly. It made her feel like a little kid, but she kind of loved it, too.

Dr. Wilde smiled. She reached over Charlie to tuck the blankets in on the far side, then secured them on the near side, so she was nice and snug. It made her feel warm and safe.

When her mom turned out the bedside lamp and kissed Charlie on the forehead and said "I love you, little bunny" like she always used to, Charlie balked. "Mom," she said. "Enough."

Charlie's mom laughed softly and hugged her through the blankets. "Okay. Good night. Tomorrow will be better."

"Night, Mom."

Mom got up and left the bedroom, closing the door softly behind her. Charlie stared into the darkness after her.

The next day Charlie navigated her own way to first period. She got there early and found Kelly talking to Maria about soccer tryouts. She joined them.

"Charlotte plays soccer, too," Kelly said to Maria, raising an eyebrow.

"Yep," said Charlie. She wasn't sure why Kelly was calling her Charlotte all of a sudden, but it was just one more thing that bothered her about Kelly.

"That's fantastic!" said Maria. "We'll have fun at tryouts." It looked like she really meant it.

"Thanks," said Charlie with a cautious smile. Maria seemed like a cool person. And Kelly didn't have anything bad to say about her. That had to mean something, though Charlie wasn't really sure what.

Charlie made it through the morning on her own, though sometimes she naturally fell in step with Kelly since they were always going in the same direction. She joined Kelly for lunch again and sat quietly like she'd done the previous day, content to observe and try to find people who might be better friends for her. But the others at the table all seemed to have their own best friends already, which wasn't surprising. Several of them politely asked Charlie a question or two, but then went back to conversations with their friends about horse shows or various clubs they belonged to, which Charlie wasn't really into.

Kelly was superpopular, and she reveled in attention, but she didn't actually seem to have any close friends. Charlie was sure she was not going be one either. Halfway through lunch, she began to scout out the rest of the cafeteria to see where she might sit in the future, because she really didn't see herself fitting in with these students. Just as she shoved the last of her food into her mouth, she spied Maria a few tables away, sitting with a boy who was constantly messing around on his phone while they talked a little now and then. And there were open seats at their table. Charlie smiled to herself. She'd look for Maria tomorrow.

On Wednesday Charlie stopped shadowing Kelly and went to her classes on her own. She strode more confidently through the buildings and across the courtyard, saying hi to a few familiar-looking people now and then. At lunch she stopped short of Kelly's table and went to the one where Maria was sitting across from the boy.

"Hi, Maria," said Charlie, eyeing the open chair next to her.

"Hey, Charlie," said Maria. "You want to sit?"

"Sure," Charlie replied, relieved. "That would be great." She set down her tray, glanced at the boy, who was furiously typing on his phone, and sat in the chair next to Maria.

Maria wore her hair in a ponytail. The corners of her mouth turned up naturally, which made her look like a very pleasant person even when she wasn't smiling. But she was smiling now. "That's Mac Barnes," she said, pointing to the kid across from her.

The boy, who had braces and an impeccably perfect squared-off Afro, leaned forward on one elbow and looked up. "Hey. How's it going so far?"

"Pretty good," said Charlie. "You're in my first class too, aren't you? You sit near me."

"Yep," he said. "One row over." He went back to his phone.

Maria butted in. "Are you excited for tryouts tomorrow?"

Charlie perked up. "Yeah! But where do we go? My mom got an email about it when I signed up, but I forgot to ask her about that."

"Behind the school," Mac said, still typing. "The field inside the track. The goalposts aren't up yet, but they should be soon."

"Do you play too?" Charlie asked him, surprised. "I thought it was a girl's team."

"No," said Mac, glancing at her. "I just come to watch Maria once in a while."

"That's really cool," Charlie said with a grin, and then she looked slyly at Maria and back at Mac. "Are you two . . ."

"No," they both replied, a little hastily.

"We're just friends," Maria told Charlie. "We've been friends since we were really little." She frowned at Mac. "Anyway, for soccer we'll all go to the locker rooms to change first—just like for PE class."

"Cool. I know where that is."

"And be prepared—Coach Candy is tough, and she works us really hard. Our team was undefeated in the fall, so we want to keep up the perfect record."

"Okay," said Charlie. A shadow of doubt entered her mind. Maybe tryouts would be tougher than she expected.

Mac took a bite of his salad, then turned his attention to his cinnamon roll and started painstakingly picking the raisins off it.

Charlie resumed eating and watched him curiously.

Mac glanced up at her. "The raisins look like bugs," he said. When he'd gotten them all, he shoved half of the roll into his mouth. "Arfopaws ow isgussee."

Charlie frowned. "Arfopaws? What?" She laughed.

Maria rolled her eyes as Mac chewed. "He said arthropods are disgusting."

"What's an 'arthropod' again?" asked Charlie. It sounded familiar.

"Bugs, lobsters, junk like that," said Maria dismissively. "It's a word on our science vocab list this week."

"Ah, that's where I saw it," said Charlie.

Mac swallowed. "I mostly just hate bugs."

"He's terrified of them," Maria said.

Mac shrugged, unapologetic. "I like snakes, though. Go figure."

"I can't stand snakes," said Maria. She shuddered. "Give me a bug any day." She hesitated. "I mean, don't *actually* give me a bug. . . ."

"I won't," Charlie said, laughing.

Maria picked up her last bite of cinnamon roll and smashed it on top of Mac's raisins, then shoved the whole sticky mass into her mouth. "'hanks!" she said, chewing.

He wrinkled his nose and sighed. "I seriously hate raisins. They're almost as bad as peas."

"Raisins are okay," said Charlie, "but I agree, peas are disgusting."

"Right?" said Mac. "They're literally the worst."

"They squeak between your teeth."

"I hate that." Mac shuddered. "Peas are *estúpida*."

"*Estúpido*," Maria corrected. "*Peas* are masculine. Own the peas, Mr. Man."

"Whatever," Mac muttered. He glanced around the cafeteria, then said abruptly, "I gotta go." He stood up and shoved his chair under the table, and with a nod, he was off to return his tray and join a group of boys who were leaving the cafeteria.

Maria frowned and licked the frosting off her fingers. If she was bothered by Mac's brisk departure, she appeared to get over it quickly. "Anyway," she said, "are you coming to practice after school?"

Charlie looked confused. "What?"

"Some of us are getting together to practice in the field after school today—didn't Kelly invite you?"

"Um, no," said Charlie. Her face grew warm.

"Oh," said Maria. "Well, can you stay after school? It'll only be for an hour or so."

"I—I don't have my gear with me." Charlie desperately wished someone had told her. "Maybe I can have my dad bring it," she said automatically, like she'd always done back in Chicago. But then she remembered her dad had a job now, and neither parent was around to help her out. She'd have to run all the way home to get her stuff, then come all the way back. And, if her mom hadn't, she'd have to find it all first. She chided herself for not looking for her gear before. "Actually, never mind," she said, disappointed. "I can't make it."

"No worries," said Maria, standing up. "It's not a big deal." She smiled reassuringly and gathered her tray and utensils.

Charlie wasn't sure what to do. Was she invited to hang around with Maria? She hastily downed her milk as Maria started walking away.

Maria looked over her shoulder. "You coming, Chuck?" she asked.

Charlie grinned at the nickname and jumped to her feet. "On it."

Things were looking up. Now all Charlie had to do was make the soccer team. And from the way Maria spoke about it, it might not be easy. Tonight was definitely going to be a practice night, even if she had to practice solo.

CHAPTER 7

A Mysterious Gift

"Mom!" Charlie yelled when she walked in the house after school. "Have you found my soccer stuff yet?" Jessie bounded over and jumped up to lick her face. Charlie pet the dog's neck distractedly, then gently pushed her to the floor.

Mom didn't answer. Charlie set her empty water bottle on the kitchen counter next to a long to-do list, with very few items crossed off. Charlie noticed "find Charlie's soccer stuff for Thurs" was penciled at the bottom in her mom's handwriting. But it wasn't crossed off. Charlie sighed and went upstairs to her room. Fat Princess was curled up and sleeping soundly on her bed. Big Kitty, who'd come out from behind the stove days ago, slunk down the hallway ready to jump at any noise.

"Mom?" she called again.

"She's still at the hospital!" Andy hollered from his bedroom. "She called and said she had to stay late again."

"It figures," muttered Charlie. She tossed her backpack on her bed and, remembering the science vocab she needed to brush up on, considered doing her homework. But she went down to the garage instead.

Jessie followed her out the door, eager to nose around. Charlie flipped on the light, revealing stacks of boxes everywhere. They couldn't even fit their car in there yet. The family was planning on tackling it all this weekend, since Mom and Dad were too busy with work to do anything else these days. But Charlie was nervous. She needed her stuff. She hadn't kicked a ball around in months. Why had she waited until now to prepare for tryouts?

She started pawing through boxes, looking inside them and closing them again. "Welp, I found the kitchen," she said to nobody in particular. "Not that Mom and Dad have time to cook anything anymore." She glanced up and scanned the garage. There had to be a better way to find what she needed.

Andy appeared in the doorway. "What are you doing?"

"I need my soccer gear. Tryouts tomorrow."

"Most of your stuff is in the back corner. Me and Dad separated the boxes when we unloaded the truck."

"Dad and I."

"No, it was Dad and *me*," Andy said. "I should know. All your books were really heavy."

"I meant— Aw, forget it." Charlie scratched her head and wove through the stacks to the back corner. "Thanks."

"I have a couple of friends coming over," Andy said, "so if you see them, let them in."

Charlie scowled. Andy already had friends at the coming-over-to-the-house stage? Whatever. "Let them in yourself," she said.

"Okay, cranky butt. Sheesh." Andy disappeared, and Jessie bounded into the house after him.

Charlie started peeking inside boxes again. She and her mom had packed the soccer stuff all together with other sports equipment, she remembered. She started moving things around, finding all her summer clothes, three crates of books, a container with FRAGILE written all over it that contained some of her electronics, and a big lightweight box of Halloween costumes. As she tossed the costume box onto another pile, a small package slipped to the floor at Charlie's feet.

She bent down and picked it up, then turned it over and saw her name, Charlie Wilde, and her old address. There was no return address and no stamp on it. Was this the package that she saw by the door when they were getting ready to leave the old house?

"Hmm," she said. She worked at the flap, trying to rip off the tape, and finally managed to get it started with her teeth. She tore it open the rest of the way and looked inside, then held her breath and carefully slid the contents onto the top of a box. Out came something encased in bubble wrap, and a folded piece of paper. Charlie unrolled the bubble wrap and pulled out a bracelet.

"Sweet!" Charlie turned the bracelet over in her hand. It had a solid, silvery-metallic band with a small, square, black screen. Tiny buttons protruded from both sides. It kind of looked like one of those expensive health-monitoring bracelets that athletes wear.

She pressed a button, and then another, but nothing happened.

Probably needs a battery, she thought. The bracelet was cool but not flashy, and it might even make Charlie look like a more serious soccer player at tryouts tomorrow, which wouldn't hurt. She turned it over again. It had a metal clasp with a release button. She pressed it. The clasp separated, but it immediately tried to stick together again, as if the two pieces were magnetic. "Ooh, cool," she breathed.

Charlie slipped the bracelet on her wrist, securing the clasp. It fit just a little bit loosely. If she wore it partway up her forearm, it was snug enough that it wouldn't bounce around.

"I bet the magnetic clasp is for balance or something scientific like that," she mused, twisting her wrist this way and that, admiring it, then held her arm out. She liked the bracelet a lot, probably even more because it was so professional looking. It was the kind of thing Charlie's soccer hero, Alex Morgan, would wear. Or Jessie Graff from *American Ninja Warrior*. She picked up the folded piece of paper and opened it.

Charlie, it's time. You know what to do.

There was no signature.

The handwriting kind of looked like Charlie's grandma's.

Charlie's grandma was sciency like Dad, so she might think a bracelet like this was interesting. But why would Grandma leave a gift on the doorstep like that without coming in or saying something?

Maybe it was a going-away present from Amari and her other

soccer friends in Chicago, and they tried to disguise their handwriting so she'd be surprised. Charlie pulled out her phone and texted Amari. "Did you leave a sports bracelet at my house as a gift?" She took a quick photo of it and sent that to Amari too.

"Nope!" came the quick reply. "But I wish I had—that's cool! Just pretend it's from me, haha. Are you doing better?"

"A little. I miss you, though."

"Me too," Amari replied, with four rows of crying emojis.

"I've got soccer tryouts tomorrow," wrote Charlie. "Wish me luck!"

"LUCK!!" replied Amari. "Don't worry. You're a superstar! You know what to do."

Charlie smiled forlornly. *You know what to do.* Amari had written the same words that were in the note. Maybe the mysterious gift was a sign that she'd do well.

But not if she didn't find her gear. Reluctantly she replied to Amari with a variety of hearts and put her phone away. It was almost easier to handle the loneliness when she didn't talk to Amari. Then she could pretend her life in Chicago never really existed.

Charlie turned back to the bracelet and examined it more closely, studying some etchings near the clasp. "Well, thank you very much, whoever you are," Charlie said, and shoved the paper and bubble wrap back into the package. With the recycle bin already overflowing, she left it on top of a stack of boxes to take care of on the weekend. "That's one emptied," she said, looking over the piles of boxes filling the garage. She pulled her sleeve down over the bracelet in the chilly garage. "Only forty thousand more to go."

With renewed energy Charlie began her search once more, tossing boxes left and right with little effort, even the ones full of books. "And Andy said these were heavy," she scoffed. "Weakling." She made it all the way to the bottom of the second stack before she found what she was after. "Finally!" she exclaimed, tearing open the box. In her excitement, the flap ripped off in her hand as easy as a piece of paper. She tossed the hunk of cardboard aside and pulled out her favorite soccer ball, her shin guards, and the brand-new cleats her parents had bought right before the move because her old ones were too small. She didn't have much time to break them in.

With her gear in hand and the new bracelet on her arm, Charlie left the wreckage and went to the grassy area in the neighborhood to practice dribbling. She wished doubly hard now that Kelly had invited her to the after-school practice on the field, and wondered why she hadn't. Maybe she'd forgotten. And maybe Kelly was just being Kelly.

Charlie shook her head as she missed a shot in her imaginary goal, trying to get the negative thoughts out of her brain. She focused on the bracelet and reminded herself that she was an excellent player. And that she *did* know what to do. And even if she had butterflies inside, the bracelet made her look like a pro. "Okay," she said under her breath. "Let's do this."

"How'd today go?" Charlie's dad asked the kids as they sat at the table to eat. His voice had taken on a hint of anxiety since the move. He loosened his necktie and rolled up his sleeves. "I told my students you were settling in."

"What?" moaned Charlie. She still wasn't used to her dad having students, and now he was talking to them about her. "Please don't do that."

"Where's Mom?" asked Andy, eyeing the take-out pizza on the table. "She said she was going to be home for dinner." It was the third pizza night they'd had since they'd gotten here.

"She's on the way," their dad explained, "but said to start without her."

"Good. I'm starving," Andy said. He grabbed a slice. "My day was great. Juan and Zach came over to play video games for a while."

"That's cool," Dad said. "How was school?"

"Fine."

"And how about you, Charlie?" he asked cautiously.

Charlie looked at her mom's empty chair and sighed. "Feeling guilty again, Dad?" She reached for a slice.

"No-o-o," he said, making a face.

"My day was okay," she said.

Dad's face cleared. "Good! How are things with, um . . . Katie?"

Charlie glanced at him. "Who? You mean Kelly?"

"Sorry. Yes."

"She's fine, I guess. I didn't hang out with her much today."

"Oh." He pressed his lips together and spread a napkin on his lap. "Have you found any other friends yet?"

"Dad, please." Charlie took a bite of her pizza and wrinkled her nose. The crust tasted like the desert itself. Arizona pizza makers could sure stand to learn a lesson from Lou Malnati's or Connie's.

"Please what? I'm just wondering about your life."

Charlie chewed and swallowed, and gave her father a bored look. "Yeah, okay, I met a girl named Maria and her friend Mac. Maria plays soccer, too."

"Wonderful!" said her father.

"Oh, and after school I found my soccer stuff, so you can cross that off the to-do list—I saw it on the counter."

"Great job handling that one on your own!" Dad exclaimed as Charlie's mom came walking up the driveway from the bus stop. "And look, Mom's home." He paused, and his voice softened. "I'm very glad you found a friend, Charlie."

Charlie rolled her eyes. "Yeah, yeah, you make it sound like I'm in first grade, Dad." They all looked up when they heard the door open, then Charlie continued. "You'd better not go around telling your students that you're so glad your kid finally found a friend. That's embarrassing."

"What's embarrassing?" asked Mom, walking into the kitchen.

"Dad is," Andy piped up. "He needs to stop talking about us in class. It's weird."

Charlie's mom laughed. "You just aren't used to your dad talking to anybody but you kids. But I talk about you all the time at the hospital—I always have. Back in Chicago, too. Just today I was telling the mom of a young patient about the awful diaper rash Andy had as a baby."

"Mom!" Charlie and Andy said together. Andy covered his face with his hands and fell dramatically back in his chair. Charlie shook her head.

"What?" their mom asked innocently. She joined them at the table. "I only do it if it helps me connect with a patient. Besides, every baby has a diaper rash once in a while. Andy's was just . . . exceptional." She grabbed a slice of pizza and winked at her husband across the table. "Wasn't it, honey?"

"Mother, stop!" Charlie said. Andy pretended to faint off the chair. He crawled under the table.

"It won first prize in the diaper rash contest," Dad said, chuckling.

Reluctantly Charlie laughed too. She had to admit, diaper rash was kind of funny—unless you're the baby who has it. And when your mom is a doctor in the emergency room, you end up talking about embarrassing stuff like that a whole lot.

CHAPTER 8

Escape

Far from Arizona, a scientist in a white coat entered a heavily guarded office across the hallway from his laboratory. "Good evening, soldiers," he said to the black-suited figures inside. "You've had a busy week."

"Good evening, Dr. Gray," said the two nearest him.

The scientist's gaze was drawn to the center of the office by his desk, where the burglar who'd broken into the facility sat. The man's hands were tied behind his back and his ankles were bound. He had a gag in his mouth.

"How's my old friend Jack today?" asked Dr. Gray, walking over to him. He pulled the gag out, then stepped back and leaned against the desk. "Tired of the interrogation yet? Ready to talk, just the two of us?" He studied the man, a curious, almost sympathetic look on his face. "Soldiers, please give me a moment with Dr. Goldstein."

Without question they slipped out, leaving the two men alone.

Dr. Jack Goldstein looked angry and unkempt. He had bruises on his face. "You can't keep me here, Victor. People are going to notice I've gone missing."

Dr. Gray reached into his lab coat pocket and produced the prisoner's passport. He pulled out a folded, unused plane ticket and waved it at Jack. "People think you're in Peru doing research. Isn't that right? They won't miss you for quite some time."

"They'll check in," Jack said through gritted teeth. "How long are you going to hold me here? If you really think I've wronged you by trying to take back what's rightfully mine, then have me arrested! If not, let me go." He narrowed his eyes, glanced at the doors to make sure the soldiers were gone, and wriggled his wrists inside the rope. He'd been working at the knots since the soldiers had brought him to this room. His skin was covered in rope burns, and every movement was excruciating, but the knots were getting looser.

The scientist frowned. "Not until you tell me what you did with the other device."

"I don't have it."

"You keep saying that." Dr. Gray shifted. "But we both know that's not true."

"You've searched me. It's obvious I don't have it."

"Not on you." Dr. Gray clucked his tongue. "You always were so literal." He crossed his legs in front of him and then leaned forward and looked Jack in the eye. "Where is it?"

Jack's head fell back and he let out a deep, ragged sigh. "Victor."

Dr. Gray slammed his hand down on the desk. "Answer the question!"

"Isn't it clear by now that I'm not going to tell you or any of your . . . your new . . . *soldiers?* Or whatever they are." Jack pretended to shift indignantly in his seat, tugging at the ropes at the same time. With searing pain, he managed to pull out one hand. A wave of hope coursed through him, but he knew he couldn't let on. Now he just had to find a way to distract Dr. Gray. He kept his voice steady. "Why do you want it so badly anyway? It doesn't work."

Dr. Gray scowled.

"No, really. I mean it. Why? Are you on the verge of something? A breakthrough? Is that why you added the extra security?" Slowly, carefully, he slipped his other hand out of the rope and grabbed on to it so it wouldn't fall to the floor and give him away.

Dr. Gray stood up and shoved his hands in his pockets. "Look, Jack, I know what you're doing."

Dr. Goldstein's hands froze. "What am I doing?"

"You're changing the subject. And I need an answer from you. So I'll ask you one last time. Where. Is. My—"

Jack jumped to his feet and threw the rope at Victor's face. With his ankles still tied, he lunged at his former friend, knocking him down, and then struggled to yank his feet free, trying to hop over to the door at the same time.

"Soldiers!" cried Dr. Gray. "Quickly!"

Jack kicked his shoes off and forced his feet out of the ropes, then ran for the nearest door, stumbling and catching himself as he went. When the soldiers rushed in, Jack barreled into them, knocking them off balance. He dived to the floor between them and scrambled on all fours to get through the door. If only he could make it outside the building, he might have a chance!

Another soldier came running at Jack as he got back to his feet. Jack dodged her and twisted away, just barely out of reach. "Help!" he shouted, running for the stairwell. But the woman was quick and shot after him. At the top of the steps, she tackled him around the legs. Arms flailing and body teetering, he crashed to the stairs. He made a desperate grab at the soldier's bodysuit as he fell, dragging her with him. They thudded all the way down the stairwell, while a pack of soldiers who appeared at the top of the stairs raced after them. Jack and the woman hit the landing, both of them dazed by the fall. After a second to regain his bearings, Jack rolled out of her reach and got to his feet, limping and trying to run as fast as he could. The woman groaned and didn't move.

But the pack of soldiers was in hot pursuit. Jack turned down a long hallway, gunning toward the double-door exit. The clatter behind him grew louder. He pushed harder. Almost there!

When he reached the first door he slammed into the handle at full speed. His face and body smacked the glass. He gasped in pain and crumpled to the floor, stunned. The door was locked.

The soldier from the stairwell reappeared, zigzagging past the others and taking the lead. They all closed in on Jack. Quickly he got to his feet and tried the other door. It opened! He burst through it to the snowy sidewalk as the woman dived after him. She grabbed him around the waist and knocked him flat on the ground, landing on top of him. Within seconds, they were surrounded.

Defeated, Jack let his body go limp. Dr. Gray's soldiers grabbed him by the arms and hauled him back into the building. They dragged him down the hallway and up the steps as if he were as light as a feather, and brought him back into the office.

There, as Dr. Gray silently watched, the soldiers tied up Jack again, much more securely this time. The doctor stared down at Jack for a long moment, fists clenching and unclenching, lips pressed hard into a white line. Then he turned away. With a heavy sigh, he walked to the door. When he reached the soldiers, he looked back. "Ramp up your interrogation efforts. I don't care what you do. Don't stop until you have the information I want."

CHAPTER 9

Doubt Creeps In

Charlie bumped into Maria the next morning on the way to first period and walked with her. Mac trailed behind them with another boy, examining his cell phone.

"He's kind of a tech genius," Maria said, tossing her head in Mac's direction. Seeing the phone, she pulled hers out of her pocket. "I meant to get your number yesterday," she said as they entered the classroom. "Quick, before the bell rings."

Charlie gave it to her.

"Texting you now so you'll have mine," said Maria.

"Cool," said Charlie. She squelched a smile, trying to be cool, but she was thrilled that Maria had asked for it.

Kelly came in and joined Maria and Charlie at the front of the room. "Hello," she said, sounding a bit aloof.

"Hey, Kel," said Maria.

"Hi, Kelly," Charlie said. "How was your soccer practice yesterday?" She tilted her head slightly, then looked at Maria too.

"Good," said Kelly, twirling her necklace. "Sorry I forgot to invite you. It just slipped my mind, I guess. The other girls and I were saying how surprised we were that you play. Are you ready for this afternoon?"

Charlie didn't know what Kelly meant by being surprised, but she didn't ask. She lifted her chin and clasped her hand over the bracelet under her sleeve, drawing confidence from it. "I'm ready," she said. She tried to take comfort in the fact that this was a smaller school, so she probably wouldn't be up against eighty-five other girls vying for twenty spots.

"What position do you play?" asked Kelly. "I hope we don't have to compete for a spot on the team." She was wearing the fake smile that Charlie had seen plenty of. It made her uneasy.

"Halfback or forward," Charlie said. "How about you?"

"Defense," said Kelly. She brightened.

So did Charlie. "Good, then there's nothing to worry about."

Kelly laughed. "Oh, *I'm* not. I was just concerned for you."

Charlie grew flustered. "Oh."

Maria balanced on the corner of her desk as other students came pouring into the room. "The truth is, everybody's excited to see how you play. We can use another big scorer."

"I suppose every team can use that," Charlie said, trying to laugh, but it came out hollow. What if she wasn't as good as Maria was expecting? What if Kelly was right to be worried for her? "I wish I'd had more time to practice, but there's been a lot of snow back home," said Charlie. "And . . . we're still unpacking, so I've been pretty busy," she added miserably. She remembered what a disadvantage she had. Here in the Southwest there was no snow. Kids could play year round. And maybe they had been. Charlie's one attempt at brushing up her skills last night suddenly seemed extremely weak.

The late bell rang, and everybody rushed to their seats as the teacher strode into the room. Charlie, whose seat was at the back of the room next to Mac's, darted to it and sat down fast. Her desk skidded. "Whoa," she muttered.

"Dang," said Mac.

"Yeah," said Charlie. "That was . . . really weird." She scooted her desk back in line, her cheeks burning.

Soon her mind wandered to soccer tryouts again. What if she wasn't good enough to make the team? But she knew she had to keep her attitude in the right place. Think positive. Be strong. Focus on the ball. And run like she was being chased by a pack of wild animals. Or like the late bell just rang. *You know what to do.*

Charlie stared down at her bracelet. She undid the clasp and held it in her hand, wishing it actually worked. Maybe this weekend she could look for a battery for it. Then she slipped the bracelet back on. Top athletes used these, and now so did Charlie. She was going to be like Alex from the US women's team and show everyone she had the right to wear it. This bracelet would help her keep her mind focused on being the best player she could be.

But Kelly's words still bothered her, and she had to work hard to push the doubts aside. If only she could stop feeling so jittery.

CHAPTER 10

Tryouts

After school Charlie sped to the locker room to change. She wanted to arrive at the field as soon as possible so she could get in a few kicks and dribbles and maybe calm her nerves a little. She waved to Maria as she left the locker room and made her way past the athletic storage building, which several guys in hard hats were working on, and across the track to the grass, where some orange cones and a mesh bag full of balls sat. Charlie grabbed a ball, did a few stretches, and began a slow dribble up the field before coming back and stretching some more. This would be a bad time to pull a muscle. As she held her stretches and listened to the steady pounding of hammers nearby, she pulled up her sleeve and used her bracelet to keep her focus strong.

When Kelly, Maria, and a bunch of other girls reached the field, Charlie was all business. She nodded politely but didn't join in the joking and laughter. Instead she went over her best moves in her mind and began to jump in place, warming up and trying to get her new shoes to bend and give a little more. The bracelet slid around on her wrist, and Charlie shoved it up her arm to secure it.

Soon the coach joined them. "Gather around!" she shouted,

and clapped her hands a few times. The girls moved to surround her.

Coach was young and tall and muscular, with blazing black eyes and hair, and dark-brown skin. "It's great to have you all back again," she said. "And nice to see some unfamiliar faces, too—I look forward to getting to know you. For those of you who are new, I'm Coach Candy."

Charlie felt a wave of relief—apparently she wasn't the only new face. And then she spied an athletic bracelet on Coach's arm. Cool!

Coach explained how the tryout would go. She laid out her high expectations, making individual eye contact with the girls as she spoke so she could be sure they understood. "Everybody starts at the same level today, whether you've played on the team before or not. This is not a time to be shy with your abilities. I want to see how you move the ball, how you share it, and how you attack the goal or defend it," she said. "Is everybody clear?"

"Yes, Coach!" shouted the girls who'd been on the team before. Charlie missed the cue, but she vowed to get it next time. She felt intimidation creep in again. Despite what Coach had said, Charlie worried that the other girls knew her so well that they'd have an advantage.

When Coach Candy caught Charlie's eye to make sure she understood, she nodded emphatically.

Coach Candy split the girls into two teams and handed out red scrimmage vests to one team and blue to the other, then sent them to opposite ends of the field for some warm-up exercises. Charlie was on the blue team, and she noted ruefully that Kelly and Maria were together on the red team.

As she ran suicides and dribbled through the cones, Charlie fought her nerves and tried to let her instinct take over, but she couldn't stop thinking about what Coach said about not being shy to show her abilities. This was Charlie's chance, and she didn't want to blow it.

When Coach came to observe the blue team, she called out encouragement and suggestions to the girls to improve. "Stay tight around that end cone, Bree," she called to a tall girl dribbling through the cones in front of Charlie. "Don't let that ball get away from you."

Charlie pushed hard, her lungs and thighs burning. Her legs were shaky, a sure sign that she wasn't in top shape, but she kept the ball in control as she rounded the end cones.

"Way to dig in, Charlie!" Coach called out.

Charlie didn't let on the pride she felt, but it gave her a boost of confidence, temporarily at least.

Soon Coach whistled to announce a scrimmage between the two groups. She assigned positions, putting Charlie in the left forward spot. Still breathing heavily from the workout, Charlie took her place, and her nerves kicked in again. Compulsories were one thing—Charlie didn't have to count on anybody else to prove she was good at that. But an actual scrimmage was different. She jumped up and down a few times to keep her muscles warm, but she felt jittery. "Calm down," she muttered. She was doing fine so far. Plus, Coach already knew her name—that was a good sign, wasn't it?

When Coach put the ball in play, Charlie kept her eye on it and advanced with it, staying in her invisible lane. She stumbled once over her new shoes but thankfully didn't fall. The play went along for several minutes with no action for Charlie, but her team was dominating. When Bree, who was playing center forward on Charlie's team, popped the ball up in the air for a goal shot, Kelly, as a fullback for the red team, headed it. It hit off somebody's knee and flew sideways toward Charlie.

Charlie dug in, but after pushing so hard earlier, her muscles were still weak. She felt slow getting to the ball, like her alertness was lagging a second behind where it should be. And her nerves kicked in, making every movement seem slightly out of control. She dribbled awkwardly, almost losing the ball—it wasn't going where she wanted it to go. Try as she might, Charlie couldn't get in the groove. Soon the red team swarmed in and stole the ball out from under her, racing in the other direction and leaving her breathless and empty-handed. She stared and shook her head, angry at herself, then started back toward the centerline, hoping she didn't just give the other team a chance to score.

Coach soon subbed out half of each team, including Charlie,

to let other girls play. Disappointed, Charlie headed for the bleachers, knowing she hadn't had an opportunity to show Coach what she could really do. She wiped the sweat from her forehead and took a drink of water, then sat down to try to get her head in the right place. She couldn't fail tryouts! How awful and embarrassing would that be? Not only would she have to face Kelly, but she'd have to tell Amari that she didn't make it. No matter how hard Charlie tried to push the thoughts aside, they began to consume her.

After a while Coach called Charlie back in. She jumped up and raced to her position, knowing this might be her last chance to make the team. She had to hustle.

The whistle blew, and the girls exploded. Charlie had to make her own magic happen if she was going to leave a good impression. When at last the ball soared toward her, Charlie didn't waste a moment. She sprinted for it, trapped it, and started for the goal, trying to turn her anxiety into action. Immediately a girl from the red team was on her tail, and then another. Charlie felt her heart racing—she couldn't lose the ball now. This was her chance! But the other team was closing in.

Charlie lunged forward with a burst of adrenaline and pulled away from her competitors faster than she'd ever done before. A thrill rushed through her. She dodged around another girl who was coming toward her, chipped the ball over her outstretched leg, and sped after it. She blew past a halfback and looked around wildly for a teammate, but everyone was too far behind her—she was going to have to take it to the goal alone.

She ran over the field, keeping the opposing team's fullbacks and goalie in sight as their halfbacks and sweeper reversed directions and started charging after her. Seconds later, she closed in on the goal box. The fullbacks thundered toward her, and before Charlie realized what was happening, Kelly's blond braid was swinging in her face.

Charlie ducked and slid around the astonished girl. She tipped the ball out of Kelly's reach, then recovered and sprinted with all her remaining power toward it. A circle of red jerseys closed in around her. With a giant leap, Charlie reached the ball and slammed her foot into it. It soared over Kelly's head at bullet speed. The goalie dived. Her fingers nicked the ball and it flew up, skimmed the bottom side of the goalpost, and bounced into the net.

The blue team cheered. The flabbergasted red team stared. Charlie stared too, breathing hard, almost unable to believe she'd scored a goal. Then she caught Kelly staring intensely at her, and she wasn't smiling. Charlie stopped short, a little shocked by the glare, then decided to ignore it. She turned around, pumped her fist in the air, and started jogging back to her position.

"Nice one, Chuck," Maria said as she passed her. "Girl friend can run like the wind! How'd you do that?"

Charlie grinned. She wasn't sure how she'd done it, and she also wasn't sure she could do it again. "Beginner's luck," she said.

But for the moment she felt invincible. The sluggishness was gone, and her confidence was back. Things were looking up.

The game continued, with Charlie feeling stronger than she'd ever felt. After a few more plays Charlie's teammates began passing the ball to her, and it wasn't long before Charlie was being pursued down the field once more, leaving everybody in her dust except a few teammates who began to anticipate her moves. She passed the ball to Bree as she came sprinting up toward the goal, and the blue team scored again, Charlie taking the assist.

When opposing team members chased after her, Charlie felt a spike of adrenaline—she could play forever! Maybe it was the crisp air, or the different climate, or the fact that Charlie wanted it so badly, she wasn't sure which, but she hoped the feeling would stay.

But the third time Charlie broke away with the ball and raced for the goal, Kelly was ready and waiting, wearing a look that said she was going to get possession no matter what it took.

Charlie didn't see the look. She barely saw Kelly, who came charging toward her. Instead Charlie dodged and wove through the layers of defense. As she maneuvered, Kelly drew near, pulled her leg back, and let it fly. Charlie quickly nudged the ball to a teammate, but with sickening speed, Kelly's foot smashed into Charlie's leg, just above her shin guard. Their bodies collided. The impact rattled Charlie's teeth, and searing pain shot through her. With a horrible scream, Charlie collapsed onto the field.

CHAPTER 11

A Strange Turn of Events

"Foul!" Coach yelled, and came running over.

Kelly slowly got to her feet and staggered over to Charlie. "Are you okay?" she asked.

Charlie writhed on the ground clutching her leg. Pain blinded her. She couldn't breathe, and she felt like she was going to throw up.

Maria rushed to Charlie's side as Kelly melted into the background to walk off her own injuries. Coach knelt down in the grass and examined Charlie. The other players crowded around.

"My leg," Charlie gasped.

"Back up, everybody, please," Coach said, carefully removing Charlie's shin guard and pushing down her sock. She looked at Charlie. "Any other pain besides your leg?"

Charlie shook her head. "No," she whispered. "I'm okay."

"Did you black out or hit your head?"

"No."

"Stomach pain?"

"A little queasy when I look at my leg."

"Yeah, it's swelling up fast, Charlie—I'm worried it could be broken." She glanced quickly at her watch. "The nurse will have left by now. Are your parents around? We should call them and get you checked out." She pulled a cell phone from her pocket.

"My mom's a doctor—she works at the hospital."

"Okay, good. What's the number?"

"I can't remember. It's in my phone, though," Charlie said. "In the locker room." She tried hard not to cry and failed miserably, but the pain was intense. She'd never broken a bone before. Plus, she was surrounded by strangers staring at her, and that just made her feel worse. And what about soccer? A broken leg meant she wouldn't get to play this spring at all. The one thing she was looking forward to in this boring nothing town. She closed her eyes and put her arm over her face.

Coach looked up at the other players. "Any of you know where Charlie's stuff is? We need her phone."

"I'll get it," Maria offered.

Charlie told her the lock combination. Maria broke through the crowd and ran for the building.

Coach looked at Charlie. "You're going to be okay. It might just be a bad bruise, but we should make sure. Do you want to try to stand up? Let's see if you can put any weight on it."

Charlie wiped her eyes with her sleeve and nodded, grateful for the distraction. She pushed herself to a sitting position, and Coach and another girl helped her to stand on her good foot. She slung her arm around Coach's shoulders and tried putting some weight on her bad leg. She yelped in pain but gritted her teeth, and slowly Coach helped her hop to the sideline and sit down in the grass. Coach Candy ran to grab her emergency kit and returned to Charlie's side. She broke open an ice pack and handed it to Charlie, who held it gingerly against the swelling bruise. Not long after, Maria burst out of the school and ran toward them.

"Are you hanging in there with me?" Coach asked. She searched Charlie's face.

"Yeah," said Charlie. "I'm okay."

"Keep the ice on it."

Charlie nodded. She tried not to look at the other players, who were all stealing glances her way. She wished they would stop.

Maria reached them and handed over the phone.

Charlie turned it on and hesitated, staring at her contacts and trying to focus through the threatening tears. She glanced at the staring players, and her lip trembled.

Coach Candy leaned closer. "Do you want some privacy?" she asked in a quiet voice.

Charlie nodded numbly.

"All right," said Coach. "I'll keep the other girls occupied. Maria, stay with Charlie until her mom comes, okay? I'll be nearby if she wants to talk to me."

"Got it, Coach," said Maria.

Charlie nodded again.

"You played great, Charlie. I'm impressed."

Charlie swallowed hard as more tears came. "Thanks." She dialed her mom's new cell phone number and held the phone to her ear.

Coach Candy stepped a few yards away, staying close enough to monitor Charlie, and called out to Kelly, who was dribbling the ball nearby. "You okay to play, Kelly?"

"I'm good, Coach," Kelly said.

Coach yelled to the other girls and clapped her hands. "Okay, everybody! Let's get this game moving. Direct kick blue!"

Charlie's mom's cell phone rang five times and went to voice mail. Charlie hung up and texted her mom to call immediately because of a soccer injury. Then she tried the ER desk and left a message for her mom to call Charlie's cell phone right away.

When Coach Candy saw Charlie set her phone in her lap, she checked in. "Still doing okay? Were you able to reach your mom?"

"I talked to the receptionist," Charlie said. "She's going to tell my mom to call as soon as possible."

Coach nodded and went back to watching the scrimmage.

Maria put her hand on Charlie's shoulder. "Are you doing okay?"

Charlie let a shuddering sigh escape and wiped her eyes with her sleeve. "I just hope it's not broken or my life is over. Kelly can really kick, that's for sure. I hope she didn't do it . . ." She trailed off and shook her head. "Never mind." Of course Kelly wouldn't kick her on purpose—she was just playing the game. It could happen to anybody. Charlie's leg throbbed.

"She's a tough player," Maria said grimly. "I'm sure she feels bad, though. Your leg is swelling up like a balloon. It's horrible."

Charlie squeezed her eyes shut. She leaned back against the bleachers and wondered why her mother was taking so long to call.

A few agonizing minutes later, Charlie's phone rang. "Mom!" said Charlie, fresh tears springing to her eyes. "Finally."

"I got your message. Are you still at school? I'm on my way." She sounded like a doctor. "What's the injury?"

Charlie told her.

"I'll be there in ten minutes," Dr. Wilde said. "Elevate it!"

"Okay, Mom. Gosh," Charlie said, her lip beginning to quiver again, "you don't have to yell."

Charlie's mom's voice softened. "You're right, sweetie. I'm so sorry—I've got my work brain engaged. I bet it hurts a lot."

"What if it's broken?" Charlie's voice pitched upward, and she started crying again. "What if I can't play? This is seriously the worst." She pressed her fingers over her eyelids, trying to stop the tears.

"Hey, at least it wasn't your head," Dr. Wilde said with a laugh. That line was a running joke in their family whenever anybody got hurt, and it annoyed Charlie and Andy whenever their mother said it. "I sure hope we don't have to amputate."

"Not funny, Mother," Charlie said. She rolled her eyes and

looked at Maria, and mouthed, "Doctor humor."

Maria smiled and shrugged. "I'll go tell Coach your mom's coming," she whispered, and Charlie nodded. Maria slipped away.

"You're totally right," Mom said. "I was just trying to keep your mind off the pain. How is it? Do you have ice on it? Is it elevated like I told you?"

"Yeah," said Charlie, wincing as she swiveled around to put her foot up on the bleacher seat. She lay back on the grass. "It's feeling a little better. Just . . . just hurry. Please." Charlie wiped her eyes.

"I am, sweetie. I'll see you soon."

They said good-bye and hung up as Maria came back.

"She'll be here soon," Charlie said. "I'm okay sitting alone if you want to get back in the game."

Maria frowned. "No, it's okay." She sat on the bottom bleacher next to Charlie's foot and looked out over the field, watching the action. "I still can't believe how fast you are. Do you have like Olympian relatives or something?"

"What?" Charlie laughed despite the pain. "No. I was just having a good run, I guess. Until Kelly decided to play like a . . ." She glanced at Maria and bit her lip. "Sorry. I know she was aiming for the ball, not my leg. But jeez, this hurts!" She paused. "How close are you and Kelly?"

"We get along okay," Maria said. "We don't hang out much, but she lives by me, so we carpool if it rains. And we'll watch

76

movies together or kick the ball around or whatever when we're bored. I've known her since preschool."

"Oh."

"She's . . . a lot more fun when there's not an audience," Maria added carefully. "She acts differently when I'm with her one-on-one."

Charlie looked at the sky, remembering the other day when Kelly seemed almost like she was going to confide in Charlie. That was a different Kelly from the one who swept through a crowd of adoring fans, then dissed them behind their backs.

"Anyway," Maria continued, "all I'm saying is, she wouldn't try to hurt you. She's pretty competitive, though, so my guess is she was going to get that ball no matter what, and your leg got in the way."

"That's good to know." It didn't make it better, but Charlie knew she'd been guilty of the same thing in the past. It just hadn't resulted in injuring somebody this badly.

Charlie's mom arrived still wearing her hospital scrubs and carrying the first aid kit she always kept in the car.

"You didn't change?" Charlie asked, surprise in her voice.

"No time for that when my girl is hurt," Dr. Wilde said with a smile. She knelt down in the grass next to Charlie and took her wrist in one hand. Her eyes locked on Charlie's as if she was already assessing the level of pain.

Charlie was familiar with that look.

"All right," said Mom, turning to Charlie's leg, still elevated on the bleacher seat. "Let's see what we've got here." Maria scooted out of the way to make room.

Charlie propped herself up on one elbow and lifted the ice pack. Her mom examined the injury, running her deft hands over the bones from ankle to knee.

"Wow, the swelling has gone way down already," Charlie said, surprised. "You should have seen it twenty minutes ago."

Maria nodded in agreement.

"How does it feel?"

"It hurts," Charlie said, "but it's actually feeling a lot better."

Dr. Wilde nodded. "It's a really nasty contusion, but I'm sure nothing's broken. I don't think we need an X-ray—let's see how the next few hours go." She looked up. "You've got strong bones."

Charlie sighed in relief. "So I might have a soccer season after all? If I make the team, I mean."

"You'll need to take it easy for a few days, but as soon as you feel good putting your full weight on it, you should be fine to play." Charlie's mom looked up as Coach Candy approached.

"Did I hear good news?" Coach asked. She held out her hand to Dr. Wilde. "Hi, I'm Candy Mason, the girls' soccer coach. Sorry to meet under these circumstances."

Mom stood up and shook Coach Candy's hand. "Pleasure. And everything checks out okay. I'm pretty sure it's not broken."

"That's what I thought I heard you say. Everyone will be glad to hear that."

"I think she's done for today, though." Dr. Wilde looked at Charlie. "Did you have a chance to show Coach what you could do?"

"She did," Coach assured her. "The team roster will be posted on my office door before school tomorrow."

Charlie bit her lip and glanced at Maria, who was standing a short distance away. Maria gave her a reassuring nod and made a face.

"Maria can help you get Charlie to the car," Coach said.

"That would be great." Dr. Wilde smiled at Maria, then held out her hand to Charlie to help her get up. Maria smiled back and came over to assist.

Charlie tested her leg and found she could put a little weight on it now. She limped between her mom and Maria, officially introducing them to each other along the way. They chatted about the scrimmage, and once they reached the car and Charlie was safely inside, Maria said a hasty good-bye. "I'll call you later to see how you're doing," she said.

Charlie's face lit up. "Okay."

Maria waved and bounded back to the field.

At home Charlie's mom helped Charlie change into sweats and a T-shirt, and then got her settled on the couch with her leg propped up. Charlie automatically pushed her bracelet up her arm.

"Is that new?" asked Charlie's mom, pointing to it.

Charlie glanced at it. "Yeah. It was in a package on the front step with my name on it on the day we moved away. Do you have any idea who it's from? Grandma, maybe?"

Dr. Wilde studied the bracelet. "What a thoughtful gift! No, nobody said anything to me. Maybe Amari sent it?"

"No, I asked her already."

"I guess it's a mystery," Mom said with a smile. She turned and took another assessment of Charlie's injury. "Wow," she said, surprised. "It's looking remarkably better. You must be a fast healer. Have you been eating extra veggies?"

Charlie laughed, thinking of all the pizza they'd had lately. "Not exactly."

Charlie's mom squeezed her hand. "Well, whatever you're doing, keep doing it." She smiled and picked up the TV remote, setting it on the coffee table between Charlie's backpack and her glass of water. "There, now you're all set for a while. If you need anything before Dad gets home, just yell for Andy."

Charlie's face fell. "Aren't you staying?"

Dr. Wilde sighed, looking truly sorry. "I have to get back to the hospital."

"Oh." Charlie turned her head away.

"I'm sorry, honey. I really hope it feels better soon." She brushed a strand of hair off Charlie's face.

"It's okay," Charlie mumbled. "You know, it's kind of weird— it hardly even hurts anymore."

When Maria called to check in, Charlie was cozily snuggled in her own bed, reading her favorite fantasy novel.

"Hi, Maria," Charlie said.

"Chuck! You sound happier than you did."

"My leg feels a lot better," said Charlie. "I've been icing it. And my dog, Jessie, has been licking it. Which is kind of gross, actually, but thoughtful, I suppose."

"Oh cool, you have a dog? Me too. A couple of them. Big ones."

"Yes! Jessie is the best. We also have two cats."

"I wish we could have a cat," said Maria, "but one of my step-brothers is allergic."

"You can borrow ours if you want to come over sometime."

"Sure!"

They talked for almost an hour about all sorts of things they had in common, and about their differences, too, like in what they enjoyed reading.

"Do you like horse books?" asked Maria.

"They're okay," said Charlie. "I like books with fantasy more, though, and I just started reading graphic novels."

"Ooh, I love comics!" said Maria.

"Well, I've never read an *actual* comic book," Charlie admitted.

"But I'd like to try one. I just . . . I'm not sure where to start, I guess."

"You should try Spider-Gwen or Ms. Marvel," Maria said. "They're about high school girls, not stupid old guys. I'll lend them to you when Mac is done reading. He and I trade comics all the time."

"Thanks," said Charlie, beaming.

By the time they hung up, Charlie was feeling so much better that she forgot to text Amari about her injury.

Maybe living in Navarro Junction wasn't going to be so bad after all.

CHAPTER 12

The Roster

When Charlie woke up the next morning, she walked all the way to the bathroom before she remembered her injured leg. It didn't hurt at all. There was barely any swelling. The red and purple bruising had faded to green and yellow on her skin. Only fifteen hours earlier she'd thought it was broken, and now it was practically healed.

That's so crazy, thought Charlie as she took the bracelet off her wrist and turned on the shower.

At breakfast Charlie's dad hurried into the kitchen with his tie loose around his neck and a pair of socks in his hand, looking frazzled. "Oh," he said, giving her a strange look. "You're up and about. Are you going to school today?"

"Um, yes," said Charlie, narrowing her eyes at him. "Why wouldn't I? What's going on?"

Dad started yanking on his socks. "I've got an early meeting I forgot to tell you about," he said. "Can you be ready to go in five minutes?"

"What?" Charlie dropped her spoon into her cereal bowl and stared. "Dad! Clearly not. I have to finish getting ready." She got up and started toward the stairs. "What about Andy?"

"I remembered to tell him," Charlie's dad mumbled apologetically. "He's ready."

"Dad!" she said again.

"I'm sorry. I thought you were staying home from school because of your leg."

"Are you kidding? The team roster will be posted this morning. I have to be there! Can't Mom drive me?"

"She's sleeping after pulling a double shift. She got home at four in the morning."

Charlie sighed. "Maybe she should just live at the hospital." She ran upstairs and grabbed her bracelet and earrings from the bathroom counter, putting them on as she went to her room to finish getting dressed. Her homework sat on her desk, only half completed. She'd been planning to finish it this morning.

"Just go with Andy," she called out, exasperated but trying not to shout too loud so she wouldn't wake her mother. "I'm not ready yet, so I'll walk to school."

"Are you sure? Doesn't your leg hurt? Do you know the way?"

"My leg's fine," she said, roaming around her room trying to find her shoes. "I know there's a shortcut through the football stadium. Lots of kids go that way."

Dr. Wilde bounded up the staircase and appeared in Charlie's bedroom doorway holding his briefcase and overcoat. "You're sure?" he asked.

Charlie rolled her eyes. "Dad, you don't have to worry about me. I used to take the "L" train to school, remember?"

"Yes, but—"

"So as long as I don't walk into a cactus, I'm pretty sure I'll be just fine."

Dr. Wilde looked at his daughter. "But you're just a little kid in a strange new neighborhood," he said finally, a small smile tugging at the corners of his mouth.

Charlie could tell he was having a sentimental moment. "Dad, stop," she said. "I already know how to get everywhere. This whole town is like the size of Navy Pier."

Charlie's dad let out a sigh as Andy sauntered by with his backpack. "All right. Be careful. Walk with other students. Watch for cars, and—"

"Now you're embarrassing yourself."

Dr. Wilde laughed and reached out to tousle Charlie's hair.

She reared back. "Dude, don't mess with the tresses!"

"Dude?" he shook his head. "My daughter just called me dude. Wow. Can't wait to tell the students about this."

Charlie grinned. "Get to work. Oh—by the way, I'm staying after school today to help with the set, if that's okay with you."

"The set?" asked Dr. Wilde, puzzled.

Charlie followed. "Yeah. For the musical we're doing in theater class. Is that okay?"

"Ah, sure," said Dr. Wilde. He set down his briefcase and

slipped on his jacket. Andy hollered from the front door, wondering if he was coming.

Charlie raised an eyebrow. "You didn't even remember I'm taking theater, did you?"

"Um . . . ," Dr. Wilde said absently. He whirled around, looking for something, and picked up his briefcase. "Where'd I put my coffee?" He headed down. "Love you, Charlie! Have a great day."

"Love you too," Charlie said, stepping out into the hallway to watch him descend. "Maybe if you're not being embarrassing, I'll let you drive me home."

Charlie's dad rounded the corner into the kitchen below and disappeared from sight.

"I'll text you if I need a ride," she called after him, and then shrugged. It was odd to see her dad preoccupied and rushing off to work like that. She finished getting ready, noting that she was running out of clean clothes to wear. At least tomorrow they'd be unpacking the rest of their stuff.

She hurried through the math problems she had to finish. They were harder than she'd expected. Finally she got the work done, grabbed her backpack, and left the house, locking the door behind her.

She hurried through the neighborhood toward school. Seeing some familiar-looking students ahead of her, she followed them down a path that linked Charlie's neighborhood with the ones next to it.

This must be the shortcut, Charlie thought. On the phone last night, Maria had told her that there were seven or eight neighborhoods in a circle around the junior high, and all of them were connected by walking paths. Charlie had told Maria where she lived, and Maria figured out that her house was on the opposite side of the school grounds from Charlie's—but it wasn't very far because of the shortcut. She explained that some paths led to the municipal football field next to school, where all the kids converged and streamed through the gate to the school property.

Charlie kept an eye on the time and began picking up speed. She wanted to get to Coach Candy's office before class so she could see if she made the team, and she had no idea how long it would take to walk to school this way.

After a few minutes Charlie began to worry that she wasn't going to make it in time. And then she wondered if this was even the right way to her school. She didn't actually know for sure—what if all these kids walking in this direction were going somewhere else?

Charlie knew it was silly. They were all wearing backpacks like her. She thought about asking one of the kids she passed, but she chickened out—because, what a dumb question! Instead, she moved faster along the path and remembered the first time she'd taken the "L" train to school all by herself—she'd had the same worries. But at least back then she'd traveled it with her dad several times first to make sure she was familiar with the route.

Charlie laughed to herself. Amari would totally make fun of her for being nervous about walking through neighborhoods like these. She pulled out her phone and took a quick Snapchat of her view as she hurried to school, and sent it to her Chicago friends.

Finally Charlie saw football bleachers and goalposts, and the rooftops of school buildings beyond it. Relief washed through her. She began sprinting toward them, past the other students, still anxious about making it to Coach's office in time. Her leg felt as good as ever—maybe even better than ever, if that was possible. And before she knew it, she was flying across the grass. Charlie had never run this fast before. It was completely crazy. And kind of awesome.

"Hey, Chuck!" Maria called as Charlie whizzed by.

Charlie slowed as Maria ran to catch up. Mac trailed behind her.

"Hi," Charlie said, catching her breath. "I didn't want to be late."

"I thought you broke your leg," Mac said when he caught up to the girls.

"I told you it *wasn't* broken," Maria said, sounding mildly annoyed. "We just thought at first that it might be." She turned to Charlie and linked arms with her, tugging her toward school. Charlie glanced back at Mac, who was frowning at his phone. He looked up and all around, like he was searching for someone.

"Are you coming, Mac?" Charlie asked.

"Yep," Mac said, beginning to follow. "Just looking for some-body." He texted rapidly as he walked.

"Who?" asked Maria. She slowed slightly, and Mac caught up.

"Jason Baker. He needs me to jailbreak his phone."

"What's he trying to do?"

"Apps, hotspot, text from Lock screen. The usual."

Charlie looked at Mac curiously. She had only a vague idea of what he was talking about.

"Is it really necessary to be able to text from the Lock screen?" Maria said with a hint of condescension.

"It's ten bucks," said Mac, shrugging. "Besides, you do it."

"I wouldn't pay to have it done, though."

Mac gave her the side-eye. "Because I didn't charge you for it." He scanned the students again, and his face brightened. "There he is." He ran a short distance ahead to where two paths converged. A boy handed Mac his phone and a ten-dollar bill. Mac pocketed the device and the money and kept walking with Jason.

"Nice gig," Charlie said to Maria.

"Yeah . . . kids pay him to do all sorts of tech stuff. Heck, even my mom paid him to set up our modem router thingy." Maria looked Charlie up and down. "So you're okay? You were running superfast. Your leg doesn't hurt?"

"Not really," Charlie said.

"That's . . . a little strange," Maria said. "Don't you think it's strange?"

"I guess." Charlie shrugged. "I'm just glad it feels better."

Maria pressed her lips together but didn't say anything else. They walked into the gymnasium and jostled their way through the swarm of students toward Coach Candy's office.

Kelly joined up with them as they reached Coach's door, and everyone crowded in front of the list posted there.

A few girls walked away quickly, frowning or with heads down. Others whooped and high-fived. Kelly and Maria pushed in, straining to see, and almost simultaneously shouted, "Yes!"

Charlie hopped up and down, trying to see over the others to get a look. Finally she squeezed between two girls and stood in front of the list.

She scanned over Kelly's name, then Maria's. Her eyes traveled all the way to the bottom. And there, the second to the last name, was Charlie Wilde.

CHAPTER 13

Friend Problems

Charlie brought her fingers to her lips, a grin spreading over her face. She'd made the soccer team in spite of the injury. What a relief!

"Yes!" she whispered. She skittered out of the way of other girls who were trying to see, and ended up face-to-face with Kelly.

"Congratulations," Kelly said.

"Oh," Charlie said. "Thanks, you too."

"You made it?" squealed Maria.

Charlie laughed. "I made it!"

"Of course you did! You played terrific!" Maria whooped and threw her arms open wide and hugged Charlie, and they jumped around together in the hallway like they'd been best friends for-ever.

Kelly tilted her head, a suspicious look on her face as she watched Charlie hopping around.

When they came to a stop, Kelly put her hand on her hip. "So, Charlotte, how's your leg?"

"It's much better," Charlie said.

"That's really great to hear. Because Coach sort of ripped

into me after tryouts for playing rough, so I really hope it wasn't because you were faking it. Because then we'd have a problem."

Charlie stared, the smile fading from her lips and her eyes narrowing. "No, I wasn't faking it, Kelly," she said. "In fact, I was kind of wondering if you intentionally tried to kick me."

"*What?* Of course not!" Kelly said. "I'm just saying you don't seem very injured after telling everybody it was broken."

Charlie felt her face growing hot, and her voice became quieter. "I never said it was broken," she responded, taking a step toward Kelly so their faces were inches apart. "Coach did. And luckily for you it wasn't broken because—"

"*Cálmate, chicas*," Maria interrupted in a low voice. "Are you *trying* to get kicked off the team right now? Because Coach is just behind that door."

Charlie glanced over her shoulder at the clouded-glass inset in the door. She could see the shadow of Coach's upper body sitting behind her desk inside. Charlie's mouth twitched in anger, but she relaxed her posture and took a step away from Kelly. "I'm going to class," she muttered as the bell rang.

"Good call," Maria said with a slight shake of the head. She flashed a puzzled look at Kelly and went with Charlie to first period.

Kelly dropped her gaze. She hesitated a moment, but the three girls were all going to the same class, so she had no choice but to follow.

* * *

At lunch Charlie found Maria and Mac. Kelly sat at the popular table a short distance away as usual. Now that a few hours had passed and Charlie'd had time to cool off, she felt a little silly about how defensive she'd been. She set down her tray across from Maria, then went up to Kelly and apologized. "Hi . . . I'm sorry for getting in your face this morning."

"Oh, no problem!" said Kelly with a smile. She raised an eyebrow at her friends, who watched the exchange with wide eyes and too-innocent faces.

Charlie hesitated, a sense of dread filling her. She knew what that meant—Kelly would be talking about her later. But there was nothing she could do about it. If she said anything else it would just give Kelly more to talk about. So she went back to her table. When she glanced at Kelly, she saw her lean over and whisper something to her tablemates that made them snicker.

"Blurgh," said Charlie, flopping into her chair. Mac's head was down and his food untouched as he worked on Jason Baker's phone under the table.

"What's wrong?" asked Maria.

"I don't know. I'm not sure what Kelly's deal is."

"What do you mean?" Maria asked. "Are you talking about this morning?"

Charlie bit into her cheeseburger—she was starving. She chewed, swallowed, and said carefully, "I can't figure her out. I don't think she likes me very much, but I'm not sure why."

"Well," said Maria, "you did kind of get in her face."

"She did?" asked Mac, looking up. "Dang, I missed it."

"Yeah," Charlie admitted. "But I just apologized."

"Do you get in people's faces a lot?" Mac asked.

Charlie turned to him and pretended to be tough. "You wanna find out?"

"Whoa," said Mac, leaning back. He laughed.

Charlie grinned sheepishly. "I learned how to fake being tough in Chicago in case I ever got into a scary situation on the 'L' train. But yeah, I mean, I'd much rather avoid conflict if possible."

"Oh," said Mac, sounding a bit disappointed. He went back to work under the table.

Charlie shrugged and turned to Maria, her face clouding. "Anyway, it made me mad when Kelly said I was faking. She really kicked me hard—as hard as . . . as hard as a . . ." Charlie struggled to find a comparison.

"Kangaroo?" suggested Mac, not looking up.

"Yeah! And everybody at tryouts saw how bad it looked."

"Sometimes you have to ignore Kelly," Maria said.

"Maybe." But Charlie wasn't ignoring her now. She watched as several people from Kelly's table looked over at her. She lowered her voice. "Now they're talking about me. Look."

Maria leaned forward and put her hand on Charlie's arm. "Can I give you some friendly advice?"

"Sure."

"Try not to get too caught up in things with Kelly—she's . . . well, she's not the easiest friend to have right now."

"Oh," said Charlie, confused. "Okay."

"Truth is, she was probably just embarrassed that you got past her defense. And it's no fun when Coach has a talk with you, you know? Kelly's not all bad. And things will be better when you're on the same team as her, working together." She smiled. "But for now you've got me." She glanced at Mac, who was eating Tater Tots and staring at Jason's phone. "Us, I mean. Right, Mac?"

"Yeah, sure," Mac said, not looking up. He pushed his chair back, picked up his tray, and stood. "I need to plug in to finish Jason's jailbreak, and then we're going to check out some new apps. Later."

"Wait!"said Maria, shoving her chair in his path so he couldn't get past her. "We haven't talked all day. Are you coming over after school?"

Mac grinned. "Of course. Plus, I told your mom I'd defrag her ancient desktop, so I'll get that started if I beat you there. You get the new Avengers yet?"

"Yeah, it's on my desk. Are you finished with Ms. Marvel or Spider-Gwen? Charlie wants to read one."

"Yep, I'm done. They were both actually pretty awesome. I'll bring them tomorrow." He looked at Charlie. "You like comics?"

Charlie nodded and then blushed. "I mean, I think I will. Maria convinced me I should try one."

"You should," Mac said. He looked around and spotted some-one, then tapped the back of Maria's chair impatiently so he could pass. "Okay. See you after school."

"Bye." Maria pulled in her chair, and Mac skirted around it and went to the tray drop-off.

Maria watched him go and sighed. "Whatever."

"What's wrong?"

Maria shook her head. "I don't know. . . ."

Charlie studied her. It seemed like she did know. "Something with Mac?" she asked.

"I guess. I don't think he likes hanging out with me at school anymore. Not much, anyway."

"Why not?"

Maria shrugged. She finished her milk and smashed the carton. "We've had lunch together almost every day since second grade, but things have been different lately," she said glumly.

"Well," said Charlie, "he seemed happy enough to be going to your house after school. Does he do that a lot?"

"Yeah, he acts normal there. He's practically a member of my family. He even hangs out with them when I'm not home."

"That's cool." Charlie watched through the cafeteria window as Mac slapped hands with Jason Baker and another boy and they set off together. "Maybe he just wants to hang out with some guys too?"

"Maybe," Maria said. "Oh well. Hey, do you wanna come over after school too?"

"I can't," Charlie said. "I told Mr. Anderson I'd help with *Bye Bye Birdie*. We're building the set."

"That dude's such a nut ball. Isn't Kelly acting in that show? Will she be there too?"

"No idea. She might be too big of a star to do crew work." Charlie grinned.

Maria gave a sympathetic smile. "She's probably the last person you want to face with a hammer in her hand at this point. Is she one of the leads again?"

"Do you even have to ask?"

They giggled and got up to put their trays away.

"Maybe tomorrow or Sunday would work to hang out, though," Charlie said.

"Oh good. I'll text you my address," Maria said. "Have a good one. Break a leg! Or wait—maybe not."

"Ha-ha. I'll try not to," Charlie said.

CHAPTER 14

A Powerful Shock

After school Charlie made her way to the auditorium and found Mr. Anderson. Soon he had her wielding a saw, cutting planks for a train station platform. Sara, the stage manager, came by and checked her work, and the two chatted for a few minutes. But most of the time Charlie happily focused on her task and was content to listen while the others joked and sang bits of songs from the musical and talked about their plans for the weekend. Apparently some of them were going to the Phoenix Zoo, which was having a big event. It was weird to think about going there in February. She wondered if the zoo had penguins and polar bears and other animals that might prefer cold to heat. And if they did . . . did those animals miss their old homes too?

About a half hour into her work Charlie heard a familiar voice. She looked up, and her shoulders slumped. The queen had arrived.

"Hi, everyone!" Kelly said. "I just couldn't stay away when I knew you were all here working hard." She walked to the wing, addressing a few of her adoring fans. "I'm finished rehearsing my songs with the accompanist, and I'm here to help." She wore her blond hair down today and flipped it over her shoulders.

Kelly put down her music folder, rolled up her sleeves, and started working right away. Charlie watched her and was surprised to find that the girl seemed to know what she was doing backstage as well as onstage. And she definitely knew how to get along with everyone—at least to their faces, Charlie thought sarcastically.

When Sara called for help sweeping up sawdust, Kelly went right over to her and grabbed a broom. Maybe Maria was right, and Kelly was a decent person. Maybe Charlie had been a little too quick to judge. Maria obviously saw something good in her.

Charlie decided she could start trying harder to be friendly next week. After all, she'd apologized to Kelly earlier. Now it was Kelly's move. Charlie quickly began sawing the next plank with renewed gusto. Things were coming along well with her work. It was going to be so cool to see the finished platform onstage during the show and know that she'd built it! She texted her dad, letting him know the set building was going well and not to pick her up on his way home from work because she wanted to finish—she would walk home when she was done with everything.

Kelly left Charlie alone, or perhaps she didn't realize she was there. Whatever the case, their coexistence was working fine until the other crew kids started trickling out the door to go home, or to practice, or to piano lessons, or to whatever else they had going on. Charlie was finished cutting the boards for the entire train platform, and she had just a few more planks to nail into place, when Mr. Anderson called to her.

"Charlie, can you give Kelly a hand with this bed? We need to move it offstage to the back corner where all the 'Kim's bedroom' props will be."

"Sure," Charlie said. She got up and wiped the sawdust off her jeans, then pulled back the curtain and went to where Kelly waited by the foot of the bed. On top of the mattress was a frilly comforter and pillow set.

"I guess I'll take the heavy end," Charlie said, going to the headboard side.

"Don't hurt yourself," Kelly said sweetly.

Anger bubbled in Charlie's gut, but she remembered her vow. "I'll try not to," she said. She bent her knees, gripped the bottom of the headboard, and on the count of three, the two girls lifted it up.

"Jeez," Kelly said. "This thing is made of bricks."

"Beggars can't be choosers," sang Mr. Anderson from somewhere backstage.

"Whatever that means," said Kelly under her breath.

"I think it means we got the bed for free," said Charlie.

They heard the main doors to the auditorium open, and Mr. Anderson went to see who was coming in.

Charlie began to walk backward with the heavy end. "Watch your step here," she called out as she led the way down the ramp backstage. It was dimly lit. Charlie looked over her shoulder for the glow tape that marked the corners and edges of the steps so she wouldn't lose her footing.

Kelly struggled on the other end. "It's so dark back here. This thing is heavy."

"Quit whining," Charlie muttered, but Kelly wasn't listening— her ears were attuned elsewhere.

Mr. Anderson gave a joyful greeting to whoever had entered. Kelly quit complaining long enough to listen, and they could hear the sound of a young man's voice floating through the auditorium.

Kelly's eyes opened wide. She stopped walking, which nearly pulled the bed out of Charlie's grasp.

"What the—" Charlie began, fuming and trying to get a better grip on the bed, but Kelly shushed her.

"It's Hickory James!" she hissed. "Last year's Gaston from *Beauty and the Beast*. He's in high school now. Oh my gah—how's my hair? I have to go say hi! Dropping this now, bye!" And with that she let go of the bed and ran to the stage.

Charlie lunged forward, cringing. *Rude!* Then she stared at the bed, stunned, as she realized something even more horrifying than Kelly's behavior.

Kelly's end of the bed hadn't fallen to the floor.

Charlie was holding it—all of it. The entire bed.

All by herself.

CHAPTER 15

OUT. OF. CONTROL.

Charlie stared at the bed, held suspended by her own two hands. "What the—!" She let go of it and instinctively jumped backward as it thudded to the floor. She stood there a moment in shock. Had that really just happened? Had she been holding an entire bed by herself? It wasn't possible.

A cold sweat broke out on her forehead, and her stomach roiled. She whirled at the sound of Mr. Anderson and Kelly laughing in the auditorium. "I have to get out of here," she murmured. She took off out the stage right exit, went down the hallway, and ducked into the girls' bathroom.

Once inside, Charlie ran into a stall and slammed the door behind her so hard that the top hinge broke off. The door swung wildly and came to an abrupt stop, hanging limp and at a strange angle from the bottom hinge. Charlie didn't notice. She dropped to her knees in front of the toilet, hands shaking as she gripped the seat—she felt sick. She closed her eyes and felt her heart pounding, her breath becoming more labored, her stomach churning as she thought about all the strange things that were happening to her. Because they *were* strange—very strange. Running faster than she'd ever run before. Healing from a serious injury virtually overnight. Being strong enough to hold that entire bed by herself? That was insane! She couldn't brush the incidents off anymore. They weren't normal. Nothing about her was normal lately.

She clenched her jaw, wanting to scream. What was going on? Her grip tightened on the toilet seat as the frustration grew inside her. Her skin burned, and she could feel herself losing control. "Why is this happening?" she whispered. "Why? Why?" With each plea, she gripped the toilet seat tighter, and with one final cry, she pounded it with her fists.

The seat shattered, and the pieces fell all around. Water splashed up in her face.

Charlie stared. "How is this even possible?" she cried. "What is happening to me?" She backed out of the stall and lunged toward the sinks, grabbing hold of one and staring at herself in the mirror above it. A stranger with her own face looked back at her—or at least it felt that way. The girl in the mirror looked normal. Scared, sure, but ordinary. Yet inside Charlie felt like some strange force had taken over her body.

She twisted the faucet so she could splash clean water on her face, but the handle broke off in her hand and a stream of water sprayed from it. "Ugh! No!" she cried. With a surge of strength and frustration coursing through her, she slammed her hands down on the sink. It gave a loud groan and broke loose from the wall, coming away in her hands. Water spurted out of the pipe behind it. Charlie's jaw dropped as she stared at the devastation, barely comprehending what was happening.

The water continued to spray everywhere, soaking her, but Charlie hardly felt it. Instead she threw the sink against the wall, yelling incoherently. The sink cracked and fell to the floor, breaking in half.

The shock of the noise finally brought Charlie to her senses. She put her hands up to her face and pushed her wet hair from her eyes. Water kept coming down on her. What was happening? Her left arm ached. At first she thought she'd injured it. She pushed up her soggy sleeve to examine it but soon realized it was throbbing with heat beneath the bracelet.

"The bracelet!" she whispered. She punched the button to release the clasp, but it wouldn't open. She tugged at it as hard as she could, but it held fast. At the same time, with water streaming down her, she finally realized the full extent of the damage she had caused. She knew she had to get out of there before someone saw her.

She raced to the door and flung it open with far too much strength. The handle hit the wall, leaving a chunk of tile crumbling to the floor. But Charlie didn't stop to look at it. She ran.

She went past the distant voices of Mr. Anderson, Kelly, and the high school guy. Past the dark box office window and the banner that hung overhead, greeting visitors. Charlie pushed through the exit doors and out into the cool evening air, but she didn't stop.

She ran across the empty parking lot, over the track and soccer field, through the line of mesquite trees that bordered the municipal football field. Finally, when she was safely far away from school, she stopped running and began pawing madly at her wrist, trying to get the bracelet off.

It wouldn't budge. It was stuck.

If she was strong enough to rip a sink out of a wall, why couldn't she get this stupid bracelet off her arm? Charlie didn't know what to do. She didn't know where to turn. All she knew was that ever since she'd started wearing the bracelet she had somehow gained ridiculous speed, extraordinary strength, and the power to heal herself. She dropped to her knees, put her face in the grass, and yelled—she had to yell. She had to get out her frustration. She could only hope that the earth muffled her yells enough to keep others from hearing her, because she was totally OOC right now. Out. Of. Control.

After a few minutes of breathing deeply and trying to get a handle on things, Charlie sat up. She got to her feet. There was no one around. Slowly she continued walking toward home. Guilt flooded her when she thought of the damage she'd done to the girls' bathroom. It was so insanely impossible that she wondered if she'd only imagined it. Maybe she was so stressed out from moving that her mind was messing with her. How could this be happening? And how could she make it stop if she couldn't get the bracelet off?

She'd have to cut it off somehow. Maybe the saw that she'd used to make the platform would be sharp enough. On second thought, that was probably a really bad idea. Maybe her parents had a safer tool that could break through the metal band. Though the location of the toolbox in their garage at the moment was anybody's guess.

As Charlie neared her neighborhood, she grew calmer, and her thoughts began to come together. Who could even make a device like this? And why would someone send it to her? She shook her head, marveling at the abilities she'd gained from it. Superspeed, amazing strength, crazy healing powers . . . it sounded good when she thought about it, anyway. But it wasn't so great if she couldn't control it.

By the time she neared the driveway she was calm enough to realize she'd have to explain her sodden appearance. Not to mention her missing backpack, which she'd left backstage, filled with the weekend's homework assignments. As she began to think of an excuse, she looked up and stopped short. Sitting on her front step was Maria, who was staring incredulously at her phone screen.

"Oh," Charlie said. Her hand flew to her hair to smooth it. "Hi. I, um . . . you found my house."

Maria looked up and studied her, a strange expression on her face. "What happened to you?" she asked. She stood as Charlie approached.

"I got a little wet," Charlie said.

Maria frowned and folded her arms. "Explain."

"I—well, I was working on the set for the play."

"Yeah?"

"And I got hot," Charlie said carefully. It wasn't a lie.

Maria tilted her head.

"And, uh, I got sprayed with water, and I feel cooler now. Gotta stay hydrated here in the desert. I'm learning."

"Is that right?" Maria stared her down.

"Yep," Charlie said weakly. "So, what are you doing here?"

Maria clicked her phone off and shoved it into her back pocket. "I got a text message from Kelly that the girls' bathroom by the auditorium exploded. And there was water everywhere." She crossed her arms.

Charlie blinked. "Oh, really?" she said, feeling the blood drain from her face. "That's horrible."

Maria didn't waver. "She said you'd been there, but you just disappeared." When Charlie didn't offer any further comment, Maria uncrossed her arms and put her hands on her hips. "Spill it, Chuck," she said. "I'm on to you. I know what's up. You might not read comics, but I do." Her eyes threw out a challenge. "And I know exactly what you are."

Charlie's heart thudded. Her voice faltered. "Y-you do?"

"Please. I'm not stupid," she said. She leaned forward, a joking smile playing at her lips, and said quietly, "You're a superhero."

CHAPTER 16

The Secret's Out

"I'm a—what?" Charlie said, and then she laughed in spite of her situation because the thought was so ridiculous. "No, I don't think so."

"I'm serious," Maria said, with mock sincerity. "You know what I mean—you're, like, what do you call it? Emerging. Just realizing your powers, like Peter Parker after he gets bitten but before he figures out he's Spider-Man." She punched Charlie lightly in the arm. "I can't believe this is happening right here in our little town. Superheroes usually live in big cities. . . ." She trailed off, scratching her head. "Hey . . . *you're* from a big city." She wagged her eyebrows. "See what I mean?"

"Maria, stop."

Maria narrowed her eyes. "Okay." She studied Charlie for a long moment, and then tilted her head in earnest. "Wait, though. The more I think about it . . . and you . . . and the strange things you're doing . . ." She paused, deep in thought. "Nooo," she whispered. And then slowly she said, "But . . . seriously. Do you have any other explanation for the weird things that are happening?"

Charlie dropped her gaze and didn't answer.

"Have you always been able to run really fast?" Maria asked. "And heal overnight? And . . . and did *you* break the bathroom? I mean, look at you." Her voice softened. "You can trust me."

Charlie stared hard at the driveway. "I don't know what you mean."

"Come on," Maria said, putting her hand on Charlie's arm. "Were you born like this? Or did something, you know, *happen* to you? Is that why you moved here, because people were on to you? 'Cause you're kind of freaky."

"No, that's not why we moved!" Charlie said, offended. But she knew by now there'd be no skirting around the issue or pretending it didn't exist. Maria had figured her out. Maybe she could help her decide what to do. Charlie sighed heavily. "Can you keep a secret?"

"Yes, of course."

"It—this all just started the other day." She sighed and glanced at the house. The car was in the driveway, and the light in her dad's den was on. "Come on. Let's take a walk."

"Yeah, sure," said Maria with a look of concern. "You okay, Charlie?"

"I . . . I'm not really sure, to be totally honest."

The two girls walked down the driveway and turned onto the road. Charlie hesitated, thinking about what to say. Everything sounded so bizarre in her head—it was hard to explain. But she also knew Maria wasn't going to take some lame excuse for an answer.

Maria remained quiet, waiting for Charlie to begin.

Charlie blew out a breath and absently tried to comb through her now-dry hair with her fingers, but soon gave up. "Okay, well, this is going to sound extremely weird," she said finally, "but I don't know what else it could be. I think the problem is this bracelet." She pulled up her sleeve and held out her arm for Maria to see.

Maria gripped Charlie's arm and studied the bracelet but didn't touch it. "What about it? Is it radioactive? Did an alien give it to you?"

"Stop," said Charlie, annoyed.

"I was being serious," said Maria.

"No. It was a gift . . . I think," Charlie said. "I thought it was one of those athletic bracelets that records heart rate, distance, speed—that kind of stuff. I put it on the other day for the first time, and nothing changed." She hesitated, wondering about Thursday morning when she ran to her desk in first period and it skidded into the aisle—but she wasn't sure that was so out of the ordinary.

Charlie went on. "I felt pretty normal until soccer tryouts, I guess. I didn't really realize anything was happening. Not at first, anyway. I mean, I figured I was just having a good scrimmage, you know? I didn't really pay attention to how fast I was running because I was just playing the game. But looking back now I know you're right—that was crazy. And my leg . . ."

They approached a streetlamp, and Charlie stopped under it.

She pulled up her pant leg. "See?"

Maria gasped. "There's hardly anything there! That's insane. I saw it—I saw how bad it looked. I thought it was broken too." She looked closer. "Are you sure that's the leg she kicked?" Immediately after asking, she apologized. "Of course you are. That was a dumb question."

"It's okay. I doubted it too." Charlie dropped her pant leg, and they resumed walking. "I don't understand it. And then today . . ." She buried her face in her hands, mortified by what she'd done to the bathroom. It was such an impossible thing that she didn't even know how to claim responsibility for it. No one would believe that a twelve-year-old girl could rip a sink from the wall. And it's not like it was her fault. She didn't try to wreck anything! It was the stupid bracelet.

She glanced at Maria. "Did Kelly say she thought I did that to the bathroom?"

Maria shook her head. "No, she just mentioned you'd left. I . . ." She flashed Charlie a guilty look. "Once she told me what was happening in the bathroom, I sort of asked her if you were still there, because, well, that's the first question that came to mind, I guess, after seeing the other weird stuff that you were doing. And when you came up the driveway all soaking wet . . . How the heck did it happen, anyway?"

Charlie recounted the after-school events, telling Maria how shocked she'd been at being able to hold the bed all by herself when Kelly ran off to see that Hickory James boy. And she talked about how confused and angry she'd felt with all the weird stuff that was happening to her. "I never meant to break anything," Charlie said. "You have to believe me. I felt like I was in a bathroom made of newspaper and toothpicks—that's how easy it was to wreck things." She glanced sidelong at her new friend. "Look, I know you don't know me very well, but breaking up bathrooms is totally not my style."

Maria put her arm around Charlie's shoulders as they walked. "Of course I believe you. If it helps, Kelly said the janitor was still on campus and got the water shut off right away, so at least there won't be any damage from that."

"That's a relief."

"But I don't get it—why don't you just take the bracelet off?"

"That's the problem," Charlie said. "It's stuck on me! I tried to rip it off after the bathroom thing, and it's totally impossible. I don't know what happened. I've taken it off before a bunch of times."

"Maybe it's jammed." Maria looked at the bracelet again. "If I touch it, is it going to, like, do anything to me?"

"I don't think so."

Gingerly, Maria examined the bracelet. "What's this pentagon-shaped symbol with the logo inside?"

"What are you talking about?"

Maria pointed. "Here."

Charlie squinted at it, barely making it out in the darkness. "No idea."

Maria shrugged and tried to undo the clasp. She yanked and tugged and even tried to bite it, but nothing happened. Then she tapped the screen. "What's the deal with this?"

"I don't know. There's never been anything on it. I haven't been able to get the buttons to work either. I think it just needs one of those little watch batteries. I was planning to buy one this weekend."

"Hmm," said Maria. When they passed under another streetlamp, she held up Charlie's wrist and pressed her cheek against Charlie's arm, trying to peer under the face of the bracelet. "It doesn't look like there's a place to put a battery." Then Maria attempted to twist the bracelet around Charlie's wrist, but because of its oval shape, it couldn't rotate. "I doubt you'll be able to slip it off either."

"I haven't tried with soap yet, but I don't think it'll budge . . . unless I slice off my thumb first."

Maria cringed. "Ick."

"I'm going to see if I can find something to cut it with."

"Good luck," Maria muttered. "This thing is solid metal. Don't do anything stupid that would cut your hand off."

"That *would* solve the problem, though," Charlie said.

Maria smiled and let go of Charlie's arm. "Yes, but then you'll probably have to sit out soccer for the season."

"Not the way I heal," Charlie said. "I'll be out a day, maybe two, tops."

"That would be really funny if things weren't so awful." Maria grew serious. "Are you going to tell your parents?"

Charlie was quiet for a long moment. "I don't know," she said quietly. "They've got a lot going on right now. My mom's working all the time, and my dad's trying to figure out his new job. . . . They're a little too busy for me right now, I guess." Charlie's face clouded, but then she added, "I don't want to bug them with this if I can figure it out myself."

Maria squeezed Charlie's shoulder, faced her, and made a promise. "Whatever happens, Charlie, I'm here for you. I'll help you get through this."

Charlie felt a wave of relief. She had never needed a friend as much as she did right now. It was exactly what she'd hoped to hear.

CHAPTER 17

Minor Mishaps

Charlie felt a lot better after talking things through with Maria, and now she had the weekend to figure out what to do. She was glad she didn't have to worry about school stuff for a few days. But she had a lot bigger worries than homework.

She stopped by her dad's study after she cleaned up. Her father was typing intensely and didn't notice her standing there. "Dad?" she asked tentatively, not sure if she should be bothering him.

He stopped and looked up with a weary smile. "Hi."

"Working hard on a Friday night, huh?"

"I'm trying to get ahead so next week isn't so hard," he said, sitting back in the chair. "Turns out I've really got to brush up on my biology before I can teach it—Imagine that." He chuckled. "It's been a long time since my days in the lab."

"How old was I?"

"Just a baby."

"Are you sad you left that job?"

"Not at all."

Charlie dropped her gaze and said in a softer voice, "Did you just get tired of staying home or something?"

"No, I loved it." Charlie's father was quiet for a moment. "I was very lucky to get to spend all that time with you and Andy when you were young, and to be there for you when you got home from school. But you don't need me as much anymore. And I think it was time for all of us to try something new."

"I guess." Charlie flashed a forlorn smile and traced her big toe along the wood floor in a pentagon shape. "I hope you relearn biology fast."

"I'm trying, honey," he said.

"When is Mom coming? Isn't she supposed to be home by now?" Charlie tried not to sound too whiny or impatient, but her mom was never on time. It was getting really annoying.

"She's running late. But I told Andy I'd stop working at eight so we can get the TV set up. He wants to watch that sea monster movie while we wait for her to come home. Want to join us?"

Charlie wrinkled her nose at Andy's idea of a fun Friday night. "Yuck. No, thanks. I've got stuff to do."

"Next time you can pick the movie."

"Thanks." It wasn't much consolation. She went to her bedroom and closed the door, then got on the internet and searched "How to get a bracelet off."

The number of results was absurd. Clearly this was a huge problem for a lot of people. Somehow that didn't make Charlie feel any better.

She clicked on the first link, a video, and watched as a woman put a plastic vegetable bag from the grocery store over her hand and threaded it under her stuck bracelet, then slowly guided the bracelet to come off her hand.

Charlie paused the video and went to the kitchen. She rummaged around for a plastic bag.

"What are you doing?" called Andy, who was lying half upside down on the couch, playing his DS.

"Nothing," she said, and ran back up to her room. She closed the door again and rewatched the video, trying to copy what the lady was doing. The bag threaded under her bracelet without too much trouble. But when it came to sliding the bracelet off, it wasn't happening. "Your hands are really small, lady, you know that?" said Charlie, frustrated. "Or mine are giant beefy ones."

She set aside the bag and read another article, then went back to the kitchen to see if she could find liquid soap, ice, glass cleaner, and cooking oil. But no one had hooked up the ice maker yet, and there was no glass cleaner anywhere that Charlie could see. It was probably still packed. And instead of cooking oil, all she found was some oil and vinegar salad dressing in the fridge, left over from a take-out meal. She grabbed that along with a bottle of soap, hid it under her shirt, and ran back to the stairs.

"Now what are you doing?" asked Andy in a bored voice. He was still upside down on the couch, trying to pick up his water glass from the coffee table and drink from it without spilling.

"Nothing. Leave me alone," said Charlie. She ran up the steps to the bathroom that she shared with Andy and locked the door, then put the soap and salad dressing on the counter. She tried the soap first, lathering it generously over her wrist and hand and pushing some under the bracelet, letting the excess drip into the sink. Then she pulled on the bracelet with all her might, trying to slide the thing off. But it wouldn't go.

Where's my superstrength now? she wondered. She rinsed off the soap, then opened the container of salad dressing. It stank. But it was oily. Breathing through her mouth, Charlie poured the concoction on her arm above and below the bracelet, then massaged it in. Little flecks of herbs and spices freckled her skin. She tried again to remove the bracelet.

Andy knocked on the bathroom door. "What are you doing?"

Charlie gasped and dropped the container on the counter, half of what remained spilling out. "Go away!"

"I'm sooo bored." She heard a series of dull thuds, like the sound Andy's forehead might make thumping against the door.

Charlie picked up the salad dressing container and set it in the sink, then grabbed a wad of toilet paper to wipe up the counter. "Go bother Dad! I'm busy." She cleaned up the spill, then looked at the toilet paper. What was she supposed to do with it now? Hastily she threw it in the toilet and flushed.

"Why does it stink like cheese and dirty socks?"

"Ugh, GO AWAY," Charlie yelled again. "Why don't you call one of your new friends?"

"Oh, hey," said Andy, "that's a good idea." He left.

By now the bathroom sink was coated in salad dressing, and so was a good portion of Charlie and the bracelet. She strained to slide it off, but the more she tried, the redder and more painful her wrist became. At one point her hand slipped and she splattered salad dressing over the bathroom mirror.

"Good thing we don't have any glass cleaner," she muttered. She looked at the bracelet, and then at her smelly, slimy self, and decided she'd had enough. The bracelet wasn't going to come off this way. The internet was flat-out wrong.

Charlie cleaned up the bathroom, smearing the dressing on the mirror using Andy's towel to get off the drips. She opened the window to air out the stink, then took a shower to clean off the rest of her and the bracelet. When she was done, she brought everything back to the kitchen, unnoticed by Andy, who was finally sitting with her dad watching that movie.

Back in her room, Charlie's mind returned to something she'd thought about while trying to get the bracelet off: What had happened to her amazing strength? It was gone.

She looked around her bedroom, wondering if she could test the bracelet somehow without anyone noticing. Her bed and desk had been hastily set up last weekend when they moved in. But everything else was still in the garage. Charlie had been wanting to move her bed to the other side of the room, but her parents were never around to help her. If the bracelet was working, Charlie wouldn't need help. She closed her bedroom door and pushed the desk into a corner. And then she took a good grip on the foot of her bed and lifted as hard as she could.

It made a squeaky noise and moved about an inch. With a huff, Charlie set it back down. She tried again, and it barely budged.

"What the heck," she muttered. Her strength had definitely stopped working.

Having to change her room around the old-fashioned way was much less appealing, so Charlie decided to skip that for now and test her speed instead, to see if that part worked.

"Going for a walk," she called to her dad in the family room. "I'll stay in the neighborhood." She slipped outside and began jogging just to see if anything had changed. When she didn't notice anything special, she sped up, then started sprinting. But her speed was its usual pace. Had she somehow turned off the bracelet? Or perhaps it needed to be recharged. But how?

Maybe everything was solved and life was back to normal. It was funny—a part of her was a little disappointed.

Charlie's phone vibrated with a group text from her mother.

"I'm on the way home!" it read. She'd sent it to her dad and Andy too.

"You were supposed to be home three hours ago," said Charlie. She pushed her phone back into her pocket without answering. She'd let her dad and brother respond.

With her thoughts on her parents and Andy, Charlie slowed

to a walk. Tonight was supposed to be the first full evening that everyone was home since they'd moved. And obviously that hadn't happened—at least not yet. It definitely wouldn't happen often now with their mom's schedule. Or their dad's—apparently starting in the middle of the semester wasn't easy for him either. Almost overnight, life at home had become really different.

Andy was the lucky one. He'd had no trouble making friends in the neighborhood and at his new school, which kind of bugged Charlie because it came so easily for him. But even he had complained a few times about their parents being too busy—it was tough for both of them. And all of them were just trying to get through a long first week in Arizona.

As Charlie turned back toward home, she saw her mom walking up the street from the bus stop. Finally! Charlie quickened her step and followed her inside. Her annoyance with her mother melted a little now that she was actually here. Charlie hesitated, then snuck into the living room and squeezed onto the couch between her mom and the cats to watch the rest of the movie. Her mom kissed Charlie on her head and put her arm around her.

This was what it was supposed to be like. Charlie could worry about getting the bracelet off tomorrow. For now she was just happy that her family was together.

CHAPTER 18

A Mind of Its Own

The entire Wilde family planned to get up early the next day so they could tackle the boxes in the garage. Charlie set her phone alarm for 7:00 a.m. and was in a deep sleep when it went off. The music blasted at top volume, and Charlie almost jumped out of bed. She lunged blindly for the phone to silence it, and then she collapsed into her pillow again and rested there for a moment, catching her breath. When she got over the shock and remembered who she was and what day it was, she turned on her bedside lamp and looked at her phone. The screen was cracked.

Charlie gasped. "Oh no!" Her wrist was warm under the bracelet. Her strength had returned. But her phone! Luckily it hadn't shattered, and it still worked. But she'd have some explaining to do when her parents found out. She'd only had the phone since the beginning of sixth grade, and her parents had warned her that if she lost it or broke it, they wouldn't replace it, so she'd better be careful. She'd done so well with it—until now. That stupid bracelet was going to make her look really irresponsible if she wasn't careful. She had to find the tools today so she could get the thing off.

Until then she would have to be very careful not to break anything else. From that point on, Charlie tiptoed around the house trying not to touch anything, which was very hard to do, and also made her look weird. She cringed when she pictured herself trying to handle anything fragile. Today was about to get interesting.

After breakfast Charlie and Andy headed out to the garage while their parents cleaned up the dishes.

"I'll start with my stuff," Charlie said, thinking that if she broke anything, nobody else would have to know about it. When Andy opened the door, Charlie darted around him. Apparently her speed had returned, too.

"What the—" Andy said. "Um, *excuse me.*"

"You're excused," Charlie replied with a smug grin. She forced herself to walk carefully through the aisles to the back where her boxes were. A few sat open from when she'd searched for her soccer equipment, and the empty package that had held the bracelet was there, too. Charlie picked it up and examined it for a second time. It was just as she remembered. No return address. And no other clues.

Charlie pulled the note from inside, reread it, and tried to figure out whose handwriting it could be. She had to admit that none of her friends wrote like that—all loopy and old-fashioned—but maybe they had their parents send it or something. She pulled out her phone and texted Amari carefully so she wouldn't crack the screen further. "Hi! I miss you!"

"Ack!" came the reply. "At the Laundromat with my dad. Pipes froze, and the one connected to the washer exploded and flooded the basement—you shoulda seen it."

"Yikes!" wrote Charlie.

"Yeah, it's a mess—check my photos online. How are you?"

"Better. I was wondering if anybody from the team might have said something to you about that bracelet I mentioned."

"Nope. But why don't you just group text?"

"Okay, yeah. Good idea."

Charlie started a group message with all her friends from her old school, which kept her phone buzzing with replies for the next several minutes. It was fun to hear from everybody, but they fired lots of questions at her about how she was liking the new school.

"Ahem!" Andy called from the opposite corner of the garage. "You're not getting much done over there."

Charlie abandoned the flurry of responses and questions, and put her phone and the note that had accompanied the bracelet into her pocket. "Worry about your own junk." She discarded the packaging and gingerly lifted the top box from one of her stacks. It was filled with outdoor things: jump rope, skateboard, sidewalk chalk from when she was five—stuff like that. She moved the box to the corner since it would stay out here.

She peeked at the next two and found clothing in them. Keeping them stacked, she carried them both into the house. Andy passed her in the kitchen on his way back to get another load.

"Must be full of feathers," Andy said, pointing to her load.

"Like your head," replied Charlie.

Andy made a face and skirted around her. "Why are you walking so weird?"

"Why are you even allowed in the house?" Charlie said, and then they both cracked up. Andy was annoying sometimes, but he could take an insult as easily as he could give it, and that was cool.

Charlie continued on methodically, worried about bumping into things for fear of breaking something. She saw her parents coming down the stairs to get more boxes and let them pass before she went up to her room.

"That's the way," her mom said approvingly. "We'll have this done by lunch if you keep that up."

"If we get pizza again, I'll pass," Charlie muttered. She never thought she'd be tired of fast food, but after a week of mainly eating takeout, Charlie longed for her dad's special recipes. Maybe he'd be able to cook something now that it was the weekend.

In her room she emptied the boxes of clothes into her dresser drawers, broke down the cardboard, and went back to the garage.

Andy made a few more obnoxious remarks while she continued unpacking. Her phone buzzed continuously with responses from her friends, all saying they didn't know anything about the bracelet and asking even more questions, so she kept having to stop to answer. As much as she liked hearing from them, she wished she had picked a different time to text everyone. She let the phone vibrate while she took another trip up the stairs.

Every time she passed Andy, he made another remark about the way she was opening doors or moving boxes. It had been funny the first few times, but now it was starting to get annoying. He didn't know when to quit.

Once Charlie finished with her unpacking, she started on the containers marked Linen Closet, figuring there wasn't much in them she could break. As their parents began carting some furniture inside, Andy returned to the garage. "Oooh, you moved all the feathers one at a time, and now you've graduated to washcloths. Congratulations!"

Charlie sighed impatiently as she opened a large plastic storage container of throw pillows. "Seriously, Andy. Shut it." Her phone continued to vibrate like crazy in her pocket, so she stopped and yanked out the phone, remembering at the last moment to be gentle turning it off so she wouldn't destroy it. It was growing increasingly frustrating to be so careful with every move.

"My mistake," Andy said sarcastically. "Not washcloths. Pillows. Don't break your back lifting too many of those—"

"Enough already!" Charlie impulsively grabbed a pillow and launched it at him. It whizzed through the air and struck Andy in the stomach, sending him soaring into a stack of boxes.

"Oof!" said Andy. The boxes were heavy. The top one slid and teetered, then fell off the pile. Files spilled out over the garage floor.

Charlie's hand flew to her mouth, but she soon relaxed when she realized Andy wasn't hurt.

Andy lay there for a minute, dazed, and then sat up and stared at her. "Sorry. Gosh."

Charlie gaped and went over to him as heat pulsed around her wrist. And then a small smile tugged at her lips. "I warned you, ya little butt squeak," she said. Holding back a laugh, she thought about throwing another pillow, but instead she carefully gathered up the files, straightened their contents, and put them back.

Talos Global—Charles's Study, she read on the side of the box. Her dad's old work stuff. She lifted the box and set it back on the stack. When everything was neatly put away again, she went back to the container of pillows and carried it—very delicately—into the house.

Maybe this bracelet was worth keeping after all.

CHAPTER 19

A Broken Promise

As mysteriously as the powers had come, they were gone. By Sunday Charlie was pretty sure that the bracelet was functioning only when it turned her arm warm, but she still didn't know how to trigger it.

Andy had acquired a sudden new respect for his older sister, which was an added bonus because he stopped bugging her when he was bored. Charlie's group text messages with her friends back in Chicago eventually lessened, and once Charlie had time to reply she had a lot of fun catching up with everyone. Chatting with them made her a little homesick, but it was nice to be able to tell them a little bit about where she lived now. Once she'd learned that none of them had sent the bracelet, Charlie called her grandma to see how she was doing, and ask if she had dropped the bracelet off.

But Grandma hadn't done it either.

Charlie called Maria to update her. "Still no idea who gave this to me," Charlie said, talking softly in her room so nobody would overhear.

"That's so weird," said Maria.

"Yeah," said Charlie. "I found the garden toolboxes, so I'm

going to try to cut the thing off this morning." She nibbled at her bottom lip, wondering if her new friend wanted to get together but not quite daring to ask outright. "So, do you have a lot of stuff going on later?"

"We always have a big family lunch on Sundays," said Maria. "My stepbrothers are here until three, then they go to their mom's. I'm free after that. Want me to text you? Maybe we can hang out."

"That would be great," said Charlie happily.

"Cool, I'll check in with you later!"

They hung up.

Charlie slunk around the house to see where everybody was. Andy was working on an old Lord of the Rings Lego set that he'd unearthed during the unpacking, which would keep him busy in his room for hours. Mom was at the hospital for who knew how long. And Dad was holed up in his study with the door closed, working on lesson plans for the coming week. Charlie finally had a chance to open the toolboxes and dig around to try to find something that would cut through the bracelet.

She found a wire cutter, but it barely left a scratch. In the crate of yard tools there was a branch cutter, but it didn't do anything either. The stronger, more elaborate cutting tools she found were too big or too heavy to give Charlie a decent grip on their handles since she could only use one hand. Not to mention the blade points were sharp enough that they made her think twice about pressing them against her skin. She didn't care how quickly she could heal—those suckers could really hurt if her grip slipped!

Out of options, she gave up. The bracelet would have to stay. Despite its disasters, Charlie had also seen some of its benefits, like keeping Andy in check. So she wasn't totally disappointed about it. Maybe it could help her in other ways, too, if she could ever figure out how it worked.

With no homework to do and Maria busy for at least another hour, Charlie grabbed her soccer ball and went to the vacant football stadium near school to run drills and to see if she could activate the bracelet. But no matter how hard she tried to get her speed ability to turn on, it wasn't happening.

After a while Charlie's cell phone vibrated. It was a text from Maria. "Come to my house! Let's do some research." A second text gave Maria's address and directions on how to get there.

Charlie studied the directions, oriented herself, and realized she was almost halfway there already. *Research, huh?* she wondered. She wasn't sure what Maria had in mind, but she was curious to find out.

She dribbled the soccer ball to the path, texting her dad as she went along to let him know where she'd be. When he gave the okay, Charlie picked up her pace and soon found herself in a neighborhood on the other side of the school, walking up the driveway to Maria's house.

She rang the doorbell. There was a series of thumps coming from inside, and then an intense amount of barking. Maria opened the door and commanded two large dogs to sit. They obeyed, unlike Jessie, who didn't bark much but always jumped on people. Charlie wasn't positive what kind they were, but she thought the brown-and-black one looked like it was part German shepherd, and the other had the distinct red coat and floppy ears of an Irish setter.

"Come on in!" Maria said. In a softer voice she asked, "Are you doing okay? Anything horrible happen since I saw you last?"

Charlie put a fist out for the dogs to sniff and showed Maria her cell phone. "You could say that."

"Yikes," Maria said. "How'd you do that?"

Charlie grimaced. "Turning off my alarm yesterday morning."

"You broke your screen just touching it?" Maria asked. "No luck cutting the bracelet off, I see."

"Nope." Charlie looked around Maria's house. It was cozy and warm, painted in a palette of browns and tans, and furnished with the kind of traditional Southwest design that Charlie was still trying to get used to: horseshoes and cowboy hat throw pillows, brown leather furniture, small potted cacti. As Maria led Charlie through the house, she could hear the clatter of pots and pans. The warm scent of spices lingered in the air. They entered the kitchen, where three adults were cleaning up on the other side of a large island.

"Mamá," said Maria with a hint of an accent. "This is my new friend, Charlie, I told you about." She straightened and pushed in the bar stools as she talked. "Charlie, this is my mom, Maytée; my stepdad, Ken; and my grandmother, Yolanda."

The older woman said something to Maria that Charlie couldn't understand.

"*Sí*, Abuela," said Maria. She turned to Charlie. "Grandma's visiting from Puerto Rico."

"We're so pleased to meet you," said Maria's mother, who was very pretty and looked like a grown-up Maria. Her hair was black and silky, and hung straight down to the middle of her back.

"Pleased to meet you," echoed Maria's equally striking grandmother with a bright smile and a heavy accent. She waved her dish towel in greeting.

"Welcome," said Ken warmly. "Are you hungry? We have leftovers—unless Mac ate them all."

"Oh," said Charlie, pleased and a little overwhelmed by how friendly Maria's family was. "Thank you! I already ate lunch. It's nice to meet you too."

"Come on," said Maria. "I'll show you my room." She ushered Charlie through the dining room and down a hallway to the last door on the left, and hesitated in front of it. She touched the handle but didn't open it. "Um . . . there's something I should probably tell you. I hope you don't mind," she said, looking guilty.

"Mind what?" asked Charlie.

Maria pushed open the door, and Charlie looked inside. Mac was sitting at Maria's desk, holding an iPad.

Charlie was confused. Why would Maria think she'd mind Mac being there? But then her lips parted, and a wave of dread came over her. She gripped the doorframe and turned to Maria, fire in her eyes. "Did you tell him?" she whispered. She could feel the wood starting to give way under her fingertips.

Maria bit her lip and nodded. "Yes. I'm sorry. I hope you're not too mad."

Mac turned around in the chair. "Hey, Charlie," he said.

Mad? Charlie was absolutely furious. Betrayed by the only person who knew the truth—her friend who said she could keep a secret, not tell the whole world! The bracelet grew hot on her forearm as a jumble of emotions built up inside her. She closed her eyes and, with effort, loosened her grip on the cracking doorframe and clenched her fists at her sides. She couldn't destroy anything else. Not even the house of a traitor.

CHAPTER 20

Maria Has a Plan

"Back out in the hallway," Charlie ordered, glaring at Maria.

They stepped outside the bedroom door, and Maria closed it. She spoke quietly, the clatter of dishes in the background reminding them both of the nearness of grown-ups. "I know you're mad. But listen—"

"No, *you* listen," Charlie said in a harsh whisper. "What were you thinking? What if he tells other people? My life will be ruined!" Tears stung her eyes, which made her even angrier. "Jeez, Maria—don't you know it's hard enough being new here? Now everyone will know I'm a freak. I thought you were my friend." She turned away and covered her eyes with her hand, trying to maintain control of herself. But it was hard. She really liked Maria, but now all she wanted was to go back home to Chicago and never see these people again. "What a disaster," she whispered, slumping against the wall. "I hate it here."

"Oh, Charlie!" Maria started to reach out her hand to comfort her but then clearly thought the better of it and pulled back. She pursed her lips, her face filled with regret. After waiting respectfully to make sure Charlie was finished speaking, she cleared her throat. "Charlie," she said earnestly, "I promise you Mac won't tell anyone. And I only told him about the bracelet and the weird powers because he can help us."

"Us?" Charlie asked, her voice full of contempt.

"You, I mean, obviously." Maria shook her head, frustrated with herself. "I'm really sorry I hurt your feelings. And I'm also really sorry I didn't check with you first before talking to Mac. I should have."

"No kidding," Charlie muttered.

"I'm totally the worst."

Charlie hesitated. "Yes. You totally are."

"I'm worse than a barrel full of peas. Squeaky ones."

Charlie made a noise. It almost sounded like a laugh, but she quickly snarled to cover it. "Yes, you're much worse than that."

Maria let out a breath. "Won't you peas forgive me?"

Charlie groaned.

"Because seriously, Mac won't tell anybody. I promise. And we really do need him."

Charlie was quiet for a long moment. "To get the bracelet off, you mean?"

"Maybe. Or at least figure out what it is and why it has this crazy effect on you. And maybe even try to hack it."

Charlie peeked at Maria. "Do you think he can?"

She nodded. "He's the best. You've seen him—people pay him to do junk like this. Only of course he'll help you for free."

Charlie blew out a breath. Maria had a point. "All right," she said, resigned. "I guess there's nothing we can do about it now. We can't untell him." She slid her forefingers under her eyes in case any of her tears had leaked out, and sighed. "Let's do this."

Maria smiled. "You're awesome." She opened her bedroom door. "Yo, Mac. Come on. We're going out to the shed."

Without a word, Mac grabbed his iPad, tucked it under his arm, and followed the girls out through the back door to a little shed in the yard.

"Welcome to my hideout," Maria said. The shed smelled faintly of motor oil. In one corner was an old lawn mower and a gas can with a funnel on the spout. In another, three bikes of various sizes. There was a workbench with several cupboards on the wall above it and a number of tool drawers below, and a tidy desk area with a lamp and a recycled soup can for pencils.

Maria pulled out the desk chair for Mac to sit in, then rummaged around for another item for Charlie to use as a chair.

Mac sat down and laid his iPad on the table as he responded to a text message on his phone. In the awkward silence, Charlie glanced at the tablet. He had the Animal Planet website up and a Dr. Jeff: Rocky Mountain Vet tab open. Another tab read "12 Secret iPhone Hacks." His search bar had the question "When is Shark Week?" in it. Charlie raised an eyebrow and folded her arms over her chest.

Maria returned with a rectangular wooden crate and set it on end next to Mac. "Here you go," she said.

Charlie perched on top of it. Mac set his phone on the desk and looked at the girls.

"Okay," Maria said. "First of all, Mac, can you please promise that you won't tell anyone about Charlie's bracelet or about the strange things that are happening to her? Or about anything we discuss or discover here today or in the future?"

"Yeah, sure," Mac said.

"Say it," Maria prompted.

Mac gave her a slightly annoyed look but turned to Charlie. "I won't tell anybody anything about any of this. I promise. And," he added, "I think it's actually pretty cool you've got these powers."

Charlie gave him a hard look, then nodded, satisfied. "Okay. Thanks."

"You're welcome. Can I see it now?"

"What?"

"The bracelet. I need to see it."

"Oh," said Charlie. She stretched out her arm and rested it on the table next to Mac's iPad. He snapped a couple of pictures with it, then pulled out his cell phone and took a few more, zooming in and using features on his camera phone that Charlie had never seen before. "Flip your arm over, will you?" he asked.

Charlie did it. Mac took more photos. He lifted his head and glanced around. "You got any more light in here, Maria? This flash isn't doing it."

Maria reached for the flexible work lamp from the corner of the desk and brought it as far as its cord would reach. She flipped the switch, and light flooded the area. Mac took a few more pictures, and then he narrowed his eyes and studied the etchings. "What's the pentagon symbol all about?"

"I don't know," said Charlie.

"It looks like a logo inside. Are those letters? It's like a letter *T* and a . . . a *C*. Or is that an *O*?" Mac twisted Charlie's wrist, holding it to the light. "Maybe it's just a circle," he muttered.

"Ow," said Charlie.

"Sorry." Mac straightened her arm and examined the dark screen, then tapped it. "Does this work?"

"No."

Mac looked at the buttons on the side. He pressed one, then another, then two at once. Nothing happened. He pushed the remaining buttons in much the same manner, then continued without any pattern at all.

Charlie watched him. "You're just pressing them randomly."

Mac looked up. "Yeah. So? Did you try that already?"

"Not really," Charlie admitted.

"Okay then. I don't tell you how to play soccer, now do I? You got me?" He continued.

Charlie made a face.

Maria shrugged. "He really is the most tech-smart person I know," she said.

"Yeah, he's really something," Charlie said drily.

Mac ignored them and kept messing with the buttons.

Charlie looked around the shed. "Do you do your homework in here?" she asked Maria. It was kind of cool to have a quiet place like this to go to. It was like a secret little house.

"Sometimes. I've got three stepbrothers, so when they're here, the house gets a little crowded. It's complicated—don't ask." Maria hopped up on the table nearby.

"They're cool," Mac said, not looking up from his task. "We hang out."

Maria nodded. "True. Mac's here practically more than I am."

"That's nice," said Charlie. She was getting bored, and it was weird having Mac pawing at her arm and breathing all over it. "I just have a younger brother," she said. "I hit him with a pillow yesterday. Threw it so hard he flew backward into a stack of boxes."

"No way," said Mac. He looked up.

"Seriously?" Maria asked.

"Yeah." Charlie laughed a little, remembering.

Maria and Mac looked at each other, and Mac raised an eyebrow.

"What?" Charlie asked.

"Nothing if I can't get this thing to work," Mac said. He kept pushing buttons, and then he pressed two of them and held them down.

"And what happens if you can?"

Mac didn't answer—he was counting under his breath as he held the buttons. Maria just shrugged, but she looked like she was hiding something.

Charlie frowned, wondering what they were plotting. But she didn't have much time to spend thinking about it, because a moment later, Mac gasped.

"Whoa!" he breathed. "Check it out." As Maria and Charlie bent toward him to look at the bracelet, he read the message that now scrolled on the screen:

CHIMERA MARK FIVE . . . DEFENSE MODE INITIATED . . . KEY IN ACCESS CODE TO DEACTIVATE.

CHAPTER 21

Defense Mode

"What's that supposed to mean?" Charlie asked. "Chimera Mark Five? Defense mode? Access code? What?"

"Mark Five," mused Maria. "Like Iron Man and his suits! I wonder if that means there's a version four out there somewhere? And a three?"

Charlie didn't know much about Iron Man, but she too wondered why the bracelet would be called a Mark Five. "Yeah—maybe it's like how new versions of phones and programs are named. Like iPhone 7 or Windows 10."

"So, you think there might be other bracelets out there?" asked Maria, eyes widening.

Charlie thought about it. "Don't people just get rid of their old phones when they get an upgrade?"

Maria shrugged. "I guess."

"Hmm." Mac had been studying the phrases as they flashed across the bracelet's screen, and while the girls discussed the meaning of Mark Five, he turned to his tablet, typed "Chimera Mark Five," and hit Enter, then sat back and frowned as the search engine produced no results. "Nothing? Seriously?" He shrugged and deleted the last two words, then hit Enter again.

"Chimera," he said, reading the page in front of him, and then he clicked on the audible pronunciation. "ki-MEER-ah," it said.

Mac read the description and summarized, "Basically, it's a creature from Greek mythology made up of different animal parts."

Maria looked horrified. "Different animal parts? Sorry, but that's just gross."

Mac glanced at her, confused at first. "What? No! Not chopped-off limbs glued together, Maria."

Charlie laughed out loud as Mac continued. "The parts are, like, naturally grown or whatever. A chimera is a supercreature with the most powerful features of a bunch of—" He stopped abruptly and looked at the bracelet.

Charlie leaned over his shoulder and read the tablet screen. "The most powerful features of a bunch of animals," she finished softly. The shed was dead silent.

Maria's eyes widened. "Oh. You mean like the speed of one animal."

"And the strength of another," Mac said slowly, looking at Maria.

"And the healing power of one too," Maria said. The two turned to stare at Charlie.

"That's insane," Charlie said. Her heart raced, and a wave of panic moved through her. "*Really* insane." She stood up and shook her arm in front of Mac's face. "You have to get this thing off me. Now."

"I can't," Mac said. "Like the message says, we need a code to do that. Did it come with a code? Any instructions? Anything?"

"No, I didn't see any code. Nothing like that," Charlie said. "Just a note." She scrambled to produce it and held it out to Maria. "Here."

Maria unfolded it and read aloud: "'Charlie, it's time. You know what to do.'" She turned it over, saw that side was blank, and looked at Mac. "There's no signature. No code. Nothing. That's it."

"I thought it was about soccer," Charlie said, agitated. "But now I'm sure I don't have a clue what to do." She pulled her arm away, but Mac grabbed it.

"Hang on," he said. He tapped on the screen, and a number keypad came up. Below the numbers was a Shift key and a space bar. He pushed the Shift key, and a new keypad came up, this time with the first half of the alphabet. Once again Mac pushed the Shift key, and the second half of the alphabet appeared.

He hit the Enter key.

An ERROR screen popped up, then disappeared, returning him to the scrolling words asking for an access code.

"Okay," he muttered. "But how many characters?"

Charlie gave Maria a tortured look.

Mac let go and turned to his iPad and started a new search.

"I'm going to need time to figure out this code. It could be all numbers, all letters, or a combination. And I can't figure out how long it is."

"How much time?" Charlie asked anxiously.

"I don't know. Since we have no idea who sent it, we can't start with the usual common passwords: family and pet names, birth dates, and stuff like that." He looked at Charlie. "Can I see it again?"

Charlie held out her arm, and he tried entering a few random combinations and hitting the Enter key. All of them resulted in the ERROR screen, giving him no further indication of how many characters the ID code had. When he let go, Charlie got up and started pacing. *A chimera bracelet?* Thinking about it was really unsettling.

Maria hopped off the table and went to Charlie's side. "It's going to be okay, Charlie. Nothing has changed—you just know more about it now. I get that it's stuck on you, but you've been surviving all right with it on you this long, so maybe take a few deep breaths, okay? And *you're* not a chimera, or whatever that thing is. You just have the powers of some animals, right? Which is actually extremely cool, if you think about it."

"It's still creepy." Charlie took a deep breath, almost afraid to let it out in case fire burst from her mouth or something, but nothing happened. She felt human, like always.

"You look totally normal," Maria assured her.

"Except for your fangs," Mac added.

"Fangs?" Charlie cried, her hand flying to her mouth.

"Mac!" Maria said. "Not cool. Can't you see Charlie is freaking out?" She looked at Charlie. "You don't have fangs. You look the same as you did your first day of school. And seriously, you have great powers. I mean, think about it."

Charlie glared at the back of Mac's head, but he was looking at his phone, flipping through his code-hacking apps. After a minute she relaxed a little. "Maybe it's not so bad," she conceded. Mac's joke was kind of funny. And having these powers didn't actually make her an animal.

"Not so bad?" Mac said. "What are you talking about? It's terrific." He sounded a bit envious.

Charlie pursed her lips. "Maybe. I'd like it a lot more if I could take it off when I wanted to, though."

"Mac will figure that out," Maria said. "Don't worry."

"Yeah," warned Mac, "I hope so anyway. I've got to let these programs run and see what codes they come up with. And then I'll have to enter them one at a time, since there's no way to hook the bracelet up to my tablet. So it'll take a while."

"That sounds . . . exciting," said Charlie with zero enthusiasm.

"Hmm," said Maria, an impish smile playing at her lips. "Maybe it's time for the fun part."

Mac shrugged, then nodded.

Charlie eyed Maria suspiciously. "What fun part?"

"You'll see. Come with me." Maria smiled and put her hands on Charlie's shoulders, turned her in the direction of the door, and gently pushed her toward it. Mac, still working on his phone, got up, grabbed his iPad, and followed them.

"Where are we going?" Charlie asked. She stooped to pick up her soccer ball as they went.

"To the soccer field."

Charlie stopped and frowned. "Why?"

Maria's eyes twinkled. "Because, my friend, I think it's time to see exactly what this sweet bracelet can do."

CHAPTER 22

Figuring Out the Trigger

"No way!" Charlie said, planting her feet in the doorway of the shed and blocking Maria and Mac from getting past her. "Tell me what you're planning or I am out of here. I mean it."

"Tell her, Maria," Mac said. "She's right. She's not our test subject."

Charlie was glad to have Mac backing her up, but then she did a double take. "Your test subject?"

"Bad choice of words," Mac said. "What I meant was that you're not a chimera. You're a person, so you decide things about your own . . . self. About your own powers. Whatever we're calling them."

"You're totally right," Maria said sheepishly. "I'm sorry. I was just thinking that since it'll take some time to crack the code, maybe we could learn more, you know? Test your abilities. See how fast you can run, how much you can lift. Stuff like that. And who knows—maybe we'll accidentally figure out how to control the powers, too."

Charlie narrowed her eyes. "That's it?"

"Yep. That's all I had in mind. I mean, aren't you curious to find out?"

Maria was pretty convincing. It *would* be cool to know how fast she could run. "I guess so," said Charlie. "Yeah." She stepped through the doorway, and the three started walking toward school. "But I don't know if we'll be able to get it to do anything," she added. "The bracelet doesn't work all the time. Sometimes it doesn't do anything for hours."

Mac looked up from his cell phone. "What do you mean?"

"I mean it gives me powers sometimes and not others. I tried running fast the other night, and I couldn't get it to work. It's like . . . like a lightbulb that's not screwed in all the way, you know? Sometimes it's on, sometimes it flickers and goes off. . . ." It wasn't the best way to describe it, but it was the only thing Charlie could think of.

"So . . . do you think there's a short circuit in the bracelet or something?" Mac wondered. "Some sort of glitch?"

"I don't know. Maybe."

"Hmm." Mac lifted Charlie's arm once more and pushed a few buttons on the bracelet, but the message continued scrolling as before. He shook his head, puzzled, and gave up—for the moment, at least.

At the field, Maria had Charlie stand at the boundary line behind one goal, ready to run as fast as she could to midfield, which was forty yards away. Mac stood prepared to film the run on his phone so he could be absolutely precise with calculating speed. He wasn't looking for Charlie's average speed over the forty yards—he wanted her top speed. Once he broke down the footage and analyzed it, he'd be able to pinpoint the exact number.

"Ready over here," Mac said. He started recording.

Maria looked at Charlie. "Ready?"

Charlie nodded.

"Go!" Maria said.

Charlie sprinted over the grass as fast as she could go. She crossed the line and slowed down, breathing hard, then circled back to where Mac stood.

"Well?" she asked.

Mac watched the replay and did some quick calculations in his head. "Well, you run a decent forty-yard dash, but you're not breaking any records."

"So you're saying it didn't work."

Mac smiled patronizingly. "I'm going to go with no. Try again."

"That's what I thought." Charlie walked back to where Maria stood and got ready to run.

Maria waited for Charlie to signal that she was ready and shouted, "Go!"

Charlie dug her feet into the ground and pushed off, putting everything she had into the sprint. But when she crossed the line, she knew instinctively that her running power just wasn't there.

"Meeting!" she called between breaths, and Maria came running over.

"Are you still running normally?" Maria asked, though it was clear from her face that she could tell it was just average.

"Yeah. And I'm not sure how long I want to do this. It's great conditioning and all, but I already had my workout today."

"I hear you," Mac said. "But I'm not sure what to do. I mean, can you give us any hints? What happens when you *do* have the strength or speed? Do you feel different? Did you shake your wrist a certain way or push the buttons or . . ." He trailed off, trying to think of anything that could possibly trigger the device.

"It gets warm when it's working," Charlie said. She clasped her other hand over the bracelet and moved the bracelet up her arm. It was cold.

"Well, that's something," Mac said, typing notes into his phone.

"I don't always notice it, though. Not right away, anyway. I guess I'm usually distracted when it happens."

"Distracted," Maria repeated, tapping her chin thoughtfully. "Hmm. Let's talk through all the times when the bracelet actually gave you powers. When was the first one?"

"I'm not positive, but I think the first time something felt a little off was when I rushed to my seat in first period a few days ago after the late bell rang, and I sent my desk skidding into the aisle. Do you remember that, Mac?"

"Yeah, actually, I do," Mac said slowly. He tilted his head, thinking. "I mean, those desks are heavy. Something like that might happen with a big kid. So it surprised me. Of course I forgot all about it five seconds later."

Charlie nodded. "The first major thing I remember happening was during soccer tryouts," she said. "Not during warm-ups or even in my first round on the field in the scrimmage, though, because I started out pretty sluggish, and I was kind of jittery and anxious. The ball went sailing my way. I trapped it and started dribbling at a normal speed, I think." She tapped her chin. "Nothing much happened until after Coach subbed me out."

"So when did an ability kick in?" Mac asked.

Charlie thought back to the scrimmage. "A little while after I went back in to play. I dribbled a bit, and then saw the opposition coming at me from all sides. I remember getting that scared thrill I get when I have a challenge and the defense is chasing me. You know what I'm talking about?"

"Not really," said Mac, but Maria nodded.

"And . . . I don't know," Charlie continued, "it just happened. I started flying across the field, and I left the defense behind."

"In a big way," Maria added.

"Was the bracelet warm?" asked Mac.

"I—I don't remember. I suppose so."

"It was a really impressive run," Maria added. "And later in the game—was it the same? You got the ball, and it just clicked sometime after that?"

"When I was surrounded by defense, yeah. I had to get out of there or be trampled—that's about when it happened, I guess."

"Hmm," Mac said, typing furiously. Then he raised an eyebrow. "What about strength? Maria told me you picked up an entire bed by yourself. How would you even know to try that?"

"I didn't pick it up myself," said Charlie. "I was helping Kelly move it. I had the headboard side, and we were carrying it backstage, and then she got distracted and just dropped her end without any warning and ran out to see some high school guy."

"And it didn't fall to the ground?" Mac asked.

"Right, it didn't. I just held it like it was no big deal, and then I realized that I was holding an entire bed by myself, and I started freaking out. That's when I dropped it."

"And you ran to the bathroom?" asked Maria.

"Yes."

"Superspeed run?" Mac asked. "Or normal?"

"I don't know. I was really freaking out."

"And you tore the bathroom apart," Mac said, still typing.

"Not the *whole* bathroom."

"Right. Part of the bathroom." Mac looked at Charlie, fingers hovering over the keys, waiting for her to go on.

"Aren't you going to change that in your notes?" Charlie asked him. "I don't want anybody thinking I wrecked the entire bathroom."

"Nobody's going to even see this, remember? I'm sworn to secrecy," Mac said.

Charlie put her hands on her hips and stared.

Mac stared back at her, and then reluctantly changed it in his notes. "Fine," he said. "What else?"

"My alarm went off, and I broke my phone screen just by touching it."

Maria studied Charlie intently. "Did the alarm surprise you? Or were you sort of awake already?"

"It scared the heck out of me," Charlie said, remembering. "The volume was on full blast. And the bracelet got warm then, I remember." She thought through all the instances, trying to find a common theme. Mac and Maria were silent, doing the same thing.

After a minute Maria held her finger in the air, closed her eyes, opened them again, and said, "I've got it."

Charlie and Mac looked expectantly at her.

"Well?" Charlie prompted.

Maria lifted her chin. "Necessity," she said. "And fear, in a way. Like with animals. The chimera thing."

"Um, what?" Charlie asked. "You lost me."

"Sorry," Maria said, laughing. "I mean, when the device some-how senses you are in trouble, or in danger, it activates and gives you the powers you *need* to deal with the situation."

"Aha," Mac said, nodding at Maria. "I get it. Like when Charlie was being surrounded by the other team in the scrimmage—she needed to get out of there, like an animal that feels trapped. Fear stimulates necessity. So the bracelet sensed Charlie's change in adrenaline or whatever and gave her the ability to flee—the power of speed kicked in."

"Exactly," said Maria. "And Kelly dropping her end of the bed gave Charlie an immediate sense of urgency to stop the bed from falling. Her strength turned on so she could keep holding it."

Charlie looked skeptical. "That makes sense for those instances, but what about the bathroom? Are you saying I had an urgent need to rip out that sink?"

"No," Maria said, growing excited, "but the ability was already activated from the bed incident, and you didn't know to be careful until it turned off. And it probably doesn't turn off until your body's natural indicators tell the bracelet that you are safe. Like your heart rate and pulse going back to resting levels."

"It's like when you move cats across the country and when you let them loose they bolt and hide behind the stove in your new house for a whole day until they feel safe," Charlie murmured.

"Yes, like that!" said Maria.

"And," Mac said, "maybe the bracelet went into overdrive because you freaked out about it—so it didn't know to turn off when you started destroying the whole bathroom."

"Part of the bathroom."

Mac just looked at her. "Okay, look. You broke a toilet seat, a stall door, pulled the sink from the wall and then smashed it. . . ."

I'm just saying that's a heck of a lot of destruction to call it 'part' of the bathroom."

"There were two sinks and two stalls I left completely untouched!" Charlie said.

"Plus the water damage . . . ," Mac went on.

"Guys!" Maria said. "Drop it. Focus."

Charlie scowled. It was one-third of the bathroom at most, and Kelly had told Maria that the custodian had turned off the water right away, so she doubted there was any damage from that. But she dropped it. "So what about my cracked screen?"

Mac shrugged. "Easy. The alarm flipped the switch that time. It startled you from a sound sleep, and *bam*, the strength was there, even though you didn't need it or want it."

It was all making sense. If Charlie could keep these triggers in mind, she'd be able to be more careful when they happened in the future. But there was something else on her mind, too. She shook her arm in frustration. "Why won't it come off now?"

Mac pursed his lips. "When was the first time you tried to take the bracelet off and it wouldn't unlatch?"

"In the bathroom."

"When the powers were activated?" he asked.

"I guess."

"Had you ever tried taking it off when it was activated before?"

Charlie thought back. "I don't think so. I've only ever taken it off when it was cold."

"Maybe doing that triggered a permanent lock or something as a defense mechanism."

Maria sat up. "Ahh, defense mode," she said, nodding. "The bracelet must have gone into lockdown—it detected that someone was trying to remove the bracelet when you clearly needed it to fight off the evil toilet and sink."

"Very funny," said Charlie. But that explanation made sense. "So why won't it open now that I don't have any powers activated?"

"Because you need to enter the secret code to tell it that you're safe and all is good?" guessed Maria.

"Either that, or it's a glitch," said Mac.

"Oh. Well, either way, that stinks." They stood in silence for a moment. Then Charlie shrugged. "So, now what?" she asked, idly walking along the halfway line as she gathered her thoughts. "I'm not being chased. I have no need to run. So we can't test it."

When neither of them responded, Charlie looked up. "Guys?"

Suddenly, from behind, Maria grabbed Charlie and screamed in her ear.

Charlie gasped. "What did you do that for?"

"Run!" Maria shouted. "Mac! Video! Now!"

Charlie ran. Maria chased after her.

Charlie left her in the dust.

CHAPTER 23

Testing, Testing

"Rough estimate," Mac said, staring at his phone and then at Charlie in disbelief, "is seventy miles per hour. I have a feeling I know which animal that matches."

Charlie blinked. "Seventy? Are you sure?"

"It's right around there," he said, picking up his iPad.

"That's insane," Charlie said.

Maria whooped. "It's incredible!"

"I'll have to do all the calculations to get an exact number. But meanwhile . . ." Mac worked on the tablet for a moment, then he looked up, shaking his head a little in disbelief. "Yup, my suspicions were correct. Congratulations," he said. "You're tied with the cheetah as the world's fastest animal. Er—*land* animal, anyway, according to this," he added. "You're nowhere near the speed of a peregrine falcon. But unless you can fly, that hardly matters. Wait." He looked at her dubiously. "*Can* you fly?"

Charlie looked stunned. "Fly? Um, no, I don't think so. Did you say . . . ?"

"As fast as a cheetah?" Maria stared at Charlie, and then started jumping up and down and hugging her. "That's as fast as the speed limit on the highway! This is so awesome!" she cried. "Wow!"

"I can't believe it," Charlie said. It was scary and exciting at the same time.

"You're totally sick," Mac said with a huge grin.

"Charlie Wilde, you are officially the coolest person I know," Maria declared, beaming. She flung her arm around Charlie's shoulders. Charlie's laughter rang out.

Mac's enormous grin faded. "Wow, okay," he said quietly. "Thanks a lot." He turned and scanned the horizon like he was looking for something.

Charlie and Maria didn't notice him as they talked excitedly about the amazing speed and all the things Charlie could do with it.

"But we have to figure out a different way to activate the powers," Charlie said. "You probably won't be able to sneak up on me and scare me like that again—I'll be expecting it, so it won't work."

"Yeah, I figured that," Maria said. "Plus, I can't go around doing that in front of people. But I was thinking about whenever I watch a scary movie or bring up certain memories. They can be strong enough to get my heart racing. Does that ever happen to you?"

"I guess," Charlie said. "I'm kind of a lightweight, though. A scary Goosebumps book can mess me up, especially if I read it in the dark. Oh—and one time I saw a bad car crash—" She stopped abruptly. The horrible image of that crash was so intensely etched in Charlie's mind that she knew she'd never forget it.

Maria nodded. "Exactly. So if you feel like testing the strength ability next, maybe you could picture the crash while you're trying to pick up something heavy. See if that turns on the strength power."

"I don't know," Charlie said, doubt in her voice. She didn't like the idea of reimagining the accident. It made her stomach hurt whenever she did. But this was in the name of science. Besides, now that she knew how fast she could run, she was really curious about how much she could lift. "I guess I could try it."

"Awesome." Maria looked around for Mac. "Now we need to find something big." She rolled her eyes when she saw Mac sulking. "What are you doing?"

Mac turned and looked at the girls. He jerked his head to one side and pointed toward the small, flat-roofed athletic building that was under construction. There was no one working on it today. Beyond the building was a line of Dumpsters.

"Let's see if Super Chuck can lift one of those," Mac said.

"A Dumpster?" asked Maria. "Good idea. She probably can't destroy that. Come on." She and Mac started toward them.

Charlie wrinkled her nose. "That's disgusting." But curiosity outweighed the gross factor, and she trailed along.

When she got to the nearest Dumpster, Mac was circling it, figuring out the best angle for his video recording.

"You've totally got this," Maria said, trying to pump her up.

Charlie looked it over and stood at the front of it, intending to get a grip on its sides. But it was too wide for her arms, so instead she grabbed the long, horizontal bar that ran along the front of it. "How about I see if I can just lift this side of it," she said.

"You can do it!" Maria chanted. "Mac, you got the camera going?"

"Check," Mac said. "Go ahead anytime."

Charlie nodded, wiped her hands on her pants, and gripped the horizontal bar like a weightlifter. She tried not to breathe through her nose—the rotten stench was pretty awful.

Closing her eyes, Charlie went back to that awful day in her mind when she was nine years old. She and her mom had been driving home from the dentist. Charlie had been reading a book in the backseat when Charlie's mom hit the brakes harder than usual and said a swear word that Charlie had never heard her mother say before.

Charlie had looked up. It was almost like the crash happened in slow motion right in front of them. A green car had swerved, its tires squealing, and a blue car smashed into the side of it and flipped through the air like it was a toy.

"Hang on!" Charlie's mother had yelled as their tires squealed and Charlie was thrown forward against her seat belt. In front of them, the green car hit a third vehicle. Charlie's mom pulled safely off to the side of the road as the green car finally came to a stop.

"Are you okay, sweetie?" Charlie's mom had asked her, looking over her shoulder as she dialed 911.

Charlie had nodded, even though she felt sick.

"I'm going to see if anybody is hurt," Charlie's mom had said. "Stay in the car. Keep your seat belt on." Her commands had been firm and very serious, which somehow made the situation even scarier.

"I will," said Charlie in a small voice.

The emergency operator answered the call, and Charlie's mom went into doctor mode, speaking clearly and calmly while reaching for her emergency kit and plopping it on her lap. She reached back and gave Charlie's knee a gentle squeeze, then smiled reassuringly as she spoke. Turning to look out her window to make sure no unsuspecting drivers were barreling toward her, she took her bag and slipped out of the car.

Charlie hadn't wanted to watch, but she did anyway. The green car was like a crumpled sheet of tinfoil with smoke rising from it. The blue car sat upside down in the median. The third car, a black one, was off the road in the ditch. Then she heard the sound of someone yelling and crying.

As Charlie remembered, she felt her chest constrict. She pushed up on the bar as hard as she could, straining to lift the enormous metal container.

After a moment she opened one eye to see what happened.

The Dumpster hadn't moved an inch.

CHAPTER 24

Strength

Charlie let go of the bar and sighed. "Well, that didn't work."

Mac frowned and deleted the video. Maria patted Charlie on the shoulder. "Good try, though," she said, smiling weakly.

Charlie shook her hands out and walked away from the Dumpster, trying to figure out what went wrong. Maybe it wasn't a bad enough memory.

And then she remembered that the powers activated out of necessity. And in that memory Charlie hadn't actually been in danger herself.

"You want to go home?" Maria called out.

Charlie didn't answer. She was thinking hard. "I wonder . . . ," she said under her breath. She looked up at Maria and Mac. "I'm going to try this again."

She went back to the Dumpster, gripped the bar, and took a few deep breaths. She closed her eyes and thought back to the memory, back to the moment she looked up from her book and saw the green car careering across the lanes. And this time Charlie imagined herself in the street, next to the blue car. Now the green one was headed right toward her.

Charlie's heart raced, and in her mind she screamed. She put her hands out, her eyes like slits, barely daring to look as the vehicle neared. She caught a glimpse of the driver's frightened face. *No!* Charlie yelled. She braced her feet and leaned forward, and in slow motion, her hands met the grille of the car. She leaned into it with all her might, pushing and straining, knowing she had to stop it or it would run her down.

The car's hood crumpled under her fingertips. Charlie's feet slid backward on the pavement. And then they both came to a stop.

Charlie could feel her muscles crying out, her hands aching from gripping the Dumpster. She opened her eyes, expecting to see it in the air. Instead it was on the ground, exactly where it had been all along.

She whipped her head around to look at the others—had she lifted it and set it down?

Mac and Maria were staring intently at her. "Are you done?" Maria asked.

"Did I do it?" asked Charlie. She let go of the bar and stepped back.

Her friends exchanged an uneasy glance. "No," Maria said. "It didn't move."

Charlie's shoulders sagged. She wiped the sweat from her forehead. Her arms trembled. It certainly felt like she'd done it. "Are you sure?" she asked, knowing it was a ridiculous question. "Not even a little?"

"Nope," said Mac. He deleted that video, then clicked off his phone and put it in his pocket. "My guess is, the device can detect the difference between real danger and a memory of danger."

"So we need to find some real danger," Maria said.

"Excuse me?" said Charlie.

"Exactly," Mac said. "We need to do something different, like drop the Dumpster on her head."

"What?" cried Charlie. "No stinking way. Are you nuts?"

Mac and Maria continued their conversation as if Charlie wasn't there. "We've got rope back home," said Maria, looking around. "Is there a way to do some sort of a pulley system so that you and I can lift it?"

Mac's gaze fell on the nearby athletic building. A new section being added on to it. The building housed tools, athletic equipment, and the custodian's golf cart. Evidently it had run out of room, because weathered-looking hurdles and some football equipment were stored outside. Mac's gaze traveled up to the flat roof, where a newly placed beam jutted out from one corner. "I wonder if we can somehow use that for the pulley?" he mused.

"Hmm," said Maria.

"Excuse me?" Charlie said, more forcefully this time.

Maria and Mac turned to look at her. "What?" asked Maria.

Charlie gave them an incredulous look. "You are not dropping a Dumpster on me."

Mac turned toward Charlie. His look was just as surprised.

"Why not? You won't get hurt. Your powers will kick in, and you'll catch it."

"Oh, right," said Charlie. "You're a hundred percent sure of that?"

Maria scratched her head and glanced at Mac. "Well, not a hundred percent," she admitted.

"Even if my powers kick in," said Charlie, "we don't know if I'm strong enough to stop the Dumpster from crushing me. Besides, you two won't be able to lift it. It's way too heavy."

Mac wrinkled up his nose. "Yeah, I suppose you have a point there."

"What if we try dropping something lighter on you?" Maria suggested.

Charlie looked skeptical. "Like what?" she asked, folding her arms over her chest.

Mac went to the football equipment and hurdles. "These won't work—they're all chained together." He took a few strides away from the building, then turned and looked at the top of it. "Could we get a bike or the lawn mower or something from your shed, Maria?" he said.

"Sure," said Maria.

He squinted against the sun and put a hand up to shield his eyes. "Actually, hang on. There's lots of stuff up there: a bundle of two-by-fours and some beams and a big bucket of something." He went around to the old side of the building and spied a pallet of cinder blocks. "I'm going to take a look."

He pulled a few blocks off to make steps, then climbed to the top of the stack. From there he grabbed hold of the flat roof and hoisted himself up. He swung a leg over and rolled onto the pebbled rooftop. Then he went to where the construction supplies lay, disappearing from sight.

Charlie flashed Maria an anxious glance. "I hope he knows how to get back down again," Charlie said. She was a little nervous about getting caught, but neither Mac nor Maria seemed to be.

"He does," said Maria, sounding very sure of herself. "Mac and I have been on a few of these roofs, actually. Science building, language arts." She shrugged like it was no big deal, but Charlie could tell she was proud of her feat. It was kind of cool to have fearless friends. It made Charlie want to be fearless too.

A moment later Mac reappeared. "There's a big loose wooden beam up here," he said excitedly. "I can slide it along the roof, but I can't get it over the lip. Come up here, Maria. We can probably lift it together and push it over the edge."

Maria didn't need any urging. She ran to the pallet of cinder blocks and began climbing like Mac had done.

"But how will we get it back up on the roof?" asked Charlie.

"Your strength will be activated, so you can just toss it," said Mac matter-of-factly.

"Oh," said Charlie. "Yeah, I suppose." Part of her was still troubled about this experiment—what if her strength didn't kick in and the beam landed on her? But the other part of her was certain the bracelet would come through. Plus, Charlie desperately wanted to be daring like her new friends. She really liked that Mac and Maria just assumed she was willing to test out her strength like this—they seemed to think she was as brave as they were. She didn't want to let them down. Besides, she could always jump out of the way at the last second if she didn't sense the bracelet getting warm.

Feeling better about her options, Charlie moved closer to the edge of the building and tried not to think too much about a big wooden beam hurtling down on top of her. It was better if she didn't dwell on it.

After a minute or two of loud scraping noises, Mac's and Maria's heads appeared. With a huge grunt they hoisted the beam and balanced it on the lip of the roof.

Charlie looked up uncertainly. It was thick and long and very solid looking, with shiny metal plates on either end. "Gulp," she muttered, wondering if there were any nails sticking out of it. She flexed her hands and wished for gloves. What was it her mother had said at the dinner table once about getting cut by rusty metal? Some horrible consequence—lockjaw or something. Even though the metal on the beam was shiny and new, she pulled her sleeves over her hands just in case.

Maria peered down at her. "You okay? Are you ready?"

Charlie broke out in a cold sweat. She centered herself below them and looked up. "How heavy is it?"

Mac glanced down at her as he and Maria struggled to balance it on the narrow lip. "It's not that heavy," he said. "And it doesn't have far to fall, so it won't pick up much momentum."

"Okay," Charlie said. Her voice shook. *This is crazy*, said a voice in the back of her head. *Get out of here!* With a glance at the ground next to her, she plotted her landing spot in case she ended up chickening out and diving to safety. But she kept her feet planted.

The bracelet was stone-cold. Charlie widened her stance and raised her arms above her head, fingers outstretched inside her sleeves. "Okay," she said, so scared that she didn't even feel like she was inside her own body. "I'm ready."

Mac and Maria tilted the beam, almost losing their grip, then steadied it once again. "On the count of three," Mac said.

Maria nodded.

Charlie cringed.

Mac counted. "One, two, thr—"

"Wait. STOP!" Maria cried.

Mac stopped. Charlie peered through her fingers at them. They both looked at Maria.

"We can't do this," Maria said. "What if her powers *do* actually fail? This thing could kill her!"

Mac's mouth opened and closed. Charlie clutched her heart, trying to breathe as the absurdity of what they were about to do became clear to all of them. She sank to her knees in a daze.

"You're right," Mac said reluctantly. "Let's pull it back."

Maria let out a breath and nodded.

"Ready?" said Mac. "Go."

They both pulled hard on the beam, but the metal plate attached to Mac's end caught firmly on the edge of the roof. Mac's hands slipped off, and he went tumbling backward. Maria lunged to try to hang on, but she couldn't control the unwieldy beam by herself. It teetered on the edge of the roof for an eternal second, then dropped over the side.

"CHARLIE!" screamed Maria.

CHAPTER 25

Healing

When Charlie heard Maria's screams she looked up and saw the big hunk of wood hurtling toward her. There was no time to get up or roll out of the way. She put her hands in the air as the beam made impact. An instant later she was on her back, holding the thing above her face. The bracelet pulsed with heat on her arm.

She stared, trying to make sense of what had happened as Maria and Mac scrambled to the edge of the rooftop and peered over, their faces horrified. "Charlie!" Maria yelled again.

"I'm okay," Charlie called.

The two gaped down at Charlie, holding the beam above her face.

"Whew," said Mac. "We're coming down." They disappeared.

Charlie, still stunned, noticed the dents her fingers had made in the wood. She grimaced and threw the beam into the grass next to her, then looked at her hands. Amazingly she was unscathed, except for a few tiny splinters in her fingers. She rolled to all fours and got up, then began dusting herself off as Maria and Mac made their way down to the ground.

"*¡Lo siento!*" Maria cried, running to Charlie's side. "I'm so sorry. It was an accident. The metal caught and threw everything off balance."

"Yeah, sorry," said Mac, breathing hard and wheezing a little from the exertion. He pulled an inhaler from his pocket and used it.

"It's okay," Charlie said, rattled. "I'm glad you screamed, Maria." She looked at the long hunk of wood, then tentatively bent down and picked it up. It felt as lightweight as her backpack. She moved away from the building, holding it like a giant javelin, and tossed it as carefully as possible onto the roof. It banged and thumped and settled out of sight.

"Wow," Mac said. He couldn't help staring at Charlie. "That was pretty amazing."

"Thanks," said Charlie.

"Is the bracelet warm?"

"Yes." She showed him.

"And . . . you're not hurt or anything, right?"

"No, I'm fine." Charlie narrowed her eyes. "Why?"

Mac shrugged innocently. "I just thought you might want to see how much you can actually lift now that you've got the thing activated." He looked pointedly at the Dumpster.

"Oh yes!" said Maria. "Now's a great time to do that." She faltered, searching Charlie's face. "I mean, if you're up to it."

Charlie let out a deep, ragged sigh. She shoved the warm bracelet back up her forearm and pulled her sleeve over it, then wiped her hands on her jeans and flexed her fingers a few times. She walked over to the Dumpster.

Silently Mac got his camera cued up.

Charlie rested her hands on the bar and closed her eyes, and then she strained with all her might to lift it.

When she heard a distant sound of yelling, Charlie opened her eyes. Maria and Mac were both exclaiming unintelligible things next to her. She looked up and nearly gasped, for she was holding the Dumpster above her head, and loose pieces of trash were tumbling out. "Whoa," she said as a bag of something hot and slimy hit her in the face and fell to the ground. "Blech!"

Totally grossed out, Charlie dropped the container, which made the ground shake and the asphalt crack below it.

"Yikes," she said. She stepped back and looked at her hands. It really was possible.

Standing here with Maria and Mac witnessing everything made the powers seem more real. Charlie tried to comprehend the strange predicament she was in. These crazy things were really happening. These powers belonged to her and her alone, whether she wanted them or not. As long as the bracelet was stuck on her wrist, Charlie had a choice. She could tiptoe around telling herself the bracelet was bad, dreading the next time something happened. Or she could accept the fact that these abilities were hers to use and, in using them, try to learn how to control them—at least a little, she hoped. They'd already learned so much today. But it had opened up even more questions, like who could create a device that would do this . . . and why?

As she stood there, Maria and Mac having an excited conversation in the background, a tiny thrill raced through Charlie, conflicting her thoughts. As much as she wanted to get the thing off her arm, part of her couldn't wait to see what else she could do.

"Gorilla, maybe," Mac said as they picked up the trash and threw it back into the Dumpster. "Nah—whale. Hmm. Or maybe an ox?"

Maria and Charlie exchanged an amused glance as Mac carried on the conversation with himself, but they, too, wondered which animal's strength Charlie had adopted. Once they went back to Maria's shed, Mac researched the weight of different Dumpsters, and factoring the trash inside, he thought that Charlie had probably lifted more than six hundred pounds.

"Sheesh," Charlie murmured. "I'm amazing . . . but only when necessary."

"Amazing when necessary," quipped Maria. "That should be your motto."

Charlie laughed. "I like it."

But Mac wouldn't be distracted. "We still have one more experiment to do."

Charlie narrowed her eyes. "We do?"

"Yeah. The healing one."

"And just how are we supposed to test that?" Charlie asked warily.

"Well, I was hoping you'd get hurt by the falling beam, actually," Mac said.

"What a nice thing to say," Charlie said drily.

"Sorry. But since you didn't," he said, back to business, "I was thinking we could start with a cut, like on your arm or something. Somewhere that your parents won't notice—"

"Absolutely not," said Charlie.

"And then move on to breaking a bone. Just a small one, like a toe—"

"I don't think you heard me."

"And if we're really daring," Mac went on excitedly, "we could try cutting off a limb to see if you can regenerate—"

"Stop. Talking. Now," Charlie said, with an eerie calmness in her voice.

Mac stopped. "What?"

"Um, I'm not really interested in hurting myself, much less cutting off a limb, just to see how fast I can heal. Thanks anyway."

"But—but animals!" Mac said. "Here. Look what they can do." He searched "animal healing ability" on his iPad and started showing Charlie the various pages. "See? Lizards can regenerate limbs. And starfish—you won't even believe this, but some starfish can regenerate almost entire new bodies!"

Mac seemed way too excited about cutting off Charlie's body

parts. And testing this ability was one thing she wasn't going to give in to, that was for sure. She already knew she could heal fast based on how she'd recovered from the soccer injury. That was enough information as far as she was concerned.

"Not happening, Mac," Charlie said once he'd exhausted his resources. "Sorry. Actually, not sorry. And since you're starting to sound a little bit crazy with all of this, I think we might need to call a time-out." She got up to leave. "Maybe you can go back to actually finding out what the secret code is to deactivate this thing," she said, shoving up her sleeve and shaking her arm. "Remember? That was the plan."

"I have a program gathering a list of the most frequently used passwords as we speak," Mac said. "Once I've got them all, we'll start trying them."

Charlie stopped midshake and glanced at the bracelet, frowning. "Hey," she said. "Look at this. The screen is different."

Maria and Mac crowded around to see it. Instead of the red words declaring *DEFENSE MODE* scrolling across the screen, there was a gray-circle graphic sliced like a pie into five sections, each containing a strange line drawing. Three of the drawings were animated, like GIFs. The other two didn't move.

"How did you get to this screen?" Mac demanded.

"I don't know," Charlie said.

Mac took a short video of the screen and then randomly pushed a few buttons on the bracelet. The screen went back to the scrolling message, reminding them that defense mode was in place and asking for a deactivation code. He pushed more buttons and, after a few tries, discovered that if he held down the two buttons on the side of the bracelet nearest Charlie's hand for two seconds, the screen flipped to the chart.

"Maybe it happened when you caught the beam, or when you were lifting the Dumpster," Maria guessed.

"Hmm." Mac let go of Charlie's arm, typed a few notes into his phone, and studied the photo of the chart, zooming in on the individual pie pieces. "So what's the chart for? The drawings look like vines floating through the air or something."

"Or worms." Maria shrugged, stumped. "And why aren't those two animated?"

Charlie squinted at the device screen. After a bit she looked up. "It's a chart of the bracelet's abilities. Look at this first one." She held out her arm to Maria.

"All I can see is a bunch of swirly lines being blown side to side in the wind," Maria said.

Charlie smiled. "Focus on it. It's a cheetah running—do you see it? Here's the head."

Maria looked again. All at once her face lit up. "Oooh," she said. "I see it now!"

"Show me," said Mac, yanking Charlie's arm closer.

"Screw your eyes up a little," Charlie said. "It'll come into focus."

After a minute, Mac's face changed. "Whoa, I got you now. Cool." He squinted and said, "What are the other ones?"

All three of them stared. Charlie's arm began to ache from being held up. The second pie slice had darker-gray vine lines moving in an up-and-down pattern.

"Elephant!" Mac cried. "Darn it, I should have guessed. He's standing on his back legs and facing us. But what the heck is he doing?"

Maria tilted her head. "He's lifting a log up and down. Do you see it, Charlie? Ha! A bodybuilder elephant."

No matter what Charlie did, she couldn't see what Mac and Maria were seeing. She looked up at the ceiling for a moment, and then looked back at the bracelet. The elephant shape finally came into focus. "Oh!" she said, giggling. "I see it now. I think I was trying too hard before."

Mac pointed to the screen. "What's the third one?"

The third animated drawing was made up of lines that all met and twirled around like a pinwheel. The outer edges of the lines rolled up and then stretched out as they rotated in a circle.

"Sweet," said Maria, looking up. "This one's my favorite."

Mac looked harder.

"What is it?" asked Charlie. "A flower? The sun? No, it's got to be another animal."

"Oh, it's a starfish!" exclaimed Mac.

"Starfish are very cool," said Maria.

As soon as they figured it out, Charlie could see the third drawing was a starfish too. She turned to Mac, her eyes like slits. "Don't get any crazy ideas."

He rubbed his hands together eagerly.

"I mean it, Mac," said Charlie. "You'd better keep the pointy objects away from me!"

Maria looked at all three wedges. "So each wedge shows an animal that is part of the chimera. You have the speed of a cheetah, the strength of an elephant, and the healing ability of the starfish?"

"I guess so," Charlie said. She turned back to the bracelet. "What about these two sections that aren't animated?"

"More abilities?" Mac guessed. "Maybe they become animated once you activate them."

"I'll bet that's it," said Maria. She squeezed Charlie's forearm. "How exciting!"

Charlie's eyes widened, and she glanced back at the chart. "More?" she echoed.

"I sure hope so," said Mac, his grin growing wider by the minute.

"Whoa," Charlie said under her breath. There were two more abilities that she hadn't activated yet. She had no idea what they could be.

CHAPTER 26

Unknown Powers

The three tried to guess what the other two abilities could be by studying the wedges. One of the drawings had a tiny circle in the middle with four lines going out from it.

"Clearly that's a bow tie," said Maria, "so you must have penguin abilities."

Mac wrinkled his nose. "What?"

"Get it? You wear a bow tie with a tuxedo."

"Yeah," said Charlie, nodding, a grin spreading over her face. "Tuxedo. Looks like a penguin suit. I get it. So my special ability is . . . what? Holding an egg on my feet for like two months?"

"What are you talking about?" said Mac.

"*March of the Penguins*—haven't you ever seen it?" asked Charlie. "My dad is a freak for that movie." She shook her head in mock disgust. "Biologists."

"Parents are weird," said Mac. "My dad cries every time we watch *Toy Story 3*. But back to the symbol," he said, tapping the device, "I think it obviously represents a sneeze. Try sneezing, Charlie. Everybody stand back."

"Ha-ha," said Charlie. "Very funny. But it's not a sneeze. It's an old TV antenna. My dad has one stashed away in the garage just in case the world ends and cable goes out. With our luck, we'd probably only be able to get PBS."

"Great," Maria groaned. "So your fourth ability is broadcasting baby TV shows on public television."

"Easy, now," muttered Mac. "PBS isn't just for babies. And there's nothing wrong with the occasional *Odd Squad* when you're killing time." He sniffed. "I'm just saying."

Maria stared at him. "My little stepbrothers watch that. Since when do *you* watch *Odd Squad*?"

Mac looked defensive. "I watch it *with* them when I'm waiting for you to come home from practice. It's kind of like I'm babysitting. Your parents should pay me, actually."

"You know," said Maria, "You could come to practice once, and then you'd know when I'm done."

"Forget that," said Mac. "No Wi-Fi on the field. And your mom counts on me to try her after-school snacks to make sure they taste good."

"You don't really fall for that, do you?" asked Maria, incredulous.

"Hey," said Mac, "this dude does what it takes to live the good life. If that means I have to suffer watching *Odd Squad* with free Wi-Fi and a cookie in hand while I wait for you, then that's the price I have to pay."

Charlie laughed and shook her head, watching them. "Excuse

me, people, but what about this last drawing?"

Mac and Maria turned back to look at the bracelet. The fifth wedge had several vine-type lines to it with absolutely no distinct detail to focus on. It was just an oval-shaped blob with some lines sticking out.

Everyone was silent for a long moment.

"It's a . . . campfire?" ventured Maria.

"Definitely Bigfoot," said Mac.

"I was thinking mud puddle and sticks," said Charlie. She scratched her head and looked at her friends.

They both shook their heads. With a growing sense of dread, Charlie began to wonder what would have to happen for this latest mystery to be solved.

CHAPTER 27

Powers, Activate!

Whenever Charlie was alone over the following week, she tried triggering her abilities. She knew now that the powers would only work when necessary, like when she was on the defensive or in danger. But how did the bracelet know? Was it her heart rate and pulse that activated it? Or her sense of fear? Just imagining danger wasn't enough. But she wondered if there were other ways she could trick the bracelet into believing she was in danger. So she decided to do a few experiments of her own.

In first period she purposely waited for the bell to ring before running to her desk, hoping to trigger speed like she'd done early on. But by now Charlie knew her teacher was usually late coming into class, so she wasn't actually worried about getting in trouble. It didn't work.

She tried to get it to turn on during soccer practice that week, but the team only worked on drills and ran short plays. They didn't split into teams to scrimmage, so without an opponent hunting her down, that didn't work either.

After school on Friday she ran all the way home, thinking that maybe if she elevated her heart rate for a long enough time, it might indicate to the bracelet that she needed help. When she got home, she went into the garage and tried lifting the extra freezer they kept there, but she couldn't even move it an inch.

"There has to be a way," she texted Maria. "Parents both working until late, brother at a sleepover, so I'm home alone tonight. Gonna try the horror-movie thing."

"I've got a great one!" replied Maria. "Have you seen *Cringe 3* yet?"

"OMG no way too scary."

"Then it's perfect. I'll bring it over!"

Charlie's heart was already racing in anticipation. "Yikes— OK. Is Mac coming?"

"Nah, I'll send him home. He'll just make fun of us if we scream. See you in 15!"

"OK!"

Maria arrived with the movie and a copy of the first Ms. Marvel comic. "As promised," she said. "I thought you'd like this one first."

"Thanks!" Charlie put the comic on the dining table. She showed Maria to the living room to get the movie going, then ran through the house to turn out all the lights for an ultrascary experience. She and Maria settled on the living-room couch in the dark to watch *Cringe 3*. They turned up the volume. And they screamed their heads off. By the time the movie was over, Charlie's heart was racing. Her palms were sweating. And she was scared to death.

"Come on," Maria said in a low voice. "Let's sneak through the house with all the lights off. Maybe some murderous ghosts will come out like in the movie."

Charlie shuddered. She was still getting used to this house and the quirky sounds it made at night. In daylight she would have scoffed at the idea of creepy killer ghosts in her house, but after watching the movie and being here in the dark without her parents at home . . . well, of course she *knew* there weren't supernatural things happening, but . . . what if she was wrong? "Okay," she whispered, her voice faltering.

Maria crawled through the dark living room, with Charlie sticking close behind. They went into the dining room and on to the kitchen, inching along quietly. Charlie's heart pounded. She heard a rustling sound and stopped. "Do you hear something?" she whispered.

Maria didn't answer.

Charlie's pulse pounded in her ears. "Maria?" she whispered more harshly this time. "Where are you?" She began feeling around for her friend, who had been right in front of her a minute ago. "Come on, don't tease me."

Maria still didn't answer.

Charlie began to panic. She scrambled to her feet and tried to remember which wall the light switches were on. She ran into the garbage can, knocking it over and scaring herself even more.

"Maria!" she shouted. "This isn't funny!"

Suddenly something grabbed Charlie's leg. Charlie let out a bloodcurdling scream. Jessie came bounding down the stairs from Andy's room to see what was going on, knocking into Charlie and spinning her around in the dark.

Completely disoriented, Charlie could think of nothing but escape. She ran, stumbling over the garbage can again and slamming her shoulder into a wall before finally finding her way to the front door. She flung it open and took off out into the neighborhood with her excited dog chasing after her.

Maria came out of hiding and followed her to the yard. "Charlie, come back!" she shouted, hands gripping her hair and a worried look on her face. But as she watched Charlie move under the streetlamps, her worried look faded and turned to confusion. Charlie didn't seem to be running any faster than normal—certainly not as fast as when they'd tested her. Jessie was keeping up with her just fine.

A few minutes later Charlie and Jessie returned, breathing hard but unharmed. "Why didn't you answer me?" accused Charlie.

Maria's voice was filled with remorse. "I'm sorry. I was just trying to scare you so the bracelet would turn on like before. I didn't think you'd freak out like that."

Charlie's eyes clouded, but now that Maria was visible and penitent, she began to feel a little silly. "I told you *Cringe 3* would be too scary," she mumbled. "Anyway, it didn't work."

"Nope," said Maria glumly. "So now I'm extrasorry I scared you."

"It's okay," said Charlie, giving Maria a quick side hug as they walked to the front door. "It's weird, though. Once I could think straight, I realized the bracelet was warm. So I tried to run faster, but it didn't work. I don't understand it. Between you and Jessie scaring me, I seriously thought I was about to die. Not to mention that horrible trash can disaster," she added with an embarrassed laugh.

"I don't get it," Maria said, going inside and turning on a light. "You weren't nearly that scared when you managed to clock seventy miles an hour the other day."

Charlie whistled sharply to Jessie, and then followed the dog into the house "What's even weirder is that my wrist is actually still warm," she said, batting at the front door to close it. But it was stuck to the wall and wouldn't budge. "What the—?" Charlie gave it a little tug. It wiggled, but she couldn't get it to swing shut. She peered behind it, and to her dismay she saw that the door handle was embedded in the wall—it had broken through the drywall. Charlie's eyes widened, and she looked down. The little stopper on the floor was decimated.

"Oh no!" Charlie exclaimed. "Look, Maria."

Maria came to the door. "Whoa," she said. "How'd you do that? Should we check the device? Maybe something will show up on it."

Charlie held down the two buttons, and the pie chart graph appeared. The once gray elephant graphic was lit up in bright silver, black, and red.

"Wow," said Maria. "Full color—does that mean your strength ability is working?"

"Looks that way," said Charlie, scratching her head. "But why did strength turn on instead of speed? Isn't the natural instinct of an animal to run when it's scared?" She pulled out her phone and took a photo of the damage, then texted it to Mac so he could see what had happened, along with a selfie of her and Maria with looks of mock horror on their faces.

"Wow," he texted back, with a selfie of himself looking bored. Charlie showed Maria.

"Hmm," she said, frowning a bit at his reaction.

Charlie examined the wall, growing serious. "What am I going to do about this hole?" She tugged the door gently as pieces of drywall broke off and dropped to the floor. "Yikes."

With another tug the handle came loose, and she closed the door. "I'm not sure what to tell my dad when he gets home," said Charlie. She and Maria went to the kitchen to clean up the garbage so she wouldn't have even more to explain, and then checked the bedrooms to make sure neither of the cats had escaped during the confusion with the front door standing open. She found them both curled on Andy's bed, having slept through all the excitement. Apparently their flight responses hadn't been triggered either.

The girls returned to the front door, but before they could come up with a plan to magically fix the gaping hole in the wall, they heard the garage door open.

"That's my dad, I bet," said Charlie, pulling her sweatshirt sleeve down over the bracelet. "Maybe you should go."

"I'll stay if you want," said Maria. "I can help take the blame. It's partly my fault—I scared you."

"It's okay. Unless . . . do you maybe want to stay overnight? I mean, I know you didn't bring your stuff. . . ."

"I'd love to!" Maria said. She pulled out her phone to text her mom.

"Awesome," said Charlie as her father walked into the house.

"Hey, Peanut," he called out in a weary voice. "You're still awake?"

"Hi, Dad," said Charlie, going to greet him and pulling Maria along with her. "This is my friend Maria."

Dr. Wilde's tired eyes lit up, and he smiled warmly. "Hi, Maria," he said. "I'm glad you could keep Charlie company tonight."

"Hi, Mr. Wilde," Maria said with a little wave. Then she read his ID, which was clipped and hanging unevenly on his jacket pocket. "Wait . . . you're a doctor too?" She turned to Charlie. "So both your parents are doctors? Cool!"

"Yeah, technically he's also Dr. Wilde," Charlie explained. "But my mom's the *real* kind." She flashed her dad a playful grin, as if they'd made that joke before. "Confusing, I know."

"That's for sure," said Charlie's dad. "I'm the doctor you definitely don't want to call when you almost break your leg. You're fine just calling me Mr. Wilde. Or Dr. Wilde Two. Or Mr. Dr. Wilde. Or Charles. Or . . ." He stopped. "I think that's all I've got. Take your pick."

"Mr. Dr. Wilde is funny," said Maria, grinning.

Charlie reached out and took her father's briefcase and helped him out of his jacket, suddenly growing nervous now that she had to explain the hole in the wall. "How was class? Can I get you some ice cream or anything?" she asked a little too sweetly.

"Class was— Hold on. Ice cream?" He eyed her suspiciously. "Why? What happened?"

Charlie bit her lip as she hung the jacket in the closet. "Um, I kind of have to show you something," she said guiltily.

Dr. Wilde gave her a guarded look. "All right," he said. He glanced at Maria, who hung back, eyes wide.

Charlie took his hand and pulled him to the front door, pointing at the wall.

"I'm really sorry, Dad," said Charlie earnestly. "We were just goofing around in the dark and scaring each other, and I opened the door too hard and . . . this happened. I'll fix it if you show me how."

Dr. Wilde looked at the damage, then dropped to one knee and picked up the doorstop spring. He squished what was left of it between his fingers. It crumbled. He ran his hand over the hole in the drywall, wiping away the tiny loose bits, and then he looked at Charlie with a tired smile. "Well, I suppose the new house couldn't stay perfect forever," he said, "but I'd hoped it might make it longer than a couple of weeks."

"I know," said Charlie, cringing. "I'm sorry."

He reached out to ruffle her hair, but his voice was strained. "Just take it easy next time, please."

"It's my fault," Maria blurted out. "I scared her."

Dr. Wilde straightened up. "It was an accident. And clearly the doorstopper was defective; otherwise it would have stopped the handle from hitting the wall. So that's no one's fault," he said. He looked at Charlie. "We'll fix it some weekend once things settle down at the college, okay, kiddo?"

"Yeah," said Charlie. "Thanks, Dad." She hesitated as he walked toward the kitchen. "Um, can Maria stay overnight?"

He stopped and looked back. "Did you ask Mom? It's fine with me."

"I haven't seen Mom since Tuesday," Charlie said with a tinge of accusation.

"You forgot how to text?" he asked sharply as he continued into the dining room. "She has a cell phone."

"Okay, I'll ask her," Charlie said, trailing after him. "Sorry. Anyway, it's fine with you, right?"

"Of course," he said, picking up his briefcase from the table where Charlie had placed it. He headed in the direction of his study. "Glad to have you, Maria."

"Thanks, Mr. Dr.," Maria said meekly.

That drew a smile from Charlie's dad.

The two scampered to Charlie's bedroom and closed the door—gently.

CHAPTER 28

Best Friends

The girls awoke on Saturday morning to the sound of Maria's phone ringing. It played the theme from *Spider-Man*, which meant it was Mac calling. Maria sat up and squinted as sunlight streamed in through the space between the shade and the window. She looked around, bewildered, before locating her phone and answering it.

"Hey," she mumbled. "What's up?"

"Where are you?" Mac spoke harshly, and loud enough for Charlie to hear.

"I'm at Charlie's. I slept over. What's—"

"Well, guess where I am?"

Maria pushed her mussed hair off her forehead. "I have no idea."

"I texted you like five times."

"I just woke up," said Maria. "Where are you?"

"I'm in the movie theater lobby, waiting for you. The movie started five minutes ago."

Maria's eyes widened. "Crap," she said. "I— What time is it?"

Mac's voice was cold. "Five minutes after the movie started."

"Sorry," Maria said, cringing. She scrambled to her feet and began looking around for her things. "I'll be there as soon as I can."

"Forget it. It's too late now." Mac hung up.

Maria stared at her phone, quickly scanning the flurry of texts, and then called him back. He didn't answer.

"What's going on?" asked Charlie.

"Ugh," Maria said, pulling her hair out of its ponytail and smoothing it down. "I totally forgot to meet Mac. He's been waiting for me at the movie theater."

"I'm sorry," said Charlie, biting her lip. "He sounded mad from what I could hear. Want me to go with you?"

"Nah." Maria grabbed *Cringe 3* from Charlie's desk and slipped into her shoes. "Well, maybe," she said, grabbing a brush from Charlie's dresser and redoing her ponytail. "Do you mind?"

"Of course not." Charlie hopped out of bed and hurried to get ready, and soon the girls were on the move.

By the time they got there the movie was sold out, so they played video games in the lobby until it was over. "He'll be the last one out," Maria said. "We always stay through all the credits in case there's an extra scene."

Finally Mac rounded the corner of the theater, slam-dunking his half-full popcorn bucket into the garbage can before he saw the girls.

He frowned. "What are you doing here?"

"Waiting for you," Maria said. "We tried to get tickets, but it was sold out."

Mac folded his arms and looked from one girl to the other.

A boy across the lobby hooted at Mac. "Your girlfriend showed up after all!" he called.

Maria whirled around and stared down the boy. "Shut your pie hole, Mendez!" she shouted at him.

"Knock it off, Maria," Mac said sharply.

"What? He was being gross."

"I don't need you to stand up for me. Sheesh. Ignore that jerk."

Charlie shrank back a little and pretended to look at the display of Jujyfruits and licorice whips inside the snack case.

"Excuse me?" said Maria. "I'll stand up for my friends whenever I feel like it."

Mac snorted. "Or maybe you'll just stand them up and forget that you go to the ten-o'clock movie every Saturday morning with your best friend."

"I said I was sorry," Maria said. Her voice softened. "I am, really." She put her hand on his arm, but he stepped back, out of reach. "Come on," she pleaded. "Let's go get a slice from Barro's. It's my turn to pay."

Mac's face went through a barrage of emotions. He looked like he didn't often turn down a free slice of pizza.

"I don't know." He shrugged and pointed toward Charlie. "Is she coming?"

Charlie looked up expectantly, and then dropped her gaze again when she realized Mac didn't seem excited about the prospect. She wasn't sure why he was mad at her—she hadn't done anything wrong.

"Of course she's coming," Maria said. "Let's go." She grabbed Mac's arm with one hand and linked her other arm with Charlie's. "We've got to hurry and get there before all the tables are gone."

Mac went along with her, halfheartedly at first, then pulling from Maria's grasp once more but keeping up. "If they run out of tables, maybe Supergirl here can rip off a piece of the wall and make a new one." He looked sideways at Charlie.

Charlie grinned at him. "The problem is, we'd have to watch a scary movie first and then run around in the dark like idiots."

"Huh?" asked Mac. He seemed annoyed again, and Charlie realized she probably shouldn't have said anything.

But Maria didn't notice. She giggled and said, "If only you could activate the powers on command, all our problems would be solved."

"Not quite," Mac muttered.

"What?" asked Maria.

"Never mind," said Mac.

The next Monday at soccer practice Charlie didn't even bother trying to activate the bracelet. It was too frustrating when it wouldn't turn on, and it just began feeling like a waste of time. Besides,

Charlie wanted to focus on improving her scoring skills since the team would be playing against other schools soon—their first game was on Thursday. Charlie wanted to be a starter, not sit on the bench, and the next few days of practice would help Coach Candy decide the lineup. So Charlie became intent on doing the best she could . . . without the bracelet's help.

Of course Kelly got in the way sometimes. Ever since their collision on the field, Charlie had largely ignored her, both on the field and backstage. And Kelly kept her distance for the most part as well—especially recently. Both were nice when they were together, but it was clear that they would never be best friends— not like Charlie and Maria. And Mac, of course.

Coach divided up the team to scrimmage, and Maria and Charlie were on the blue team together this time. Kelly was on the opposing side wearing red, and after she'd been noticeably quiet at school during the day, she was burning up the field.

"Kelly's playing really hot today," Charlie remarked to Maria as they walked back to their positions after she scored another goal.

"Yeah, she's doing great," said Maria. "She was acting pretty *loco* in the locker room earlier, though. Had a screaming fight on the phone with her mom. It wasn't pretty."

"Hmm," said Charlie. Part of her wished she'd witnessed it, but then she felt bad—screaming fights with parents were never fun. And she'd had enough tension with her own parents lately to feel sympathy, even for Kelly. "I'm kind of glad I missed that."

She moved to her spot as left forward. Coach blew the whistle, and Charlie's team took the ball.

The red team's forwards and halfbacks attacked Charlie's team's advancing line in layers. Their fullbacks, including Kelly, moved up to try and gain control in case the ball went flying. Charlie stayed with her line, edging toward the middle of the field a bit more as the center forward wove around the opposition.

When the ball broke loose, Charlie dug in her cleats and went after it, dodging around the other players. One of the forwards on the red team, a tough, muscular girl named Vanessa, charged toward the ball as well. Charlie had gotten tangled up with Vanessa a few times during scrimmages, and they'd had some good-natured complaining to do about each other, but they kept it friendly. Now, with the stakes high for the forwards who all coveted the four starting spots, Vanessa had a determined look on her face.

Charlie's face matched it. Vanessa was bigger, but Charlie was a tiny bit more agile, so the race was on for the loose ball. But then, out of nowhere, Kelly rushed in and captured it. The two forwards tripped over each other and scrambled to their feet just in time to watch Kelly take the ball straight down the center and pass it off to a red-shirted halfback, who took it all the way to the goal and scored.

Vanessa cheered her team on, and Charlie went back to her position, disappointed and breathing hard.

The next time Charlie had possession, Vanessa was there again.

Simultaneously they connected with the ball, sending it soaring straight up. They jockeyed for position under it, but Charlie knew Vanessa's height would win out this time. Vanessa leaped up to head the flying ball, but she mistimed her jump and came down on top of Charlie, who caught the girl. Immediately Charlie realized that her bracelet had activated, so she dropped Vanessa and fell to the ground, both of them sprawling over the grass. Charlie flopped to her back, the wind knocked out of her. She lay there for a second, seeing stars and feeling the bracelet burning on her wrist. The ball rolled out of bounds.

When Charlie could breathe, she got to her feet. "You okay, Vanessa?" Charlie asked, holding out a hand but being careful not to yank the girl to her feet.

"I'm good," Vanessa said. She hopped up and down, keeping her game face on.

"Blue team's ball!" Coach hollered.

Charlie jogged a few steps to make sure everything was working properly. The bracelet stayed warm. She gave it a quick click and looked at the screen, seeing the elephant lit up. Only the strength ability was activated.

Charlie took a spot on the field near where the ball had gone out of bounds and waited for her teammate to throw it in. Out of the corner of her eye she saw Kelly step up behind her.

The ball flew over their heads. They both turned to run toward it, Kelly pushing off Charlie to get a head start. With only her strength activated, not speed, Charlie had to hustle to catch up to Kelly and get in front of her, but by some miracle she pulled it off. She started toward the goal, almost no opposition in front of her. But Kelly was on her heels, trying with all her might—and almost succeeding—to get the ball away from Charlie.

Charlie passed to the teammate on her right and faked left as the red team's halfbacks caught up with them. With a look of consternation, Kelly realized how far she'd strayed from her position. She abandoned her efforts, letting her teammates do their job, and turned to jog back toward the goal to protect it with the other full-backs.

As the blue team drew close, Charlie's teammate flipped the ball back to Charlie. Seeing her shot, Charlie pulled her leg back and punted the ball as hard as she could toward the goal. The ball screamed toward it . . . heading straight for Kelly. Kelly didn't see it coming until she looked up at the last second. The ball struck her hard in the side of her face, knocking her off her feet, and ricocheted directly into the goal.

Which meant that Kelly had accidentally scored against her own team.

Everyone was silent for a split second, trying to comprehend what had just happened, and then several of Charlie's teammates began cheering for the goal. Some of the girls on Kelly's team exploded in anger, while others ran to make sure Kelly was okay.

"Oh, crud," Charlie whispered. She put her hand in the air,

claiming fault—though, in truth, if Kelly had watched where she was going, she might have dodged the hit in time. Thankfully Kelly soon rose to her feet, her cheek an angry shade of red. She was furious. Charlie glanced at Maria with a look of relief once she saw that Kelly wasn't seriously hurt.

As Coach declared the blue team victorious and called an end to practice, Charlie ran over to Kelly to apologize, but the girl was surrounded.

Not wanting to fight her way through the crowd, Charlie headed to the locker room instead to change first. Maria caught up with her, and they walked together.

"Chuck, you need to be careful," Maria murmured. "Did you notice the bracelet had activated? That was a really intense kick."

"I know," Charlie said. "I wasn't aiming for Kelly—she just got in the way."

Maria shot her a sympathetic smile, and the two parted in the sea of players. They'd have to talk later.

Charlie started to get dressed amid the chatter. Some of the girls were imitating Kelly and the way she got bowled over when the ball hit her. Charlie frowned and hurried to pack up her things, wanting to get out of there before Kelly came in and heard her teammates making fun of her. Sure, Charlie didn't really like Kelly all that much, but she didn't want people to be mean to her either.

When Charlie was ready, she grabbed her backpack and phone and slipped through the locker room, then paused at the door, feeling like she should tell them all to lay off. But she changed her mind. She was still really new here. She didn't want people to turn on her, too. Besides, a tiny part of Charlie thought Kelly could use a bit of ridicule to take her down a notch. She turned to go.

As she went out the door and toward the path that led to home, she saw Kelly coming in from the field. Kelly glowered at her.

Charlie slowed, feeling guilty. "Are you okay?" she asked, trying not to stare at the giant red blotch on Kelly's cheek. "I'm sorry—I didn't mean to hit you with the ball."

Kelly's eyebrows twitched. And while her mouth remained in its angry pout, her other features softened the tiniest bit. She turned her head away. "I'm fine," she said with a cool smile.

"Good. Because we're on the same team from here on out."

"Whether we like it or not," Kelly said, and even though she still wore a smile, she didn't seem happy. She hesitated, then kept going to the locker room.

Charlie watched her for a moment, then turned away and walked home.

CHAPTER 29

Bold Moves

Ever since Saturday morning at the movies, Mac had been acting a little strange. But he seemed as excited as always when the three of them were talking secretly about the bracelet and its powers. Charlie couldn't quite figure out what was going on with him.

At lunch on Tuesday, Maria glanced over her shoulder at Kelly's table, then leaned toward Charlie, who sat across from her. "Did you see the bruise you gave her?"

"Yeah," said Charlie. "How could I miss it?"

Mac squinted at Charlie. "You gave her that? How?"

"Hit her with the ball when my strength kicked in. Not on purpose. She got in the way."

"Wow," said Mac. "Bet she was mad."

"No kidding," said Charlie.

"I wonder why your strength turned on in the first place," said Maria. "Was it another one of those weird glitches like Friday night?"

"I don't think so," said Charlie. "Vanessa fell on me, and that turned it on."

"Weird glitches?" asked Mac. He gave Maria an accusing look.

"Sorry. Forgot to tell you about that part." Maria filled him in on the things that he didn't know had happened at Charlie's house with the scary movie, and then in a quieter voice she explained to Mac how they'd expected the speed power to kick in, but the strength power had turned on for some reason.

"That's strange," said Mac. "Did you look at the bracelet at all?"

"Yeah," said Charlie. "The elephant was lit up—in color. It was pretty cool. I'll have to show you the next time it's activated. It's back to normal now." She shoved up her sleeve and held out her arm to show him.

He scooted his chair back a few inches and leaned away. "That's okay," he said, looking around. "I've seen that."

Charlie's eyes narrowed. "Ooh-kay," she said. She pushed her sleeve over the bracelet and sat back.

Maria didn't seem to notice. "You should have seen the wall at Charlie's house, though," she said, shaking her head.

"I saw the photo."

"And the doorstop—holy smokes. She obliterated it."

Mac stopped scanning the cafeteria and looked at her. "Guess you had to be there," he said, a little too lightly.

Maria picked up on his tone this time. She frowned. "What's that supposed to mean?"

"Nothing," said Mac. "I . . . I gotta go work on a thing. Meeting a friend. Later."

Mac left with his tray. Maria watched him catch up to a group of guys. "See? He's doing it again."

Charlie shrugged. "I don't know what's up with him. But starting tomorrow I'm going to help out with the set for the musical during lunch. The show is Friday night, and we're not even close to being ready. We could use some more help—do you want to come?"

"I don't know," said Maria dubiously. "Isn't Mr. Anderson kind of nuts?"

Charlie grinned. "A little, but building the set is really fun, and he's not around much. When I started here," she confided, "I picked theater class as an elective because my mom thought it would be good to help me make friends." She grimaced. "But it sounded easy, so I went along with it."

Maria laughed. "Moms," she said, shaking her head.

"I know. But it turns out theater class is way better than I expected it would be." Her face began to light up as she talked. "We get to use tools without any adults hovering over us making us nervous. And Sara, the stage manager, is really cool—she asks my opinion about the set even though I'm new."

"Sara Cortez? I know her. She's nice."

Charlie nodded and went on. "Mr. Anderson has a lot going on with the actors and musicians, so he leaves us alone and has us figure out how to do stuff on our own. He's in the building if we need him, obviously, but he keeps telling us it's *our* production, so we're in charge, not him." She pondered for a moment, trying to pinpoint what it was she liked so much about that. "He trusts us," she said finally. "So . . . do you wanna come help?"

Maria gave a small smile. "Sure," she said. "I guess if Mac is going to keep ditching me, anything sounds better than sitting here alone."

The next day Charlie and Maria met up before lunch and walked together past the cafeteria building on their way to the auditorium. As they crossed the courtyard, they ran into Mac.

"Hey," he said. "So you're working on the set?"

"Like I told you this morning," said Maria, a bit coolly.

"Okay, well, I was just making sure," said Mac, looking down. He kicked a rock off the sidewalk into the stones nearby. "Have fun." He started toward the cafeteria.

Maria watched him go, her face troubled.

Charlie felt a pang of pity for both of them. "Wait," she called after Mac. "We could use more help if you want to come along."

Mac stopped and turned back to the girls. He studied them for a second and then shrugged. "I mean, if you really need help, I suppose I could."

"Come on," said Charlie, and Mac caught up with them.

Charlie tracked down Mr. Anderson to let him know she'd brought friends, and he was very glad to have the extra help. Since Charlie knew what was going on with the set, he let her give them their jobs, and he disappeared to work with a few of the actors.

Charlie showed Mac and Maria the construction area backstage, which was opposite the side where Kelly usually hung out with a few of her adoring stagehands when she wasn't rehearsing. Charlie pointed out two towering pillars that were lying on their sides.

"I painted them yesterday during class," Charlie said to Maria and Mac. "Now we just need you to do the black trim, and then carefully carry these guys onstage and set them up on the movable platform."

"Aren't they heavy?" asked Maria.

"Nope," said Charlie. "They're made of Styrofoam, so they're light. There should be tape marking the spots where they go." She turned and pointed. "Black paint and brushes are right there on the worktable, and the trim parts that need paint are marked on the diagram next to the pillars. Any questions?"

Maria shook her head. "I think we've got it."

Mac, looking like he might be regretting his decision to help, picked up the brushes and paint, and he and Maria got started.

Charlie heard a loud thump, followed by arguing on the other side of the stage. "I'll be right back," she said. She went to investigate and found the kitchen set piece in disarray. Kelly was red faced—and not just from the bruise—and arguing with Sara. A few set changers stood off to the side, eyeing the argument but having a quiet discussion of their own.

Charlie had seen Kelly tangle with Sara before, and she didn't want any part of it. She started backing away, but Sara saw her. "Charlie, come over here. What do you think about this? Kelly— who does *not* do any set changes—thinks that the kitchen should be brought on and off the stage in pieces during scene changes. Some of the set changers and I think it'll take way too much time to do it that way, and it'll sound like a herd of elephants to have that many crew pulling off the table, chairs, cupboards, and all the dish props and appliances too."

"What did Mr. Anderson say?" asked Charlie.

"He told me to handle it," said Sara. She eyed Kelly and lifted her chin.

Charlie blew out a breath and studied the bulky set. She refused to look at Kelly, though she could feel the girl's eyes practically boring a hole through her skull. Somehow Charlie doubted that Kelly had forgiven her for hitting her with the ball. She hoped that stage makeup would cover the bruise for the show, or Kelly might explode.

"Why do you think we need to tear it down each time, Kelly?" Charlie asked carefully.

"Because it's too heavy to push it onstage, even on wheels," said Kelly. "These set people were just running through a scene change, and they made such a racket trying to push it that I could hear them from the seats. I don't want my audience listening to a bunch of grunting, sweaty cows."

The set changers stopped whispering and stared at Kelly.

"Hey," Charlie said quietly. "You wouldn't have a show without us. Maybe if you want it to go well you should try appreciating all the work people are doing just so you can sing your solo."

"Maybe all you should appreciate that it's thanks to me and the rest of the cast that you even have something to do," Kelly said.

Charlie frowned. "Are you serious?"

Kelly sniffed haughtily and looked away, folding her arms. "Nobody asked you anyway," she muttered.

"I asked her," said Sara.

Charlie shot Sara a strained look, then went back to Kelly. "I think you should let the stage manager make the call on set changes."

She turned and walked over to the set pieces. When assembled, it looked like a real little kitchen perched atop a 10-by-12 platform on wheels. There were walls on two sides with cabinets attached and painted cardboard appliances in place. A hefty dining table with six chairs filled out the rest of the space.

The platform was large and took up a lot of the backstage area, but it also held items that would be difficult to move individually.

Charlie looked at Sara. "I'll ask my parents if I can work backstage for both shows if you want me to, so I can help the set changers push it." She glanced at Kelly. "And none of us will be grunting."

Kelly rolled her eyes. "I doubt you'll make a difference," she scoffed.

Charlie raised an eyebrow and said nothing, while Sara ignored Kelly completely. "That would be great, Charlie," she said, and turned to the set changers. "Put it back together, and let's try this again."

The set changers obeyed.

Charlie pulled out her phone and hesitated. "Will I get in trouble if Mr. Anderson sees me texting them?"

"*Pfft.* Not a chance," said Sara.

Charlie sent off a quick text to her parents and turned off her phone again. "I'm sure it'll be okay." She walked around the set piece as the other crew put things in place. "Has anyone thought about greasing up the wheels?"

One of the set changers spoke up, looking a little guilty. "I couldn't find that spray grease stuff."

Charlie looked around and hollered, "Who has the WD-40?"

A girl whose name Charlie couldn't remember came over with it. Charlie got down on the floor and showed her where to spray. She could see more wheels under the center of the platform, but they were out of reach, so she hoped getting the outer ones done would be enough. They rocked the platform back and forth a little.

"Let's test it out," Sara said. She called over the other set changers. "Okay, so in the kitchen scene, Kim—played by Kelly—and her family are all eating a meal. When we kill the lights, let's have the actors exit stage left and crew enter stage right to push the platform off so we don't all run into each other." Sara turned to Kelly, who stood observing the situation with arms folded across her chest. "Will that work for you to exit stage left after every kitchen scene?"

"I suppose." Kelly watched for a moment, then walked away, the click of her shoes echoing across the stage.

"Good," Sara said, seeming relieved that Kelly was gone. "Thanks, Charlie."

Charlie smiled. "Sure."

Sara clapped her hands to get the crew's attention. "Okay, crew, let's time this. I'll hold the curtain aside so the top of the set can clear it."

Charlie, another girl, and two boys took their places along one end of the platform.

"It's too heavy," warned one of the boys, who was a huge admirer of the queen, apparently despite her insults. "The wheels under the center of the platform are the ones that get jacked up so we can't get it going."

"Let's just try this," Charlie said. "You've got me now." Knowing the bracelet wouldn't help, she hoped her regular strength was enough to get the thing rolling.

The boy snorted.

When Sara said "Go!" Charlie put all her weight into pushing. The blood rushed to her head. Her arms strained, and her hands hurt from boring into the wooden frame. The platform leaned a few inches, but the wheels barely budged. After a minute the three gave up.

"Sheesh," Charlie said under her breath. She felt her bracelet. It was stone-cold. *Big surprise*, she thought. She looked around and called Maria and Mac over, and told them what they were trying to do.

Mac dropped to all fours and peered under the platform. "Why didn't you oil the wheels in the center?"

"We can't reach them—the platform isn't high enough to get under there."

Mac squinted. "I can do it." Before anybody could protest, he grabbed the can of WD-40 and flattened himself to the floor, then began sliding under the platform, head turned to one side to fit.

Sara got down on her hands and knees and watched him. "Are you sure you should be doing that?" she called out.

"I'm fine," Mac said. His legs and feet disappeared under the set piece.

After a minute Charlie and the others heard the telltale sound of the spray can, followed by a muffled shout, "There's your problem!" followed by a sudden coughing fit. "Yuck," Mac muttered when he stopped coughing. "That stuff is lethal."

"Don't breathe that junk, Mac," said Maria, sounding worried. Charlie wondered why, but then remembered Mac's inhaler.

"Quiet, Maria," Mac warned.

Charlie and Maria exchanged glances. Sara got down to look under the set piece. "Great job, Mac," she said. "You can come on out now."

"I'm coming," said Mac. He coughed.

They waited.

Sara squinted. "Mac?"

"One second!" he called. "Oof."

That didn't sound good. Charlie and Maria dropped to the floor too.

"Are you okay?" Maria asked him.

"I'm fine," he said. "I'm just, well, I'm stuck." He started wheezing.

"What?" cried Sara. "You have to get out of there!"

"And feeling a little, uh, claustrophobic, um, at the moment," Mac added, his voice pitching upward.

Charlie's heart pounded. "Can't you slide back the same way you slid in?" she screeched.

"My shoes keep getting stuck," he said. His voice sounded scared. He wheezed some more.

"Can you take your shoes off?" Maria suggested.

"It's not . . . ," Mac said with a cough, "like I can reach them."

Charlie could hear Mac's labored breathing growing louder. She turned to Maria, alarmed. "What's happening?"

"He's got asthma," said Maria quietly. "That WD-40 must have gotten to him. She laid her cheek on the stage and looked under the platform. "You doing okay?"

Mac's eyes shone scared. "Can't . . . catch . . . my breath. . . ."

Maria sat up and looked at Charlie in alarm. "You have to do something," she whispered. "He's having trouble breathing!"

Charlie's heart thudded, and immediately her bracelet grew warm. She clicked it on to see which ability was activated, and pulled Maria close to show her the brightly colored elephant.

"Phew," said Maria, and she whispered, "Let's lift it off him!"

"We can't!" said Charlie. "Not with all these people watching."

"We could have everybody help," said Maria.

Charlie eyed the set piece. The items on it weren't attached yet. If they lifted one side of the platform, the heavy stuff on it could slide off or the walls could tip over—it would be even more dangerous. "No—we've got to roll it."

She went to the center of one side. "Come on," she ordered. "Everybody grab on! Mac, lie as flat as you can—we're going to push it."

More coughing erupted from underneath the platform.

Sara called to a group of actors rehearsing a scene nearby to help out, explaining the problem, and they quickly came over. Everyone grabbed onto the piece, and on Sara's count, they pushed with all their might, Charlie secretly lifting slightly to give Mac more room for the platform to glide over him.

This time the set piece rolled onstage—and once it got moving, it went with almost too much force.

As soon as Mac was free, he rolled to his side, coughing and wheezing. Maria helped him to his feet, but he just scowled and staggered away. "I'm fine," he managed, pulling his inhaler out of his pocket. He escaped to the boys' bathroom, leaving Maria looking hurt.

"All right!" Sara said once she saw that Mac was okay. She thanked the actors, who went back to rehearsing their scene, and addressed the crew. "Good work, team. Looks like we can move this thing after all," she said, a bit smugly, though it had taken more people to do it than would be able to help on show night. "Let's try it again with just the four of you. Maybe take it a bit easy there, actually—we don't want the kitchen rolling all the way across the stage, or we'll have to start calling it a food truck."

Nobody seemed to get her joke, but it didn't matter. The two boys looked at Charlie. "Well sure," said the one who liked Kelly, "it moves with seven of us. But with four? I doubt it." The sour look on his face seemed to be ever present.

"We'll be fine," said Charlie, annoyed. "Come on." She took her position as Mac returned and joined Maria to watch. She waited for Sara to signal them.

"Okay, timing it," said Sara. "If we're under thirty seconds, it's a done deal. Annnd, go."

Charlie pushed gently on the set piece, remembering her strength was still activated, but soon she realized the sour-faced boy had recruited the other boy to be annoying too, and they were

messing around and not pushing very hard at all, trying to prove that Kelly was right. With a burst of anger, Charlie put her full strength into it, and the piece rolled smoothly to its designated spot offstage.

"There," said Charlie. "Mac fixed the wheels. That wasn't hard at all." She glared at the boys, who seemed surprised that the platform had moved so well without their efforts.

"That was perfect," said Sara, glancing at her watch. "Twenty-eight seconds. By Friday we'll knock it down to twenty. It's settled, then. Crew, let's nail down the kitchen. Thanks, Charlie. You've been a great help. Maybe you should try for stage manager for the next show."

Charlie beamed. "Thanks! Maybe I will."

The boys just looked at her dubiously and said nothing. Which was more than enough, as far as Charlie was concerned.

She didn't see Mac frowning at her from backstage.

CHAPTER 30

Living on the Edge

Throughout the rest of the school day, Charlie realized the strength ability remained activated, so she was extracareful as she moved from class to class. The elephant stayed lit up during soccer practice, too. *This thing is definitely glitchy*, she thought. As puzzling as that was, she took advantage of the strength to make some great shots, managing to leave her friendly rival, Vanessa, without the ball more times than not. But Charlie was careful not to be too obvious about it. She didn't want to make anybody suspicious.

After practice, Coach Candy called for a team-building meeting. Charlie, Maria, Kelly, Vanessa, Bree, and all the other girls assembled in the locker room. The energy was high—everybody was excited about the first game tomorrow, and to see who was going to start.

Charlie loved this part of being on a sports team—the anticipation of the first game, everybody on the team so hyped up to go out there and play together and win. By now Charlie really felt like she was part of something—like she belonged. And it was a really good feeling. But there was a weird part to it too. Charlie had been playing against some of these girls this whole time. They had been the ones to beat. Now they, as a group, were one. Each of them had to change whatever negative feelings they'd had for some of their rival teammates into positive ones, which could be hard.

Coach Candy called for silence. "We'll keep this brief," she said. "And before I read the lineup, I want to tell you all that I'm so proud to be your coach. You are putting in your best effort, and that is such a delight to me. We are a very strong team this season, and I can't wait to see what you do."

The girls beamed from the praise and a few high-fived each other.

"This is always a tricky moment," she went on, "going from scrimmaging against one another to coming together as a team. We've had some scrapes and some tense moments." Coach Candy looked around the group, and the girls grew silent. "That indicates passion, which is a good thing. But let's all remember that now we're on the same team. Channel that passion into playing with strength together."

Charlie glanced at Kelly, who was staring stone-faced at the locker room floor. Vanessa looked Charlie's way and smiled. She grinned back. Charlie knew she could be a team player with anybody in this room—even Kelly. But whether Kelly could play nicely with her remained to be seen.

Coach Candy pulled out the roster and announced the starters. She named the goalie, the fullbacks and sweeper, and the halfbacks. Kelly's and Maria's names were both called, to no one's surprise. Then Coach called the four starting forwards . . . and she ended by calling Charlie's name.

Charlie's heart surged. She was going to start the first game! Maria reached over to fist bump her, and Coach led them all in their team chant: "Let's go, Summit! We're the TOP!"

With the meeting over, the girls began to disperse. Vanessa touched Charlie's sleeve. "Congratulations," she said quietly. Her face was filled with disappointment, but she seemed bent on pushing past it.

Charlie's eyes widened. In her excitement she hadn't realized Vanessa's name wasn't called. "Oh!" she said. "Oh, Vanessa—I'm really sorry."

"It's cool," said Vanessa bravely. "You deserved it—especially after the way you played today."

Charlie's smile faded. "Thanks," she said, dropping her gaze. "Um, I guess I'll see you tomorrow."

"See you." Vanessa moved to get her things and left.

Charlie watched her go, then lifted her sleeve and clicked her bracelet. The elephant was back to its gray, wavy self.

Maria was waiting outside the locker room for her. Together they walked to Maria's house, Charlie strangely quiet while Maria talked excitedly about the upcoming game. By the time they reached her street, Maria was so animated that she accidentally began crossing without looking for traffic.

"Look out!" Charlie said, grabbing Maria's arm as a big white van screeched to a halt a few feet away. Charlie squinted at the driver, but the sun was bouncing off the windshield, and she couldn't see. The van squealed around the girls and took off down the street.

"Rude!" said Maria, watching it go. "This is a neighborhood, you loser!"

"Are you okay?" asked Charlie.

Maria turned to her. "Yeah. Thanks, Chuck."

"No problem. Looks like that didn't even activate the bracelet."

"Well, I guess I didn't rate high enough to trigger a need to be rescued," Maria said with a laugh.

"That's probably a good thing, don't you think?"

"I suppose so."

When they got to Maria's house, they greeted her parents and grabbed a snack. Maria introduced Charlie to her three stepbrothers, who were all younger than her and doing homework or coloring at the kitchen table.

"Hi there," Charlie said to the boys before Maria grabbed her by the wrist and dragged her to her bedroom. Mac was sitting in his usual spot at Maria's desk, hunched over his iPad.

"Oh," said Maria. She acted like she was still a bit miffed about the way Mac treated her after the set-building incident at lunch. "Didn't know you'd be here."

"I'm always here," Mac said, not looking up.

"Are you feeling okay after your asthma attack?" asked Charlie.

"I'm fine," Mac said, almost angrily.

Maria rolled her eyes. "He's a little sensitive about it. Kids used to tease him back in second and third grade because he made a little barking noise."

Mac ignored her, and Charlie wasn't sure what to say. It seemed like Maria was trying to get him to react, and he wasn't taking the bait.

"Charlie saved your life, you know," Maria said matter-of-factly, even though it wasn't really true. She threw her backpack onto her bed and plopped down next to it. Charlie did the same and rolled back, staring at the ceiling.

"Some hummingbirds weigh less than a penny," said Mac, like he was trying to change the subject. "And the oldest-known clam is over five hundred years old. Guess where it was discovered."

Maria glared at him. "I don't know. Your butt? Did you hear what I said?"

"Wrong—it was Iceland. And a king cobra's venom is strong enough to kill you a hundred and fifty times over."

"What if you have a healing superpower?" asked Charlie, and then she bit her lip, not sure she wanted to enter the strained conversation.

Mac frowned and didn't answer at first. But then he looked up, skeptical. "I don't think your bracelet is going to bring you back to life," he said. "Once you're dead, you're dead."

Maria turned over to lie on her stomach. She propped her chin in her hands. "Since when do you make the bracelet rules?" she said crossly. "You don't know if it can bring her back to life or not."

Mac looked at her. "What's up with you? Are you trying to pick a fight with me or something?"

"Why can't you just say thanks to Charlie? She's the one who moved the platform off you."

"Yeah," Mac retorted, "okay, let's talk about that. Because later I heard those two guys muttering about how Charlie practically pushed the whole platform by herself. What kind of move was that, huh, Charlie? People are going to figure it out if you keep showing off like that. I hope you don't think those guys are going to push hard next time now that they're suspicious. And what are you going to do for the actual show if your bracelet isn't activated? Run out in front of a speeding train before every scene change? Huh, Charlie? Did you think of that?"

Charlie's mouth opened, and then she closed it. She thought for a moment. "If they see it's not moving, they'll help for the sake of the show," Charlie said quietly, turning to lie on her side so she could see him. "We'll be able to get it moving thanks to you greasing the middle wheels."

"Thank you!" Mac said, agitated. "It's about time I got some appreciation around here for once."

"We appreciate you," said Maria, exasperated. "Sheesh."

"How would I know?" He turned back to his iPad and muttered, "You're both too busy having sleepovers and messing with the bracelet without me."

Maria scrunched up her nose. "Maybe *you're* the one who's too busy with your other friends."

Mac scowled at the tablet. "Yeah, whatever. Anyway, I've got the master list of codes. Lemme see the device again."

Charlie got off the bed and went over to stand next to him, holding out her arm. He pushed a few buttons to get it to the proper screen. He tapped, then hit random buttons until it wouldn't let him enter any more characters. "Seven, max," he muttered. "Ridiculous." He started keying in alphanumeric combinations.

Charlie was quiet, thinking about what Mac had said. He was right. It had been a dumb idea for her to push that platform so hard. What if they couldn't move it after all? Hopefully they'd have more chances tomorrow to test it out.

Mac got through only one page of passwords before he had to leave for dinner. When Charlie got home she found Andy sitting at the table eating cereal and reading the comic book Maria had lent her.

"Where's Mom and Dad?" asked Charlie, setting down her things.

"Where d'you fink?" said Andy, his mouth full. He didn't look up from the comic.

"There's supposed to be leftovers in the fridge," she said.

Andy shrugged. "I like cereal."

Charlie grabbed a bowl and spoon and poured herself some. "How's *Ms. Marvel*?" she asked.

"It's great," he said. "Where did this come from?"

"Maria brought it for me. You can finish it first if you want."

"Thanks."

Charlie watched him read. He didn't seem to be sad about their parents working late yet again. In fact, he liked being home alone. But her big-sister instinct kicked in. "How's school going?" she asked.

"Good," he said. He turned the page and took another bite. Milk dribbled down his chin, and he wiped it away with his sleeve.

"Are you making more friends?"

Andy looked up. "Why are you being Mom?"

"I don't know. Maybe because she's never here," Charlie said.

Andy went back to reading.

Charlie ate a few spoonfuls of cereal and then said, "Are you coming to my game tomorrow with Dad?"

"No."

"But I'm starting."

"So. You always start."

Charlie shrugged and changed the subject. "I texted Dad about the musical at school Friday night. It's at seven, in case he forgets." She frowned, thinking. "Though I'm not sure he can get away two whole nights in a row just for me."

"Got it," said Andy, still reading.

"There was a big fight today at lunch," Charlie went on. "The stage manager and one of the lead actors got into it about the kitchen set piece."

Andy looked up. "A fight? Like fists and stuff?"

"No, sorry. Just an argument. The stage manager asked me whether we should keep the kitchen set on the platform or move the individual pieces on and off, and I told her we should keep the set pieces on the platform, and I would help roll it on and off. So I'll be helping backstage after school Friday until after the show is over. I won't be sitting with you for the performance or anything."

Andy didn't respond.

"That's Friday," she repeated.

Andy sighed. "Why are you telling me this boring stuff?"

"Because I don't want Dad to forget to come. And since I won't be coming home after school now, I figured I'd better tell you."

"I told you I got it. Seven o'clock on Saturday night." He grinned.

"Friday night!" said Charlie. She made a face at him and then moved her bowl aside and took out her homework, figuring she may as well hang out with Andy since nobody else was.

Five minutes later, Andy took the comic and disappeared to his room.

CHAPTER 31

Promises, Promises

Thursday at lunch Mac and Maria both helped with the set again. Neither of them said anything about the previous day's fight, though the air was a little prickly between them at first. Charlie wasn't sure what to do, but with the show looming, she didn't have time to try to help them get past it—not that they would want her to butt in anyway. She figured they'd been friends for years, and they'd probably had fights before that they'd had to work through. So she gave them some tasks to do and tried to stay out of their way. By the end of lunch period Mac and Maria were acting almost normal again.

After school, Mac sent Maria a Snapchat of himself sitting in the bleachers waiting for the game to start, just like always. Maria rushed over to Charlie in the locker room and replayed it for her to see. Charlie grinned. And even though Mac hadn't included her in his Snapchat recipients, it was good to see Maria feeling better. It really gave her a mental boost—she was more determined than ever to win the game.

The teams soon went to the field. Charlie was nervous seeing all the parents and friends in the stands, but she felt proud wearing her new team uniform that matched the others. Her teammates treated her like one of them even though she was new, and that felt pretty great. Charlie scanned the bleachers looking for her dad, but soon Coach called the starters together and she had to abandon her search.

As the game was about to begin, the first-string girls eyed their opposition. Some of them were friends with players on the other school's team and shared what they knew about their strategies. As Summit's team headed out to get into position, even Kelly fell into step with Charlie and offered an encouraging "Let's do this" before peeling off and going to her place on the field.

As Charlie waited in position for the whistle, she glanced at the bench and saw Vanessa there, leaning forward intently and shouting her support to the starters. A wave of guilt passed through her. Was she really the right person to be in this spot? Or had she only won the right to it by using the bracelet's powers?

They would soon find out. The referee started the game, and Charlie burst forward, brimming with energy. But the other team was just as hyped up. They grabbed the ball early on and dominated for the first several minutes, keeping the action near Summit's goal and leaving Charlie standing midfield with her fellow forwards, anxious and unable to help. Kelly and Maria fought to keep the other team from scoring.

When the ball rolled out of bounds on Charlie's side of the field, Kelly quickly went to throw it in. She caught Charlie's eye and hurled it to her. Charlie flew to it and punted it to an open area, chasing after it and giving her fellow forwards a chance to organize. She took it to the line of opposing fullbacks, then deftly passed it off to an open teammate, who took it to the goal for a quick score, giving Charlie an assist. Charlie pointed at Kelly, giving her credit for the excellent throw-in. And Maria was practically doing somersaults, she was so excited. It was good to all be playing together for once.

During the second half, as Charlie scrambled for the ball and felt that thrill of the chase, the bracelet grew warm again. For the moment she forgot her guilt—this was a real game, after all—and went after the goal like her life depended on it. She wove through the opposition, snaking her way deeper and deeper into the other team's defense, then pounded the ball in the goal. The stands erupted in cheers.

With Summit up 2–0, Coach Candy took Charlie out to give her a break and give Vanessa some time to play. Charlie gratefully took it and as she caught her breath, checked the bracelet to see if it had been speed or strength that had activated—she couldn't tell. To her surprise, the starfish was pulsing a beautiful fluorescent pink. Charlie almost laughed. Her healing ability was going strong for no apparent reason.

But that also meant that she had scored that goal without help from the device. She could look Vanessa in the eye once more.

* * *

Summit smoked the competition, 3–0.

Afterward the girls changed and went outside to look for their friends and family. Maria got caught up talking to some other friends, so when Charlie spotted Mac she went over to him.

"It was really nice of you to come," she said.

"I always come," he said, but seemed happy that she'd said something.

Charlie glanced around covertly, then pulled up her sleeve and showed him the bracelet with the starfish healing power still going strong.

"Wow, that's awesome," he said, looking closely at the dancing pink symbol. But then he quickly drew back as if he'd just remembered that he was too cool for girls at school functions. "I didn't realize you'd hurt yourself. Is that why Coach took you out?"

"No, that's the thing—I'm not injured. It's just another glitch, I think."

Mac frowned. "When did these glitches start? Or have they always been happening?"

Charlie thought about it. "I guess the first time was when I couldn't get the bracelet off."

"And that was after you destroyed the bathroom, right?"

"Part of the bathroom," said Charlie.

Mac pursed his lips and looked sideways at her. "Anyway," he said. "Basically everything points to the notorious bathroom incident as the moment things started going a little off the rails."

"Yep." said Charlie. She caught sight of her parents, and her mouth nearly fell open. "Wow," she said, and grabbed Mac's arm. "Come on, meet my parents! I can't believe my mom's here." She pulled Mac toward them and pretended to overlook the fact that he stepped sideways on purpose to loosen himself from her grasp.

Her parents walked up together, both of them wearing their work clothes and grinning brightly.

"You both made it," said Charlie, her face lighting up. "Did you see my goal?"

"We did," said Charlie's mom. "Amazing!"

"You nailed it," said her dad.

Charlie hopped up and down, barely able to contain her glee. After the past couple of weeks, she had prepared herself to be let down—certainly one of them, or even both, would have some work thing come up that was too urgent to miss. But here they were—and they had seen her goal. It felt better than she'd ever remembered.

"This is my friend Mac," she said, and spied Maria running toward them.

"Hi," said Mac.

Maria skidded to a stop next to them. "Hi, Mr. Dr. Wilde. Hi, Mrs. Dr. Wilde," she said.

"Hi, Maria," both replied. Mrs. Dr. Wilde laughed at the title.

Mac shot her a quizzical glance.

"They're both doctors," Maria explained. "It's confusing, so I renamed them."

"I'm really just a lowly biologist," quipped Charlie's dad.

Mac laughed. "Makes sense to me," he said. They chatted a little about the game.

Charlie loved seeing everybody together.

While the others were talking, Charlie's mom leaned toward her and said quietly, "Do you want to invite your friends to go out for froyo with us?"

"You don't have to go back to work?"

"No, we're all yours for the evening."

"Totally." Charlie turned to Mac and Maria. "Do you two want to go out for frozen yogurt with us?"

"Sure!" said Maria at the same time Mac stated, "We can't."

Mac looked sharply at Maria, unable to hide the hurt look on his face. "But we always go to The Sugar Plum. It's first-game tradition."

"Yeah," argued Maria, "but we don't have to go there."

"What if we all go to The Sugar Plum?" Charlie suggested. "Is that okay?" she asked her parents.

Charlie's parents nodded. "Of course—we'll go wherever you want."

Charlie turned back to her friends. "Well? How about it?"

Mac glowered at Maria. Then he shook his head. "Forget it," he said. "I gotta go." He waved to somebody in the distance—or pretended to—and slipped away before anyone had the chance to protest.

Maria sighed. "Well, *I'd* like to go with you," she said.

Mac was really starting to make Charlie mad.

The next day at lunchtime Charlie and Maria hurried across the courtyard to the auditorium to finish up the set—it was Friday, and this was their last chance to make things perfect before the dress rehearsal during sixth period. Mac crossed their path again, and despite his abrupt departure after the soccer game, he joined them to finish painting the set pieces he'd been working on.

There was a buzz of excitement and nerves as everyone scrambled to get things done. There would be two shows tonight: an after-school soft opening with a small audience made up of what Sara called "snowbirds." These were older people from retirement communities nearby who spent their winters in Arizona but lived in northern states or Canada the rest of the year.

"The snowbirds love this kind of stuff," Sara told her. "And they don't have to pay the five bucks for a ticket if they come to the soft opening. We invite them so we can do the full show once with a small audience before we do the real thing."

Charlie thought it was a neat idea. But she couldn't imagine how everything could possibly be ready. At least they'd get through the whole show once before everybody's parents came for the official performance at seven.

"People, please be careful," Mr. Anderson called out. "We have a lot of bulky set pieces, and our volunteer parent lighting crew from Biggs Electric is here, working on ridiculously tiny ladders. Our musical is not a tragedy—let's not make today's actions tragic either."

The few students working near him mumbled their compliance.

Apart from the adults on the lighting crew, Mac was on a ladder too, touching up the gold letters on the train station sign, which stood high above the platform Charlie had built.

Charlie was as pumped up by the excitement of the show as she was about yesterday's soccer game. It dawned on her that the two activities were similar—they were both team performances, and you really had to scramble if you messed up, but there were other people around who would help you out in a jam. Plus, the preshow butterflies felt the same as pregame jitters. Maybe this was why she'd been enjoying the class so much.

Sara had learned quickly that she could count on Charlie. She'd given her more and more responsibility as the show loomed closer, which was cool. But as time ticked down, Charlie realized there was too much to do in the little time they had. She and the other set movers had to run through all the changes one more time. The train station needed touch-up paint. The props table was a mess, and props manager Carmelita had asked Charlie to help organize it, show the actors where their spots on the table were, and instruct them to put the props back in the exact same place after each scene so the props team would know in an instant if any were missing. But the actors tended to roam and socialize when they weren't rehearsing a scene, and it was hard to locate them all.

Charlie began to race around backstage a little flustered, and knowing she needed to go fast. She wished her bracelet would activate so she could run faster. Soon she looked at the clock and saw that there were only a few minutes left of lunch hour.

"Okay, everybody finish up!" Sara called out, clapping her hands. "Get all your junk off the stage, finish painting and put your stuff away, and get the props in place! We need to be ready to start dress rehearsal the minute sixth period begins."

The cast and crew exploded to life. Charlie saw Maria coming toward her empty-handed. "What can I do?" asked Maria.

"Grab that rack of costumes and take it to the greenroom," Charlie said. "Where's Mac?"

"He's still painting," said Maria. She rushed to grab the squeaky costume rack and began pulling.

Charlie looked up and saw Mac leaning forward on the ladder, intently focused on finishing the touch-up paint. She let him be and went to make sure all the small props on the kitchen countertops were stuck down with tape so they wouldn't fall over during set changes.

In the frenzy before the bell rang, one of the lighting guys gave a shout. A rod of lights came crashing to the stage, narrowly missing students.

Mr. Anderson came running to see what had happened. He flew around a corner and caught his foot on the base of Mac's ladder, which sent him skidding onto the stage. The ladder teetered wildly, and Mac gave a yelp. His paint can and brush slid off the top of it and hit the floor, splattering everywhere. He sprang and grabbed onto the sign he'd been painting as the ladder toppled over, and he hung there, twelve feet up, his legs squirming and his hands slipping on the wet paint.

Charlie gasped. Her arm turned warm under the bracelet. She ran to the sign and stood under Mac, whose eyes were wide with fright. Students began yelling and gathering around, half of them rushing to Mr. Anderson's side. Maria came running, her face awash in fear.

"Help me put the ladder back!" Charlie cried.

Maria and Charlie struggled to set up the ladder, but it had bent and twisted when it fell, and now it wouldn't open right.

Charlie shoved it out of the way, checked the bracelet, and saw the colorful elephant lifting the barbell. She planted her feet and locked eyes with Mac. "Just let go," she said quietly, hoping he could read her lips. "You won't hurt me. I can catch you."

Mac squirmed, his grip slipping. No doubt he was picking up splinters with every centimeter they moved. "Everybody's watching," he hissed.

"Do it, Mac!" Maria shouted, desperation rising in her voice. "Worry about that later."

"Come on!" Charlie braced herself and reached up as Kelly and the other actors appeared to see what the commotion was all about.

Mac didn't have a choice. He couldn't hold on any longer. He closed his eyes and let go.

A sickening gasp arose from the students who'd gathered, followed by a split second of silence as Mac landed in Charlie's arms. Remembering his hesitation, she staggered and slid to her knees for the sake of making it look like it was difficult.

While they both caught their breath and realized they were okay, the witnesses exploded in applause, which slowly turned to snickers and laughter.

Mac scowled and jumped out of Charlie's arms. Mr. Anderson came limping over to see if everyone was okay, and Charlie hastily moved out of the limelight, sidestepping to pick up the paint can and the brush, pretending nothing out of the ordinary had happened.

But then somebody yelled, "Hey, Mac, who's your knight in shining armor?" Somebody else chanted, "Kiss the girl! Kiss the girl!" and soon others circled around Mac, Charlie, and Maria, chanting too. Not even Mr. Anderson could get them to quiet down.

Trapped, Mac grew more and more flustered as the teasing

escalated. Maria tried to calm him down, but he didn't want anything to do with her either. Finally, as Mr. Anderson began to gain control of the crowd, Mac shouted above them.

"Oh yeah?" said Mac, breaking through the circle and stepping onto the platform. "Oh yeah?" he repeated as they quieted down to listen. "Well maybe there's a little something freaky you ought to know about Charlie!"

Maria jerked around to stare at him. Charlie froze, paint can in hand, as a blanket of dread began to suffocate her. She stepped toward Mac, eyes pleading, but he refused to turn her way. Then she glared at Maria, staring her down with a hard look that said "I told you so."

CHAPTER 32

Confrontations

The students quieted. From the circle, Kelly spoke up. "Well, Mac?" she asked. "What *about* Charlie?"

Charlie's stomach twisted.

Mac lifted his chin. "Charlie is a—"

"Mac," Maria said.

Mac faltered. "Charlie has—"

"Mac, shut up!" Maria shouted.

Charlie closed her eyes, feeling faint. She couldn't breathe.

Mac looked at Maria, and then at Charlie, whose face was as white as a sheet.

"Come on! Say it!" a couple of people called out.

"That's enough," said Mr. Anderson. His face was furious. "The bell rang three minutes ago while you were all yelling. And I'm *not* writing any late passes!"

Panic ensued, and most of the students dispersed in moments. Mr. Anderson threw his hands up at the mess on the stage, then limped over to the lighting crew to ask them if any of the lights that had fallen were beyond repair. Charlie turned her back on Mac and tried to stop the tears that threatened to pour out now that all the craziness was over. She sucked in a shuddering breath, trying to keep it together, and then hurried to put the top on the can of paint even though she could barely see what she was doing. There wasn't much paint left in the stupid can anyway.

Maria put her hand on Charlie's arm. "Charlie—I'm so sorry," she whispered.

Charlie shrugged Maria's hand away. "Leave me alone," she said, her voice hitching. Then she dropped the can and sprinted out the side exit that led directly outdoors. She tore down the sidewalk, through the parking lot, and across the track and the soccer field. She kept running to the far side of the football stadium, where she could find solace alone under the mesquite trees.

She didn't care if she got caught. She didn't care if she got in trouble for skipping class. What did it matter anyway? Just when she was starting to like being here, everything became so confusing and hard and wrong again. And this bracelet was only making it worse.

Charlie's chest ached for her old life. Chicago had left a hole in her heart. Everything there had been comfortable. Amari was the most loyal friend a girl could have. And Charlie's dad had always been there whenever she needed him—not just when it was convenient for him. If she tried calling him now while he was teaching, there was no way he'd answer.

She had just begun feeling like she was fitting in. She'd made friends. She was one of the team in soccer. Sara and most of the backstage crew really seemed to like her ideas. And Mac had just ruined all of it. By now half the school would think she was a freak. She was sure rumors were flying about what Mac didn't finish saying. *Charlie is a* . . . fill in the blank. Or worse, he'd probably gone ahead and told them all about her powers.

She lay back in the prickly grass and stared at the sky, feeling desperate. She pulled her phone from her pocket and texted Amari. "Are you around?"

But she knew that even with the time difference, it was still early afternoon in Chicago, and Amari would be in class for a couple more hours. A few tears slid down Charlie's temples and burrowed into her hair. She put her phone back into her pocket.

After a while she lifted her arm, pushed up her sleeve, and stared at the bracelet. It probably didn't even matter now if she ever got the thing off. Someone she thought was a true friend had betrayed her. He was a backstabber. Way worse than Kelly, who kept to herself . . . though she'd seemed pretty eager to get Mac to spill the beans today. Charlie imagined Kelly sweet-talking Mac into telling her. Charlie's chest tightened with dread. Mac *had* to be stopped!

But Charlie was certain it was already too late to stop him. He had been so mad at her for saving him! And not only that—it seemed like he'd been mad at her for even existing lately. It didn't make sense. He should be grateful, not angry. She saved him not once but twice this week, and he didn't appreciate either of those efforts. Whatever he might want to think about her "showing off," Charlie knew he could have really hurt himself if he'd fallen to the stage on top of the broken ladder.

"He's been such a jerk lately," she muttered, thinking of him standing on the platform ready to tell all. The tears started again. "Why does Maria even like him?"

Amid the calls of mockingbirds and cactus wrens, Charlie heard the drone of something else growing louder. She realized it was the sound of voices and sat up. Her heart sank when she saw who it was.

"There she is," Maria said, pointing. She started running toward Charlie, with Mac right behind her, but they both slowed when Charlie got to her feet and started walking the other way.

"Wait!" Maria called. "Come on, Charlie. Please wait a second."

"No. Leave me alone. Go back to school." Charlie walked faster.

"Mr. Anderson sent us to find you," Maria said. "Can you stop a minute, please? We know you're mad, but just hang on, will you?"

Charlie stopped walking. She folded her arms across her chest, but she didn't turn around. "What do you want?"

Maria caught up to her. "We need to talk through some things," she said as Mac joined them. "The three of us. But we don't have time now—Mr. Anderson said if we can get you back to school before sixth period, he won't call our parents, and he'll write us excuses. But we have to get back there now."

"Why should I care if he calls my parents," Charlie said, turning around to face them. "Everything's so messed up anyway, why not one more thing?" She glared at Mac. "Or maybe Mac wants to be the one to tell my parents I skipped class, since he can't seem to keep his big mouth shut."

Mac looked like he was going to protest, but Maria shut him down with a look.

"Charlie," Maria said, "Mac didn't tell anybody anything. After you left, I told Mr. Anderson that you were upset and that it was our fault, and I asked if we could look for you. He said okay, and muttered something about performance days always being full of drama." She stopped for breath, her face earnest. "Mac's not going to tell anybody anything, are you, Mac." It was a command, not a question.

"I'm not going to tell anybody," Mac repeated.

Charlie sniffed and wiped the grass off her pants. Mac didn't seem sorry, but at least he was saying the right words.

"If we go now, we get a free pass," Maria said. "Then maybe we can meet up after school and talk all this through. What do you say? Because I don't want to lose you as a friend, Chuck. And neither does Mac." Maria elbowed Mac hard in the ribs.

Mac nodded miserably.

Charlie studied him. "You don't seem very sorry," she said.

"Well," Mac said with an edge to his voice, "I'm sort of dealing with a lot of mocking at the moment, so . . ." He shoved his hands in his pockets, his face flickering. "But I'm sorry about almost telling everybody about the bracelet," he said.

"Do you promise you didn't tell anyone? Not even Kelly?"

"No way," Mac scoffed. "I wouldn't tell her. I didn't tell anyone," he reiterated, "and I won't."

But could she trust him? He'd promised her once before, and look what had happened. Though he didn't actually tell . . . so he did keep his promise in a way. Maybe Mac wasn't the absolute worst. Charlie thought about what Maria had said. And deep down, she didn't want to lose Maria as a friend either. The part about going back to the auditorium now and getting a free pass was sounding more tempting by the minute.

"Fine," Charlie said finally. "Let's meet right after the bell rings. I'll have a little time before the first show."

They agreed on a meeting spot outside the auditorium and returned to find Mr. Anderson. He'd swept up the broken lights and cleaned up the paint, and was now on a ladder, helping the electricians reattach the strand of lights that had fallen. He came down to make sure Charlie was all right and wrote passes for them. The three quickly went to class.

Charlie sat through the rest of fifth period avoiding Kelly's inquisitive glances and dreading going back to the auditorium for the sixth-period dress rehearsal. When the bell rang, she darted out of Kelly's sight, worried what she and the other kids might say.

But by the time she got to the auditorium she was surprised that nobody was really talking about the incident at all—they were all too focused on getting through as much of the dress rehearsal as possible before they ran out of time. And when Charlie thought through all the people who'd been there to witness Mac's fall and his little speech afterward, it really wasn't that many. Twenty or twenty-five at the most. Maybe everybody had forgotten it already.

When the school bell rang at the end of the day, Charlie sighed with relief. So far she had successfully dodged Kelly, and with any luck the star would be too busy with the show to bother her.

Most of the cast and crew were staying in the auditorium to finish up last-minute preparations before the soft opening. Charlie carefully surveyed the area to make sure Kelly wasn't lying in wait to ambush her, and snuck through the auditorium to the side door to meet Maria and Mac. Only one boy stopped her along the way. "Nice catch, Charlie!" he said, and laughed.

"Thanks," Charlie mumbled. She felt a little better now. And she was really glad she'd gone back to school and that her parents weren't going to have to find out that she almost skipped class. That wouldn't have gone over very well at all. She had to give Maria credit for that.

She opened the door that led outside and peered all around. No Kelly out here either. She slipped through the doorway and, with a sigh of relief, headed to the meeting spot. As she rounded the building and began to jog, she ran smack into Kelly. Kelly's phone went flying to the sidewalk, its protective case breaking open and skittering over the stones.

"Watch where you're going!" Kelly snarled.

Charlie gasped and put a hand out to catch her fall. Once righted she quickly helped pick up the phone case. "Sorry," she said. "I didn't know you were there. Is it . . . is it broken?"

Kelly's eyes kindled as she snatched the case from Charlie's grasp and tried to fit it back together around the phone. When it snapped neatly into place, Kelly's flash of anger disappeared. She inspected the phone, turning it over. Not even a scratch. "It looks okay," she said.

Charlie let go of a held breath and inched slowly away.

Kelly wiped the phone's face on her jeans and narrowed her eyes at Charlie. "Not so fast," she said. "I think you have some explaining to do."

CHAPTER 33

Good and Bad

Kelly slid her arm over Charlie's shoulders. Charlie tried to shrink away, but Kelly wasn't having it. "You've had an interesting day, haven't you," she said.

Charlie shrugged and didn't answer.

"I'm so curious about what Mac was going to announce to everyone. Maybe you could fill me in."

Charlie's hands began to sweat. "I don't know what he was going to say," she said.

"Oh," said Kelly with a little laugh, "I'll bet you do."

Charlie shook her head, and hoped Maria and Mac would come and find her and rescue her from this.

Just then Mr. Anderson poked his head out through the stage door. "Kelly! They need you in costumes. Chop-chop!"

Kelly quickly pulled her arm off Charlie's shoulders. "I'm coming," she said as Mr. Anderson disappeared. She narrowed her eyes as Charlie turned and started walking briskly away. "We'll talk later," she called after her.

"No we won't," muttered Charlie. She broke into a run.

Maria and Mac were already at the meeting spot, and Maria was looking around anxiously. Her face cleared when she saw Charlie.

"Sorry I'm late. I ran into Kelly." She narrowed her eyes accusingly at Mac. "She wanted to know what you were about to say."

Mac's eyes flickered. "Sorry," he said.

Maria guided Charlie and Mac down a path that almost nobody from school took. It led to an older part of town, where the houses were all different from one another. They had roofs with traditional shingles, like in Chicago, instead of ceramic tile like Charlie's and Maria's houses had. Charlie's mom had explained once that tile roofs weren't a new thing—they dated back thousands of years and were common in Spanish culture. Best of all, the tiles were fireproof, which was never a bad thing when you live in a hot, dry climate where it hardly ever rains.

Once they'd made it out of earshot of other students, Maria stopped and turned to Charlie and Mac. "Okay, well," she said, sounding a little scared, "I'm just going to come right out with this—I'm really worried about our friendship. With this whole bracelet thing, I think we need to stick together as a team. We've got to be able to trust each other, or we're going to be in big trouble."

Charlie's jaw dropped. "That's exactly what I've *been* doing," she exclaimed. "I'm not the untrustworthy one." She clenched her teeth, suddenly tired of absolutely everybody.

"I know, just hang on," said Maria. She looked at Mac, who stood slumped with his hands in his pockets, looking defeated.

Maria's eyes searched his. "You're my best friend, Mac," she said earnestly. "I'd do anything for you. And I think you'd do anything for me. Right?"

"Yeah. Of course," he said quietly.

"Good. I don't want that to change. I will always have your back. Okay?"

Mac sighed. "Yeah."

"I've been feeling kind of bad lately," Maria admitted. "It's like . . . it's like you don't want to hang out with me at school anymore." She looked swiftly away and sniffed. "And you act weird sometimes when you're with me and Charlie, like you wish you were somewhere else."

Mac shuffled his feet. "I know. . . . It's not cool, but everything is just . . . I don't know. The guys . . ." He trailed off. "It's just really complicated." He remained thoughtful, and then looked up accusingly. "Besides, you two hang out without me all the time."

Maria pressed her lips together. "Yeah," she said. "I mean, I'm not mad that you don't want to hang out with me every second of every day." She pushed a lock of hair out of her eyes and sighed. "I guess I just don't understand why you're being sneaky and weird and . . ." She glanced at him. "And why you're being mean sometimes," she said. "Not just to me. To Charlie, too."

Mac stared at the ground. Charlie shifted uncomfortably, watching them.

"I just hate it when people bug me about you being my

girlfriend," Mac blurted out.

"Aw, Mac," Maria said, rolling her eyes. "They're stupid. We know that's not true, so why do you let that bother you so much?"

"I don't know," said Mac. He looked up at Maria and Charlie. "I've been acting dumb. I'm sorry." Then his eyes clouded. "But Charlie, do you think maybe you can lay off the rescuing bit a little? It's really embarrassing."

Charlie was taken aback. "Excuse me? I saved your life!"

"I could have dropped to the floor just fine if you'd moved the ladder out of the way," Mac said. "It's like you just want to be a hero all the time."

"What? No I don't. I was really scared for you!" said Charlie. She looked Mac in the eye for the first time in a long time. "You're my friend," she said, quieter. "I was worried you would get hurt."

Mac worked his jaw like he was trying to decide if he could believe her. "Oh."

Maria spoke up. "It's really cool that you have the ability to do things," she said gently. "But . . ." She trailed off and added, "I mean, people might figure it out if you're not careful, you know?"

Charlie opened her mouth to protest, but then closed it slowly, thinking about the various times the device was activated and how she'd handled it. She frowned. Had she been showing off? She thought about how she'd pushed the platform almost by herself, like she was trying to prove something to those boys. And how great it had felt to step up and save Mac, even though now she admitted he wasn't actually in *that* much danger. She thought about soccer and using the device to score when she knew Coach Candy was deciding on which girls to place as starters. And she remembered how she'd accidentally hit Kelly with the ball and knocked her down—and the tiny feeling of satisfaction she'd felt afterward.

Charlie frowned. She hadn't been using the bracelet very unselfishly. In fact, sometimes she'd actually been kind of a bully. She glanced at the bracelet, and then looked up at her friends. "You're right," she said quietly. "I've been acting dumb too. I suppose I ought to have thought things through a little more—and considered how other people would be affected if I used the abilities." She hesitated. "Even Kelly, I suppose, though she's being the worst," she said with a sigh.

"Yeah, okay, I can see why you'd say that," said Maria. "But Kelly has some rough stuff going on at home, so I also feel bad for her."

"She does?" Charlie asked. "I thought everything about her life was perfect."

"Not even close," Maria said.

"Oh," Charlie said, embarrassed. She ran a hand over her hair and took a deep breath, then looked at Mac. "I messed up," she confessed. "I should have thought about how you'd feel."

Mac shifted his weight. He looked at Charlie. "I'm sorry I've been annoying."

Charlie dropped her gaze. "Me too."

"Thanks for saving me. I mean . . . it was still pretty awkward though."

"Yeah," said Charlie. "I get it now. I didn't think about that when everything was happening. And I'm really sorry everybody teased you—I hate when that happens."

"It's okay," said Mac. "You might not believe this anymore, but you can trust me."

Charlie nodded. "Thanks." She held out her hand.

Mac hesitated, then took it, and they awkwardly shook on it.

"I need to get back soon," said Charlie, checking the time.

"And I've got to go jailbreak a phone," Mac said. "Good luck with the show."

Charlie smiled. "Thanks," she said. He took off.

"I'll walk you back," said Maria. They turned and went toward the auditorium. After a moment Maria tilted her head and said, "This bracelet really is a seriously awesome thing."

"Is it?" Charlie asked. "Lately, it seems like it's a lot of trouble, actually."

"No. Think about it. It's huge," Maria went on. "You have something nobody else has. And it's got so much power. In the comics this is the point where you decide if you're going to become evil or stay good." She grinned impishly.

Charlie laughed. "Oh, really? This is my big moment?"

"Totally," said Maria, becoming animated. "See, if you'd

decided to let the power go to your head, you'd turn bad really soon." Maria glanced sidelong and grinned sheepishly. "If you were in a comic, I mean."

Charlie frowned. "Yeah, but I'm not a comic-book character, Maria."

"I realize that," said Maria. "Obviously. And like I said, I don't think you'll turn bad because of your power. But some other superheroes? They hide their powers and don't do anything with them, good or bad. And I'm not so sure that's right either. See, the thing is—and the reason I'm acting like, I don't know, a total comic geek right now—is that I just started to realize how much *good* stuff you can do."

Charlie thought about that. "What do you mean, 'good stuff'?"

"I don't know. . . . I mean beyond scoring goals. Beyond saving someone from spraining their ankle from a fall." Maria grew more and more passionate, her hands gesturing as she spoke. "You're like a real superhero! You have the power to help people in a way that no one else can. And that's a big deal. Really big!" She gripped Charlie's arm, her eyes shining as a realization came to her. "It's . . . it's almost like an obligation."

Charlie felt a wave of panic rush through her. "What, so now I'm *obligated* to go out and save people? Like this is my life now? Look what happened when I tried to save Mac from falling—he got mad at me and almost blew my cover! That was not fun."

"Yeah," Maria said, deflating a little. She let go of Charlie's arm. "I guess that's a problem when the rescued people don't appreciate it. But is that a reason not to help? I mean, *I'm* really glad you saved Mac. I was freaking out, and the ladder was all twisted up. I was about to do the same thing you did. But both he and I would have ended up hurt that way, I'm sure. So even though he didn't seem to appreciate it, I definitely did." She looked out over the landscape and sighed dramatically. "Somebody out there will be grateful for your efforts one day."

Charlie raised an eyebrow. "I think you've had a little too much of theater class."

"I mean it, though."

They reached the stage door.

Charlie sighed. It was all so much to consider. She shrugged, not sure what Maria wanted to hear. "Look, good talk and all that . . ." She glanced down at the bracelet bulging under her sleeve. "But I didn't exactly ask for this—I'm stuck with it." She met Maria's eyes once more, then reached for the door handle. "I gotta go."

CHAPTER 34

The Show Must Go On

The after-school soft-opening performance was a total disaster. Charlie and the others did all right with their major set changes thanks to the platform's wheels all turning properly now, but that had little effect on the actors' abilities to remember their lines and the words to the songs. They seemed to have forgotten everything they had done right in the dress rehearsal. Kelly was the only one who sounded confident with her part. Plus, the show dragged, and by the time it was over, there was only forty minutes for the cast to regroup, change their costumes, and eat something before the evening show began.

While Charlie and the crew reset the stage, Mr. Anderson was in the greenroom with the cast, hollering at them. It was clear he was disappointed. When Charlie whizzed by the room to get something, she overheard him say, "I give you a lot of responsibility in this class. It's up to you to actually do something with it."

But he kept his reprimand short and sweet because of the time constraint and ended with a note of encouragement, although Sara overheard that part and told Charlie she thought it rang a bit hollow. Once they were finished resetting the stage, Charlie grabbed a sandwich from the food table and sat down on the floor next to Sara to eat.

The subdued actors filed past to change out of their end-of-show costumes and back into their beginning-of-show costumes. Charlie kept her head down when Kelly walked by, but the girl seemed in no mood to harass her at the moment. She made a beeline for the backstage door, phone in hand.

"You did a good job, Charlie," Sara said between bites. "I'm really glad you're in our class."

"Thanks," Charlie said. "I like it a lot."

"Maybe we can work on the next play together too," said Sara. "Co-stage managers, whaddya say?" She grinned. "Unless you want to try out for a part."

"I like the backstage stuff better, I think." Charlie shoved the rest of her sandwich into her mouth. "But I'm not sure I'm ready to take on your job quite yet."

They chatted for a few more minutes until another crew member scurried past. "They're opening the doors already," she said, a panicked look on her face. "Full house tonight. Anybody seen Kelly recently?"

"Not since she went outside," said Sara. They wiped their mouths and stood up. Time to get back to work.

Charlie headed for the small props table to make sure everything was where it was supposed to be. It wasn't, of course. So she tracked down the actors whose props were missing to find out where they'd set them down, and then went in search of the items to put them in place.

By the time Sara called out "Five minutes to curtain," Charlie had finished her preshow tasks. She peeked into the auditorium, watching it fill up with parents and students. Was her family there? It was probably too much to ask to have her mom at her first soccer game one day and the play the next. But her dad had said he would come. Hopefully he didn't forget. Charlie quickly texted him, and he responded almost immediately. "We're here!" He sent a selfie with Andy, both of them wearing goofy looks on their faces, already in their seats. Charlie grinned, though she was a little sad her mom wasn't there.

She shut down her phone for the duration of the show, then went backstage to see if she could help with anything.

Mr. Anderson was running around, long wispy strands of comb-over hair flying. "Where's Kelly?" he asked everybody he passed. "If you see her, get her back here now! She's not in costume." Nobody seemed to be able to find her, and the other actors were all too busy to search since they were trying to cram-learn their lines so Mr. Anderson wouldn't yell at them again.

Kelly was the last person Charlie wanted to talk to. But Maria's casual mention that things weren't going so great at home for Kelly had stayed with her. Besides, the show was about to start, and Charlie couldn't stand the thought of an even worse disaster than the earlier one. She slipped down the hallway in search of the star.

First she checked the bathroom, which was looking decidedly better than it had the last time Charlie had been in there: the toilet seat and broken tiles on the walls had been replaced, and a boarded-up spot covered the wall in place of the sink. Not finding Kelly in there, Charlie circled around the back of the auditorium and went through the stage door that led outside. It was dark, and at first glance Charlie didn't see anybody. But then she remembered Kelly had gone out here after the meeting. Perhaps she'd never come back in. She stepped onto the sidewalk and walked down it a few feet. On the other side of an overgrown, flowering plant that grew close to the building sat Kelly, still wearing her last-scene costume.

"Kelly?" Charlie called. "We're only a few minutes to curtain. Mr. A. needs you now."

Kelly shook her head. "I'm not going. Tell him to find somebody else to play Kim."

Charlie stared. The first show with Kelly had been bad enough. Doing the second one without her would be a tragedy. "Are you joking? I can't tell him that. If you're serious, you've got to tell him. And I hope you're not serious, because nobody else can play Kim. You didn't want an understudy, remember?"

"Shut up, Charlotte," Kelly said bitterly. "I don't need this crap right now."

Charlie recoiled. It was always unsettling when somebody said "Shut up" in such a mean voice. Still, remembering what Maria had told her, she didn't lash back. She walked over to Kelly and crouched on the grass next to her.

"Look," Charlie said. "You were the only thing that held the first show together. I don't know if you're upset about how it went or if something else is wrong, but we need you. There are a lot of parents out in the audience, and a lot of other actors and crew who have worked very hard for this. Everybody's counting on you. You can't let them down."

During Charlie's speech, Kelly's face grew even darker. "Why should I care about everybody else's parents?" she spat out bitterly. "Plus, the cast let *me* down by not being ready for opening. It's embarrassing."

Charlie wasn't sure what to think—something was obviously going on with Kelly that was bigger than the show. She looked around for help, but no one else was outside, so she kept trying. "Yes, it was rough—and the audience needed their pacemakers recharged, because they weren't reacting at all. But for the past thirty minutes, all the other actors have been cramming and rehearsing. We've got a full house tonight, and the crowd looks jazzed. Everybody's going to nail it."

Charlie let out a frustrated breath, then got up. "It's time. I gotta get backstage. Come on . . . please? Because it's going to be a total train wreck without you. Which will really stink, since there's an actual train scene and everything." She grinned, but Kelly wasn't playing along.

Charlie gave up and went back inside. She searched wildly for Mr. Anderson, who wasn't hard to find, since he was a walking ball of stress.

"Where is she?" he asked.

"She's outside beyond the bushes," Charlie said. "She says she's not going on."

"Oh, good grief," Mr. Anderson said, rushing toward the door. "Tell Sara not to cue the music until I say so."

"Got it," Charlie said. She saw Sara and flagged her down.

"Kelly!" he bellowed out the stage door. "Kelly, it's showtime. Come on!" He paged frantically through the script in his hand as he waited.

Charlie delivered the message to Sara and filled her in on what was happening, then the two girls watched and waited, spellbound. Would they have to do the show without Kelly?

Mr. Anderson looked up. "Sara!" he said. "Does anybody else know the part of Kim?"

Sara shook her head. "Not that I know of."

Just then, Kelly appeared in the doorway. "I'm here," she said in a quiet voice.

"Oh, thank goodness," Mr. Anderson said. He opened the door wider, and she stepped inside.

"The show will go on after all!" said Mr. Anderson. "Go change your costume, quickly! We're doing fine, we're doing fine—it's not a real performance unless we start ten minutes late. . . ." He rushed off. Kelly sped past Charlie and Sara to the dressing room without a word.

Charlie watched her go. "You're welcome, everyone," she said with a grin. Sara laughed, and the two went to their spots backstage to watch the actors look like idiots for the second time today.

CHAPTER 35

Deep Thoughts

After the show Charlie found her dad and Andy outside in the school parking lot, where the audience had gathered to greet and congratulate the actors.

"Yay, you came!" Charlie said, grinning widely and giving her dad a hug, and then throwing a playful punch at Andy's shoulder. "Was it awful?"

"The set changes were smooth," said Andy with a cheeky grin. "But some of the singing . . ." He wrinkled his nose. "The girl who played Kim was good, though."

"That's Kelly," Charlie said halfheartedly. She looked around and spotted Kelly basking in the warmth of effusive praise from fans, her laughter ever present now. Charlie couldn't tell if it was real or fake. Had she gotten over whatever had been bothering her?

They chatted about the show, Charlie keeping an eye on Kelly. There was nobody near her who looked like they could be her parents. Charlie wondered if they hadn't come. A pang of pity went through her. At least one of her parents was here, and Charlie wasn't even an actor. "Hmm," she said under her breath. "Maybe that's why she was upset."

"Who's upset?" Dr. Wilde asked.

Charlie turned her attention back to him. "Never mind. I'm ready to get out of here. Did you guys walk or drive?"

"Dad made us walk," Andy said, sounding a little cranky. "It's far. I don't know why you decided walking to school would be fun."

"There's a shortcut. Come on, I'll show you." Charlie guided them between vehicles and led the way, chatting as they went along. "What did you think of the show, Dad?" Charlie asked. "Was it a complete disaster?"

"No, not at all. It was a little long," Dad said carefully. "But you were amazing, of course."

Charlie gave him a puzzled look. "Thanks. You know I was just doing the set changes, though, right?"

"Oh!" said Charlie's dad. "Um . . ." He scratched his head and laughed sheepishly. "So you weren't in the cast?"

"No, Dad."

"Well, that's a relief. Because I was feeling pretty bad about not being able to tell which one was you."

Charlie sighed. "I told you a million times I was doing backstage stuff."

"I'm sorry. I've been a little too busy lately."

"It's okay. Just be glad you weren't at the first show. Did you see the train station platform? I totally built that whole thing almost by myself."

"You did? It was great," her dad said. "If you're that good at building things, I think you can probably fix that hole in the drywall yourself," he teased.

"Maybe I will," said Charlie earnestly. "I bet I could figure it out. I like building things."

He flashed an evil grin. "I'm sure I can find plenty of things for you to do. I could use a shed in the backyard."

Charlie laughed.

"What do you need a shed for?" asked Andy. He narrowed his eyes. "You're not going to put Jessie out there just because it's not cold here, are you?"

"No, of course not. She'll always be an inside dog. I just need a place to store my old work stuff. It's taking up too much room in my office. I miss having a basement."

"You mean those boxes with *T-A-L-O-S* on them?" Andy asked. "I knocked one over in the garage when Charlie slammed me into them the other day."

Charlie scowled at him.

Their father raised an eyebrow. "Charlie, what did you do to him?"

"Nothing. He's fine. Aren't you, Andy?"

"Yeah, fine," said Andy, shifty eyed. "So what's Talos?"

"Talos Global," said Charlie. "It's the company Dad worked with before you were born. Right, Dad?"

"That's right."

"What did you do?" Andy asked. "Were you, like, important or anything?"

Dad chuckled. "Nothing that amounted to much," he said. "My team worked on some experimental contracts for the government. Top secret stuff."

"Top secret?" said Andy, eyes widening.

"Not even your mom knows much about it."

"Wow, that's so cool."

Their father shrugged. "It's not as cool as it sounds. I had a lot more success being a stay-at-home dad, I think, looking after the two of you." He gave Andy's shoulders a squeeze. "You turned out pretty good."

Charlie linked her arm in his, and her mind annoyingly turned to Kelly again. "I guess we're pretty lucky that we had you around so much," she said. "Even if you're not around now."

Dr. Wilde looked offended. "I'm here right now," he protested. "I think so, anyway. Somebody pinch me."

Both kids gleefully obliged.

"Ouch! Yes, I'm definitely here."

Charlie hugged his arm as they approached their neighborhood. "That's true. I'm glad you made it. Even if you thought I was in the cast, silly."

"Do you wish you could go back to being a stay-at-home dad?" Andy asked him.

Dad scratched his chin thoughtfully. "Yes and no," he said.

"I miss seeing you when you get home from school and hearing about all the exciting parts of your day. But I think I might get bored. You two are gone every day, and you both stay after school for things."

"Like Battle of the Books," said Andy. "Juan and Zach and I all signed up."

"Like Battle of the Books," their father agreed. "So if you two are busy with your own things, that leaves only so much cooking, cleaning, shopping, and laundry to do. Especially now that Charlie takes care of her own stuff."

"We could definitely use your cooking," said Charlie. "And you can go back to doing my laundry if you miss it. Trust me, I don't mind."

Dr. Wilde patted her hand on his arm. "I thought you said you wanted more responsibility."

"Aw, Dad," Charlie said mischievously. "Not *that* kind."

"When do I get to do my own laundry?" Andy asked. "I'm ten and a half now. Almost."

"Believe me, you don't want to start," Charlie groaned. "It's only fun the first time."

Late that night in bed Charlie mulled over what Maria had said about her powers. She saw that Amari had texted her back to make sure all was okay, but Charlie hadn't had a chance to reply yet. Now she considered telling Amari everything about the bracelet and about what Maria had said about her responsibility to help other people. Amari was sensible and would know what to say.

But Charlie held back. Witnessing the bracelet's powers felt kind of like one of those "had to be there" moments. You had to see Charlie in action to believe what the bracelet could do, like Maria and Mac had. And you couldn't tell just anybody about something like this. Besides, the more people who knew about the bracelet, the riskier it became to have it. By the time Charlie was drifting off to sleep, she came to the conclusion that this wasn't something she couldn't talk to her old best friend about. And surprisingly, that felt okay.

The rest of the weekend was filled with chores. On Saturday Charlie did laundry and cleaned the house with Andy and her mom while their dad worked in his study on lesson plans for the upcoming week. And on Sunday, with Mom working at the hospital, Dad emerged to help Charlie fix the drywall and install a new doorstop. And then for dinner her dad taught her how to cook her favorite chicken-broccoli casserole so that when he didn't have time to do it, she could take over.

Working around the house gave Charlie more time to think about the bracelet. She remained conflicted about her responsibilities. Having special abilities was fun when it came to winning soccer games or moving stage sets. But the way Maria had talked, it was like she was supposed to go out and look for all sorts of good deeds to perform or something. And even though she and Mac had worked through their differences, Charlie was a little shy about running out to help other people now—what if they reacted like he had? Charlie would rather get rid of the bracelet altogether than deal with that again. Hopefully soon, Mac could try some more passwords, or at least give her the lists of codes so she could do some in her spare time. She thought about texting him to ask, but she didn't quite feel comfortable doing that after their confrontation on Friday. Maybe it was better for everybody to have a little space over the weekend. She'd ask him on Monday.

Sunday night, when Charlie was finishing up her homework before bed, Andy stopped by her room and tossed the Ms. Marvel comic book on Charlie's desk. "Can you get the second one for me?"

"Sure, I'll ask Maria," said Charlie. "You liked it?"

"Why wouldn't I? Ms. Marvel kicks butt." He disappeared.

Charlie glanced at the comic book. She pulled it closer and studied the cover, and then she turned the page and started reading.

On Monday Charlie was really looking forward to seeing Mac and Maria again. Their big discussion seemed so long ago, and now that the musical was over and soccer practice was down to once a week plus a game, Charlie was anxious to spend more time trying to break the code. It's not that she hated the bracelet, exactly. She just wished she could take it off and be normal if she chose to—it was getting hard to remember what that was like.

She found Mac and Maria standing together outside their first-period classroom, arguing about the action movie they'd seen Saturday morning. Life seemed back to normal for them.

"Hey, it's M&M," said Charlie, walking up. She felt her cheeks grow warm as she remembered their last meet-up. She still felt embarrassed about being called out for acting like a showoff. Hopefully they wouldn't talk about that anymore.

"Hey, Chuck!" said Maria, and Mac held out a fist for her to bump. Mendez, the jerk who'd been at the movie theater the Saturday before last, passed by them in the hallway. He wolf whistled and wagged his eyebrows at Mac and the girls. But this time Mac ignored the kid instead of getting mad. And Maria ignored him too.

"He'll shut up one of these days," said Mac after he was gone.

"Notice he never has any girls around him," Maria said with a sniff.

"Only his mom, because somebody's got to change his diaper," said Mac.

Charlie grinned. It was good to be with friends.

Lunch that day was back to normal. Mac ate with Charlie and Maria, and when he was finished, he went off with his other friends, only this time it didn't feel weird.

"Mac and I talked some more on Saturday after the movie," Maria said when he left. "He was feeling guilty about slinking away to hang out with his other friends. And I was feeling guilty for hanging out with you and not including him. Because we were so tight, we'd never actually done that before. But we both figured out that if it's something we like doing, well, what's the problem exactly?" She laughed. "Just because we're not glued at the hip anymore, as my mother would say, doesn't mean we aren't still best friends."

"That's really cool," said Charlie.

"And," said Maria, "it doesn't mean I can't have *two* best friends."

Charlie smiled. She thought of Amari back home. "Two best friends," she said. "Sounds pretty good to me."

Kelly kept to herself all day and, to their surprise, didn't bug Charlie or Mac for answers about Friday's set-building drama. She seemed especially quiet and brooding today, actually.

In theater class Charlie asked Sara if she'd noticed it.

"Yeah, I guess you're right," Sara said. "It's probably PSLS."

Charlie frowned. "What's that?"

"Post-Show Letdown Syndrome," explained Sara with a laugh. "After working so hard for so long and finally performing the show, it's over. And now," she added, with a poor imitation of dramatic flair, "we have nothing left to live for. And we have to tear it all down."

Charlie laughed. She understood the feeling. It happened in sports, too, at the end of the season. But she didn't think that was the only thing bothering Kelly. The stagehands Kelly had insulted were still grumbling about her. And others had heard about the mean things she'd said by now. Some even began to whisper about the biting things Kelly sometimes said about other people when they weren't listening. Perhaps it had finally caught up with her. And then there was the mystery of Kelly's parents and her trouble at home.

Charlie didn't spend too much time wondering about her, though. She'd probably never know what that was all about. And she needed to keep her distance—she didn't want to give Kelly any reason to harass her about her secret again. But that seemed to be forgotten along with the rest of last week's excitement as they broke down the stage.

Soon the platforms and set designs they'd put so much work into were dissembled. Charlie found herself dragging some of the trash to the same Dumpster she'd lifted a few weeks before.

At soccer practice after school, Coach Candy reviewed the highs and lows of their first game, and then had the team work on their speed drills and passing skills before letting them go a little early as a reward for their first win. Charlie headed over to Maria's house with her so Mac could enter some more passwords and try to get the device off. Mac was already there, as usual.

He looked up as they walked in. "Can I see the bracelet?" he said.

"Sure," said Charlie. She dropped her backpack and sat down

next to him, then stretched out her arm. While Mac messed around with the bracelet's buttons to get to the keypad screen and pulled up his list of the most promising options that he'd gathered from his phone apps, Charlie picked up Mac's iPad with her free hand. She checked her social media accounts and favorited a few of her Chicago friends' photos, then, out of boredom, she typed "Chimera Mark Five" into the search bar.

There was nothing that put the three words together as an item—only a list of results that had one or two of the words in the context.

"*Pfft*. Boring," she said.

Mac looked up from entering codes to see what she was doing. "Oh, I know," he said. "I searched it back when it went into defense mode. Nada."

Charlie clicked on links that seemed interesting. But none of them said anything about a bracelet. For the most part, the search landed her on gamers' message boards.

"There's no such thing as Chimera Mark Five," Charlie reported, looking at Maria.

Mac squinted at the bracelet's screen and inputted the next code. "I just said that."

Maria frowned. "Nothing at all? How is that even possible? You'd think somebody would be talking about it since it's so powerful and everything. Are you sure?"

"Well," said Charlie, "I mean, the words exist separately,

obviously. And *Mark Five* goes together in a lot of instances—like there's some sort of boat called the Mark V. And it could be a version of a device, like what you said about Iron Man's suits. But never all three words together indicating a *thing*."

"Boo. Maybe it's top secret." Maria looked up from the homework she was doing. "Did you find the right code yet, Mac?"

"No," Mac said. He went back to the bracelet, and then he paused. "You still haven't activated the other two powers, in case you were wondering."

"I know. I've been checking. I wish we knew what they stood for, at least."

Mac scrolled slowly through the endless list of codes he'd collected, typing them in one at a time. There were a gagillion options, and those were just the seven-digit alphanumeric codes. But there was no rule that said the code was seven digits. It might be six or five or four. And it was also possible that the code was strictly numbers or letters, he supposed. This task could take an entire lifetime of nonstop typing, and even then there was no guarantee of finding the right one.

After a while he let go of Charlie's wrist and sighed. "If I knew how long the code was, or if it was numbers or letters or a combination of the two, I might be able to narrow it down a little. But I don't know if it's three characters or seven or somewhere in between. And not knowing who sent it, I don't have any clues at all about what combinations they might be more likely to use. I mean,

I've entered the twenty most common pin numbers for all the various lengths, and I can go on from there; but let's be honest—it's really pointless. I'm just getting error after error."

Charlie leaned over, and Mac showed her the screen on her bracelet that flashed *KEY IN ACCESS CODE TO DEACTIVATE* at the top of it. Mac entered the next code on his list and tapped the space with his finger. An ERROR screen popped up.

Charlie sighed. "This thing is stuck on me forever."

Maria studied Mac. "How did you find out what the twenty most common pin numbers are?"

Mac tilted his head and narrowed his eyes. "That's a business secret."

"Okay. Well, maybe we don't know who sent it, but we do know who it was addressed to. What if they programmed the code to be something Charlie could figure out?"

Mac stared at her. For a very, very long moment. "You? Are brilliant," he said. "Charlie, I'm going to need some info. Phone numbers, house numbers, zip codes, birth date . . ." He found a piece of paper and started scribbling all the things he needed.

Maria shrugged. She closed her book and looked at Charlie. "And if that doesn't work, there's got to be a way to get the bracelet off if that's really what you want, Chuck. Jaws of Life or something, right? Can't your mom help? They ought to have some tools at the hospital."

"Yeah, I suppose," said Charlie. "I'm not sure if her rinky-dink hospital is big enough to have tools like that, though."

"Um, excuse me? Navarro Junction hospital has a helipad. It is not rinky-dink," said Maria.

"No?" Charlie smirked. "What would you call it?"

Mac looked up from his scribbling. "It's . . . juvenile, like a young gorilla. Still growing—and it doesn't know its own strength."

"Oh, okay," Charlie said with a smirk. "But wouldn't cutting it off destroy it? I'm not sure I want that to happen."

"That's true," said Maria. "You probably wouldn't be able to use it again, so that would stink."

"I don't know." Charlie stood up and wandered the bedroom, an uneasy feeling growing inside her. She didn't want to talk about it anymore. She was really confused about how she felt about the powers the bracelet gave her. Sometimes she wished she'd never put on the bracelet, and other times she couldn't picture her life without these new abilities.

"It's the healing power that would be a real bummer to lose," she said, remembering how she might be sitting out soccer this season with a broken leg if it hadn't been for the device. And then she shook her head, feeling horribly restless. "Ugh. I can't even deal with this right now. Let's just go kick the ball around outside or something." She charged out of the room.

Mac looked up from his list of questions, like he was about to stop her, but she was already gone. "Well," he said.

"Wow," said Maria. "She's stressed out."

"We'd better go." Mac put the paper on Charlie's backpack and they got up to follow.

Charlie forged down the hallway and past the kitchen, where Maria's stepdad, Ken, was pulling a huge cast-iron skillet from a cabinet and putting it on the stove. Her grandmother Yolanda was stooping in front of the refrigerator, taking out several butcher-wrapped packages and an armful of onions. Maria's stepbrothers were nowhere to be seen.

"Hey, Charlie," Ken said cheerfully as she raced by.

"Hi," Charlie said, not stopping. She burst through the door as if the house were suffocating her, but the feeling didn't go away once she got outside. The bracelet felt like it had turned into a huge metal body cast that was squeezing her too tightly.

She stopped in the driveway and stood there a moment, taking a few deep breaths, trying to accept the fact that if she really wanted the bracelet off, she'd have to ask for help. But if she did, would she have to tell her mother everything? What would happen?

And then suddenly she realized it wasn't that big of a deal. She didn't have to mention the powers. Her mom didn't need to know the real reason why she wanted it off—wouldn't anybody want the same thing if they had a bracelet stuck on them?

That thought calmed her. She blew out a breath. Just knowing she had the option made everything so much better.

As she heard the screen door open and close behind her, two

little kids on bikes whizzed up the street toward her. They were yelling something, and they sounded scared.

"What's wrong?" Charlie called out to them, her stomach suddenly nervous.

Maria and Mac joined her, and Maria grabbed Charlie's arm. "What's going on?"

"Fire! Fire! There's a fire!" one of the kids said.

"What?" Maria cried. "Where?"

"At the end of the street! The man said to get help!"

CHAPTER 36

Fire!

Charlie, Mac, and Maria exchanged looks. A split second later the three of them broke into a run. It didn't take long for them to detect a hint of smoke in the air.

Maria looked over her shoulder. "Mac, call 9-1-1!"

Mac was already dialing as he loped along behind them.

"Charlie, is your bracelet activated?"

Charlie didn't have to touch it to know—warmth spread up her arm. "Yes," she said. A sickening wave of fear swept over her as the bracelet grew even warmer without her having to do anything. A fire? That was way more than she could handle. She ran blindly. Numbly. She couldn't think straight. She took a few deep breaths. "You can do this," she said to herself, not even sure what it was she would have to do. Just knowing she had to do something.

She sped up. "I gotta go help," she said over her shoulder, giving her friends one last earnest look. And then, with a burst of speed, she tore down the street, not caring who saw her.

Once she rounded a curve in the road, the fire was impossible to miss. Smoke poured heavily from a two-story house, and the acrid odor of it was inescapable. A neighbor was frantically trying to attach a tangled garden hose to the spigot on the side of her house. A small crowd gathered nearby, helpless as flames licked the first-story windows. Some of the bystanders were talking fearfully on their phones, while others held theirs up to record the tragedy.

Crouched on the edge of a flat section of the roof was a screaming woman, who pointed to a nearby window on the second floor.

Someone must be trapped inside, thought Charlie. Her blood surged as she reached the scene. She had to do something! But how was she supposed to get up to the second story when flames were coming out of all the doors and windows on the main floor? She broke through the crowd and ran toward the house. Instinct took over. She leaped up in the air, grabbing on to a thin copper pipe that ran up the side of the house. Then she quickly shinnied up it to the flat second-story roof. Her mind focused laser-like on the task and shut out the reaction from the crowd below.

At the top, she hoisted herself onto the roof and sprang to her feet. The woman ran to her, hysterical, tugging at Charlie's shirt and saying something in Spanish. Charlie didn't understand.

"Come on, I'll get you down," she said to the woman, holding out her arms.

The woman shook her head and pointed inside the broken window. She started screaming again.

Charlie tuned in to someone yelling the same thing over and

over from below. "Her son is trapped! She won't come down without him."

Charlie could feel the fiery heat coming from inside. Sweat poured down her face. She peered into the window but couldn't see anything but soot and flashes of fire in the darkness. It would be stupid to go in there. But someone needed her help. What else was Charlie supposed to do? She couldn't leave them there.

Charlie closed her eyes and took a few deep breaths. No one in her right mind would enter a burning building for the sake of a stranger unless she was a firefighter. But here Charlie was. Doing it. She hoped the bracelet wouldn't glitch now and that the healing power would kick in immediately when necessary.

With a grunt, Charlie ripped a strip of cloth from her T-shirt and tied it around her head, over her nose and mouth. She took one last deep breath and dove through the broken window and over the line of flames. She landed on her back, rolled to her hands and knees, and crawled out of the room and into the hallway.

With the thick smoke and soot covering the windows, it was almost as dark as night inside the house except for the flare-ups. Charlie couldn't see anything. Her heart sank—she'd never be able to find the boy this way. She pulled her mask up to her forehead to stop the sweat from stinging her eyes and crept forward.

As she moved along, she heard strange echoing chirps and tilted her head, trying to figure out where they were coming from. Was there a pet bird in the house too? But she soon ignored the chirps because, in front of her, a shimmering outline of a hallway appeared like a silver shadow in the darkness. Encouraged, she got to her feet and, keeping low, set off in search of the boy.

The odd chirping continued and so did the shimmering silver shadows, outlining everything in her path. The air was thick. One room was fully engulfed—there was no chance of survival if the woman's son was in there. Charlie grabbed the doorknob to pull the door shut and keep the fire from getting to the hallway, and yelped in pain—the knob was white-hot. Her hand throbbed. The smoke was horrible. Charlie knew she didn't have much time before she'd have to get out.

Then she heard a small cry from behind a closed door on the other side of a fiery patch of carpet. Charlie ran deftly toward the sound. A moment later a burning chunk of the ceiling fell across the hallway behind her. She was surrounded by fire.

Panicking and knowing she had to act fast, she pulled her T-shirt mask over her mouth and nose again, then bent over, dug her fingers into the carpet, and ripped the burning section up from the floor. She rolled it down the hallway past the closed door and stomped on it to put out the fire.

Lungs burning, Charlie returned to the door and tested the knob gingerly. It was hot but tolerable. She flung the door open. With less smoke in this room, she pulled her mask off—she could breathe in here. Immediately the chirping began again, and Charlie realized that the sound was coming from her! She watched in awe

as the shimmering silver outlines of a dresser, changing table, and crib formed in the semidarkness. What was happening? Whatever it was, she didn't have time to figure it out now.

Charlie gulped at the air. Her eyes and throat stung, but she couldn't do anything for that now. She crawled toward the crib, and her chirps grew faster, more insistent. The shape of a little body standing in the crib appeared before her. She sprang to her feet, ran to the sobbing boy, and scooped him up. But how was she going to get him out of here safely?

She scanned the room, and the chirping became even more insistent. More shapes appeared before her: stuffed animals, a rocking chair, some sort of small appliance in the corner. Pulling a blanket from the boy's crib, she moved to the corner of the room to see what the item was. She felt around it, then pushed against it and got the rewarding sloshing sound she was hoping for. *Humidifier!* she thought triumphantly. She twisted the top and pulled out the mechanical part, exposing the water trough. She doused the blanket and wrapped the boy in it like she'd learned in her summer classes at the Y. Then she splashed the remaining water over her hair and on the face mask. She secured the mask over her face again. With the child wrapped up, she held him tightly to her chest and looked out into the hallway.

But the hallway was impassable now. It was fully engulfed in flames. With the boy crying, she slammed the door to keep out the fire and began to panic.

She'd have to find a different way out.

Charlie felt her way to the bedroom window, flinging the curtains aside. She ripped down the shade and threw it on the floor, opened the window, and pressed her forehead against the screen to see what was below. There were no flames, but it was a sheer drop to the backyard—no overhangs, no pipe to climb down. Only some smoldering window shutters to hold on to several feet below her. "Good grief," she muttered. She punched the screen with her fist, sending it flying, and leaned out, watching it hit the ground. Her heart was in her throat.

The house groaned, and she heard some popping noises and a crash outside the child's room. She turned quickly at the sound, the curtains fluttering near her face. And then she sucked in a breath. The curtains! Could she climb down them? She set the boy on the floor, ripped down one panel, and tied it to the bottom of the other. Leaving the other panel attached to the curtain rod, she flung the makeshift rope out the window. Then she picked up the child and hoped the strength ability was still activated so she could hold on.

Just then a window on the first floor below them exploded, and flames began climbing up toward Charlie and the boy. With the dangling curtain in danger of bursting into flames, and no time to ponder other options, Charlie grabbed it and stepped out of the window.

The people outside gasped. Holding the child with one arm, Charlie used the other to rappel down the side of the house until she ran out of curtain length. She wasn't quite sure what she was going to do next other than hang there and wait for help.

Without warning, the curtain rod broke. Charlie screamed and let go, instinctively slapping her free hand against the house, trying to grasp at anything to keep them from falling. And while the curtain fluttered to the ground, Charlie and the boy did not. They hung suspended, Charlie's hand somehow magically sticking to the side of the house.

What just happened? she thought. Both hands and feet tingled.

Once she realized they were stable, for the moment at least, Charlie quickly kicked off her shoes and pressed her tingly bare feet against the house. They stuck. Gingerly, she lifted one foot and moved it down to see if it would stick again.

It did. Slowly she slid her hand down, then her feet, then her hand again, and before anyone could comprehend what Charlie was doing, she was safely on the ground, her body shaking. Maria and Mac charged toward her. With sirens sounding in the distance, Charlie handed the child to Maria.

"That was insane!" Maria shouted. "How did you do that?"

Charlie shook her head, trying to catch her breath. "I don't know," she rasped. "I've got to go after the lady."

Mac nodded furiously. "I think you must have activated another ability!"

Charlie didn't have time to check the bracelet now. "Be right back," she croaked. Her hands and feet still tingled, but they didn't look any different. With reckless trust in the bracelet, Charlie ran toward the house and, without slowing down, flung herself at it, spread-eagle. Her hands and feet stuck. She scrambled quickly up the side to the rooftop where the woman clung as fire devoured the structure all around her.

"It's going to collapse!" somebody shouted just as a fire truck turned onto the street. There wasn't time to wait for help—the fire was uncomfortably hot on Charlie's body already. "Come on!" she said, hoping the woman would understand. She pointed down at Maria, who held up the boy so the woman could see her child was safe, then reached out and grabbed the woman around the waist. The baby's mother clung to Charlie's neck and screamed as Charlie gripped the edge of the roof, dangling over the side of the house. With the woman bigger than her and practically choking her to death, Charlie started back down. They made a strange sight. Firefighters rushed to the chaotic scene below.

"Look out!" someone cried.

Charlie didn't have to look. She felt the house shake, and then it began to crack and crumble. Flames shot out, singeing Charlie's legs. She held the woman tightly and leaped the rest of the way to the ground. The two tumbled in the rocky landscaping, and then Charlie scooped up the woman and ran away from the house until they were at a safe distance.

They both collapsed, breathing hard. Strangers swarmed around them, saying things Charlie couldn't comprehend. All she wanted was some fresh air.

"*Gracias*," the woman cried. "Thank you."

Charlie nodded, unable to speak.

Seconds later Mac and Maria were pushing through to Charlie's side. Maria handed the screaming child to his mother, and they began dragging Charlie out of the crowd to find her a place to sit down.

"Are you okay?" Maria exclaimed.

Charlie nodded. Her throat was sore from the smoke. She whipped off her makeshift mask, wiped her face with it, coughed hard into it a few times, and threw it on the ground.

Mac ran off and came back with bottles of ice-cold water from a neighbor. Charlie grabbed one with her burned hand, cringed, and poured the liquid down her throat and over her head.

"Is the baby okay?" she asked when she could speak. She watched the firefighters work to extinguish the blaze, then examined her blistered hand and legs, and found the redness was already subsiding. The pain was lessening too.

"I think so," Mac reported. "They're taking him and the woman to the hospital, it looks like. And now people are pointing this way. Here comes a paramedic."

Charlie glanced at Maria and bit her lip. "Do you think anybody's suspicious about the climbing?"

"It doesn't matter," Maria said quietly as the woman approached. "You saved people. Just play it down. You're a climber."

Charlie nodded. She peeked at her hand, wishing the blisters to disappear, and then held the water bottle in that hand again to help it along.

The uniformed woman smiled. "I hear you're a hero," she said. "Are you hurt?"

"No," Charlie said. "Just a little singed around the edges." She pointed to her clothes.

"I'm Alice. What's your name?"

"Charlie."

The woman crouched next to Charlie and looked into her eyes. "Any pain or dizziness, Charlie? Trouble breathing? Cold? Hot? Any burns?"

Charlie didn't mention her hand or the minor burns on her legs. "Nope, not really." In the distance a TV news van pulled up.

"Do you live nearby? Are your parents around? We can get you checked out at the hospital just to make sure everything looks good."

Charlie frowned. "No, that's okay. My mom's a doctor. I'll have her check me over when I get home. But I feel fine."

"How about we just take a peek at you back at the ambulance and keep an eye on you until your parents get here?" asked Alice. "We'll just listen to your lungs and look for burns, stuff like that. No big deal."

The camera operator hopped out of the news van and started setting up, and a reporter got out and began talking to the crowd.

"I'm fine," insisted Charlie. She stood up and started walking away, warily eyeing the action nearby. Mac and Maria hurried after her.

The paramedic turned to see what Charlie was looking at just as people in the crowd pointed in Charlie's direction. "Let me at least call your parents," pleaded Alice.

But Charlie walked faster. The man in the suit started coming toward her.

Alice gave up. "Stay out of burning buildings, all right?" she called after her. Charlie ignored her and looked at Maria and Mac. "We need to get out of here," she said, her voice shaking. "I don't know my way around this neighborhood. Where are we?" She could barely remember which direction she'd come from.

"On it," Mac said, taking the lead. "We'll get you out of here."

Maria ran up next to him. "There's that big cement culvert behind these houses," she said.

"Good idea. Is it dry?" He headed that way.

"Should be. It hasn't rained." Maria glanced back to see the reporter gaining on them. She grabbed Charlie's arm to help her along.

"Hi there!" the reporter called out. "Excuse me! Kids?" The reporter broke into a run, following them. He shouted out his name and TV station. "Wait! I heard one of you saved the people inside. Is that true?" In between shouts he was frantically waving at his camera operator to hurry up.

"Run," said Charlie under her breath. They turned behind the row of houses, jumped down into the culvert, and started running toward Maria's house.

Now that reality was setting in, Charlie was beginning to feel uneasy. Showing her abilities in public in such an obvious way, barely escaping being on the news . . . it made her feel like a spectacle. Did anybody get a good look at her? They weren't far from Maria's neighborhood. Had anybody from school been in the crowd? People don't just climb up and stick to the side of a house. She didn't have a good feeling about it.

After a few minutes, with Maria and Mac glancing behind them, they slowed.

"I think we lost him," Maria said.

"Thank goodness," said Charlie, dropping her pace to a walk. Her voice was still raspy from smoke, and her lungs hurt from breathing hard. She didn't tell her friends how uneasy she felt, but she figured they must have a decent idea. All she wanted to do now was hang out at Maria's and be normal again.

Affected by the smoke and the hard run, Mac was wheezing too. He pulled out his inhaler and used it.

They entered through the back door to Maria's house. The smell of delicious cooking wafted through the air. Charlie sneaked into the bathroom and cleaned up, and Maria gave her some clothes to change into. When Charlie went back into the bedroom, Maria and Mac were discussing her newest abilities.

"So you've got this new wall-climbing ability," Mac said

excitedly. "I got great video footage of it."

"Yeah?"

"For sure. Watch." He played it for Charlie.

"Whoa," she murmured. "I could totally be on *American Ninja Warrior.*"

Mac laughed. "Understatement of the year."

"Why did you take your shoes off?" asked Maria.

"My feet were tingling," Charlie said wearily.

Mac and Maria exchanged a puzzled look. Mac shrugged. "Can I see the bracelet?"

She held out her wrist to him, wishing for the millionth time she could just take off the dumb thing, if only for the convenience of letting Mac look at it without her having to hang her arm in the air. She was getting tired of Mac yanking and pawing at her all the time.

He wiped a bit of residual grime off the screen with his thumb and held down the two buttons. The screen changed to the pie chart, and now all five of the vine-like drawings in the gray slices were animated.

"Check it out!" Mac studied it and looked at the girls. "You got them both somehow. What are they?"

Maria hopped up to see. Charlie puzzled over the animations for a moment. "Oh, that one must be a lizard climbing," she said. "The four squiggly vines are its legs and feet, see?"

"I see it," said Mac.

"Yep," said Maria. "Well, we kind of figured that one out already just watching you in action." She caught Charlie's eye and gave her an admiring look. "You really were the coolest."

"Thanks," Charlie said.

"Hey," said Mac with a frown, but then he laughed. "Kidding. Maria's right—you're pretty great." He pointed at the bracelet. "Did you know geckos can hang on to a wall using only one finger?"

"I wonder if Chuck can do that," said Maria.

"I'm afraid to try," said Charlie. "And isn't hanging by one hand close enough? I almost tore my arm out of its socket. But what's the other ability?" She massaged her shoulder, though it didn't hurt much anymore.

"I don't know," said Maria. "Did something else happen inside the house?"

Charlie had been thinking a lot about that. "I'm not sure how to explain it," she said. "But when I got inside, it was dark—there was smoke everywhere. I didn't think I'd be able to find the boy."

"What happened?" asked Mac.

Charlie blushed. "I started, um, well, chirping. I guess."

Maria stared. "You did what?"

"Your fifth ability comes from a bird?" asked Mac. "That's boring. Really disappointing, actually."

"I don't think this GIF is a bird," she said, looking at the fifth wedge on the bracelet.

"Then what is it? What good would chirping do?"

"Well, when I chirped, it sort of helped me tell where things were. I know that sounds weird, but there I was in the pitch-dark, and I just started chirping in this really high voice, not able to control it at all. And suddenly a silver outline of walls and doorways shimmered in front of me and I could see."

Mac had the weirdest look on his face. "High-pitched chirping?" He snorted. "Sorry."

"Yeah, it was kind of awkward," said Charlie. "Like when you get the hiccups and you can't stop them. But I've never heard a bird do anything like that, so I don't know. . . ."

Maria looked at the bracelet. "Maybe it's some sort of sonar. Like a dolphin uses." She sat up, excited. "Yeah, that would make sense!" But then her face fell. "There is no way that is a picture of a dolphin."

"Sonar . . . ," said Mac thoughtfully. "You chirped, and the walls appeared. . . ." He scrambled for his iPad and typed in something. In seconds he was playing a video. "Did it sound like this?" He turned up the volume.

On the screen was a video of a bat chirping and diving to catch a moth. Bat chirps were inaudible to human ears, but scientists had altered the pitch on the video so that humans could hear it.

Charlie watched, fascinated. "That's it," she said. "That's the sound." She looked at the graphic on the bracelet, and the depicted animal became obvious. "It's a bat all right, flying toward us. The circle is its head, and the wavy vines on either side are wings flapping. The half-circle vines above it are . . . sound waves?"

"Echolocation!" Mac said, and then he frowned. "But . . . you mean you could actually hear your own chirps?"

"Maybe she can hear them because they're coming from her, and other people can't," said Maria. "Or maybe it's just her own lower-frequency noises echoing—I saw this video in science class once about a boy in England who is blind, and he makes a clicking noise with his tongue to use echolocation. It's really cool! I'll see if I can find it and send it to you."

Mac just sat back and looked at Charlie with reluctant admiration. "Big props. Echolocation, wall climbing, strength, speed, and healing? That is a whole mess of awesomeness."

Charlie shrugged. It was hard to fathom.

Mac turned back to his iPad. He closed out the bat video, and then clicked on his Twitter feed. He scanned it quickly, then narrowed in on a tweet. "Uh-oh," he said.

Maria and Charlie moved closer. "What?"

He clicked on a link that opened to a local news page. "'Mystery Youth Saves Child, Mother from Fire,'" he read. "'Footage of the daring rescue. Coverage at six.'"

He located the video, and they watched a slightly shaky, slightly blurry film of Charlie scaling the side of the burning house.

CHAPTER 37

Visual Confirmation

In the corner of Dr. Gray's dimly lit lab, one of his mysterious-looking soldiers watched five screens simultaneously. The large man typed constantly, recording everything he saw. Every now and then the muscles along his back rippled, and he shook his head the slightest bit, but this unusual tic didn't appear to interrupt his concentration.

At 6:23 p.m. local time, he stopped typing and stared at one of the screens, then restarted the video to watch it again. He paused it and looked at the person scaling the side of the burning house. He zoomed in, refocused, and zoomed in again, until her face and arms filled the frame. The person appeared to be a girl wearing a cloth mask . . . and a metal bracelet.

"Ahh," said the man, and then he snorted in anger. He pressed a button on the earpiece that was embedded in his bodysuit. "Zed? It's Cyke. Alert Dr. Gray. We have visual confirmation."

Shortly thereafter several doorways opened, and a dozen or so similarly suited men and women filed into the room.

When everyone had assembled, Cyke directed them to look at the screen. He pointed to the device on the girl's arm. "What do you think, Doctor?"

Dr. Gray peered at the still shot, his eyes narrowing. "I think you've got it. Run a visual test. What's she doing? How did you locate it?"

Cyke touched the screen, drawing a box around the girl's arm, and magnified the area. "This afternoon our scanners turned up a second web search for Chimera Mark Five from the same IP address in Arizona as before," he explained, "and we believe we've identified the residence from which the query took place. Our surveillance team there has been staking out the neighborhood since the first incidence. They've monitored local news as well, but nothing's turned up until this." He performed a few more operations on the magnified shot, and soon a box opened on that screen with numbers scrolling and a red bar moving across it. "Official match on the bracelet is in progress."

"How did you get this footage?"

Cyke turned to a second computer and pulled up the same website so Dr. Gray and the soldiers could see the shot unmagnified. "Local news of a fire. A bystander captured it on his cell phone. The girl climbed the side of this house to the second story and carried a grown woman down to the ground."

Dr. Gray leaned forward in alarm. "So she got the bracelet to work?" he muttered. "But how?"

"Yes, it appears to be working well, Dr. Gray," Cyke said.

"Well, who is she?" Dr. Gray narrowed his razor-sharp eyes.

"No one knows," said Cyke. His back rippled again, and his head gave a little shake. "At least no one's identified her yet."

"Play the clip."

Cyke obliged.

Dr. Gray watched in stunned silence, then ripped his fingers through his hair. "I don't understand it. Only Wilde himself could have possibly activated it—nobody else would have the knowledge. Certainly not some random child . . ." Dr. Gray trailed off, and stared at the screen, a pained look on his face.

Several soldiers shifted uncomfortably, unsure how to react to Dr. Gray's emotional outburst.

The first screen blinked, and the red bar turned green. Cyke looked at the doctor. "The bracelet matches, sir—it's definitely the Mark Five."

"What's that?" Dr. Gray said faintly, pulling away from his thoughts. "Oh, yes. Yes, of course it must be. Wilde relocated to Arizona, didn't he? I'm afraid . . . I'm afraid this is no coincidence." He blew out a breath and scanned the lab, talking more to himself than to anyone else. "Could *he* have been Jack's accomplice in the break-in? And then what—he fled to Arizona with it? Or perhaps they're *all* in this . . . together. Against me." He clutched the placket of his lab coat, his eyes flickering at the thought of being betrayed. But then he shook his head and gathered his resolve. "No matter. Now that we know the device works, we must triple our efforts."

He looked up sharply and addressed the group. "Soldiers,

I've said it before and I'll remind you again—trust no one." The expression on his face turned hard. "This location is not safe," he said. "We must guard the remaining prototypes with extreme care—we can't let this happen again. If Charles Wilde is involved and has decided to go against me, there are most certainly others preparing to do the same thing." Abruptly he pushed through the soldiers and stormed around the lab. Stopping at the far wall, he unlocked a glass cabinet, then snatched devices from it. He packed them with care in a small case, and then he returned to the puzzled group, carrying the case and muttering under his breath, "I'll just have to convince him that we're stronger together. That's all."

He placed his hand on Cyke's shoulder and took a moment to pull his thoughts together. Finally, with an air of calm, he started giving orders. "Cyke, arrange travel for you, me, Zed, and Miko to Arizona, immediately," he said. "And Dr. Goldstein too, of course." He glanced at a slight, energetic soldier nearby who seemed to have trouble standing still. "Miko," he said to her, "give Jack a little food and water so he's fit to travel, will you? Just a little, mind you."

"Yes, sir," she replied, and slipped away.

Dr. Gray turned back to Cyke. "Let the Arizona team know we're on the way. Tomorrow you, Zed, and Miko will assist the surveillance team in raiding the IP location, intercepting the girl, and grabbing the bracelet." He paused and added, with a note of bitterness, "I'll take the rest of the soldiers to see if we can locate our old friend Dr. Wilde . . . and find out what he's been up to without me."

"Of course, Dr. Gray."

"If all goes well," Dr. Gray went on, "we'll set up our lab and continue working from Navarro Junction with help from Jack and, well, whoever else we collect along the way."

He held up the box of devices to the group of soldiers. "I'm taking the prototypes with me. I want those of you staying behind to pack up the lab and tear this place down. Then follow us to the warehouse in Arizona with the gear."

The doctor emitted a strained laugh. The wounded look on his face had faded, replaced by one of pride and a hint of revenge. "A new little lab in the desert—how charming. If Dr. Wilde is behind this as I suspect, he's in for quite a shock when he finds out what I've done in the time he's been away." He looked lovingly at his soldiers. A man in the group stood up straighter and nodded, while a cunning-looking woman at the front narrowed her eyes.

Then the doctor's face clouded again, and he clapped once, loudly. "Zed, get them moving!"

The cunning-looking soldier obeyed and snarled out orders. Within seconds, and at incredible speed, several members of the group swarmed the lab instruments and began breaking them down.

Cyke turned from the computer and stood up, his muscles rippling under the bodysuit. At his full height, he stood several inches taller than the doctor, and his shoulders were a good deal broader. He looked down at the man. "Pack your things, Doctor," he said, and began gathering up some papers from his workstation. "We leave in thirty minutes."

"Just a moment!" Dr. Gray narrowed his eyes. "Get me the Navarro Junction team. All of them."

Cyke sat back down and clicked an icon on the computer screen. A moment later Dr. Gray was looking at a soldier in a full bodysuit like Cyke's standing in semidarkness inside a large warehouse. Behind him was a table with several unopened boxes stacked on top and a long row of computer monitors, similar to the ones in front of Cyke. A white van with blacked-out windows was parked beyond the table. Other soldiers were putting equipment together in the background.

"Prowl at your service," the soldier said. His voice was slow and deliberate, and contained the faintest hint of a rumbling sound, almost like a purr.

"Prowl, can you bring everyone over?" Cyke asked. "Dr. Gray wants to do a quick check-in. I see the van—is the surveillance team there too?"

"We're all here," Prowl said. He called the group to gather around his tablet.

"All present, sir," Cyke confirmed, looking at Dr. Gray.

Dr. Gray greeted the team and gave them a run-down of the plan. Then he addressed the three members of the surveillance team.

"I need you back at the IP site immediately. Be extravigilant—record every move of every person on that street so we can go in tomorrow and get the job done without any problems. Have a good look at the girl from the video so you can recognize her—she may still be wearing the bracelet. Do you understand?"

"Yes, sir," said the three.

"Does *everyone* understand our mission tomorrow?"

They all nodded.

Dr. Gray continued. "This task is more serious than I can possibly emphasize. I don't care what you have to do to succeed."

The soldiers nodded again. "Yes, Doctor," a couple of them murmured.

Dr. Gray studied each of the soldiers until he was satisfied that they grasped the urgency of the situation. "We will destroy the girl if that's what it takes," he said. "I must have that device back."

CHAPTER 38

Trying Not to Freak Out

The news segment about the mysterious youth who rescued two people from a fire ended. Charlie, Maria, and Mac stared at the iPad for a long moment.

"Oh no," Charlie whispered. Tears welled up in her eyes. She looked at Maria. "People are going to find out."

"Yeah, they might," said Mac, "though it's hard to tell it's you with that cloth over your face." He turned in the chair. "Would it be such a bad thing, though?"

"Yes!" cried Charlie. "Can you imagine the kids at school if word gets out? I don't want them coming up to me and asking me to carry them around or climb walls like I'm some circus performer. And what about the next time something goes wrong around town—are people going to expect me to show up and save the day? What happens if I'm taking a test or playing in a soccer game and I don't go?"

She sniffed and went on in a quiet voice, "I just started feeling like I belong here, and I like it that way. I don't want to stand out or have people talk about me behind my back or think I'm some sort of freak. I want to have a normal life. Besides," she said, looking at the news report, "I haven't told my parents anything about this. If they find out, they might cut the bracelet off, and it'll be ruined."

Mac saw Charlie's face and quickly looked away. "Yeah, okay, I get it. My parents would kill me if they discovered something like that about me on the news. Like I said, maybe nobody will be able to tell it's you."

They watched the footage again.

"No way people will be able to tell," Maria said decisively. "The shot is too far away. I think you're okay, Charlie."

"Can you refresh the page?" Charlie urged Mac. "Go to the bottom."

Mac did as she asked and scrolled down to the comments section.

"What are you doing?" Maria asked, alarmed.

"We need to check the comments," said Charlie, taking a determined breath and wiping away a tear. She leaned over Mac's shoulder.

"Why—you're not going to write one, are you?" asked Maria.

"Of course not," said Charlie. "But people are going to start trying to guess who the mysterious hero is. And we need to figure out if anybody recognized me, or you guys for that matter. You're in the clip, too, at the end—just the backs of your heads, thankfully. But Mac's Afro is pretty distinguishable."

"The footage is grainy," Mac said. "I don't think anybody will be able to tell. Even the still frame they blew up doesn't show your face. And if somebody notices Maria and me, we'll just say we have no idea who that person is."

"All right," Charlie said dubiously. "Maybe nobody seeing it on TV will recognize me, but what about the people who were actually at the scene? Was anybody there from school? I didn't exactly have a chance to look. Plus . . . ugh." She pounded her fist against her head.

"What's wrong?" asked Maria.

"That paramedic—I told her my first name. Stupid! What if that news guy tracked her down and she told him? Or what if she tells somebody at the ER, and my mom finds out? There's not a lot of girls named Charlie out there." Charlie got up and started pacing anxiously from the end of Maria's bed to the door and back again. "What am I going to do?" She looked up and wrinkled her nose, then took a swath of hair and sniffed it. "Oh my grossness! My hair smells like smoke. I can't go home like this!" She snatched up the plastic bag that held her filthy clothes and looked down at the clothes Maria had lent her. "May I take a shower?" she asked.

"Sure," said Maria. "Use whatever you need in there."

"Thanks." Charlie thrust the bag at her. "And can you please get rid of these clothes? Throw them away—I don't care. They're ruined anyway."

"You got it," said Maria, taking the bag. "We'll take care of it."

Charlie bolted into the bathroom.

Maria and Mac sneaked out through the back door so Maria's

parents wouldn't see them and took Charlie's ruined clothes out to the garbage can by the shed.

"Hiding evidence—it's like we're in the movies," Maria said.

"Only real," said Mac.

"What if the police come and look through the trash and find her clothes?" asked Maria.

Mac narrowed his eyes. "Why would the police come? And even if they did, it's not like Charlie did anything wrong. They'd probably give her a medal of honor or something."

Maria nodded, relieved. "Right. I forgot. We're not hiding evidence. We're the good guys."

"As far as I know, we're just throwing away really smelly, burned clothes," said Mac.

They went back inside, and Mac began monitoring the activity on the piece of news and looking for more.

Charlie came out of the bathroom clean, calm, and with a plan. "I need to establish an alibi," she said.

"Good idea," said Maria.

"Can I eat dinner here?"

"Sure."

Charlie narrowed her eyes. "Don't you have to ask?"

"Nah. They make enough food for the whole neighborhood."

"Bonus," said Charlie. She was really getting hungry after exerting so much energy. She texted her father to say soccer practice had gone well, and she was doing homework and eating dinner at Maria's. "I'll be home by nine," she told him. She looked up from her phone. "I hope he's too busy to watch the news tonight."

"It won't matter anyway," Maria reminded her. "It's impossible to tell who you are. Especially with half a T-shirt over your face. It's going to be okay."

Charlie took a deep breath and blew it out. "Yeah," she said. "You're right." She ran her fingers through her damp hair and gave the two a shaky smile. "Okay. Well, I'm sort of starving, and something smells amazing, so . . ."

Maria smiled and pointed the way to the kitchen. "You came to the right place."

"No lie," Mac said, plugging his phone into his iPad to sync and charge during dinner. "Maria's kitchen is like the best Puerto Rican restaurant in town." He snaked past the girls and led the way as a commotion of boys and dogs sounded from the front entryway. Maria's stepbrothers were home.

The whole family plus Mac and Charlie squeezed around the table to *bistec encebollado* and *tostones*: thin slices of steak with onions in a savory broth served over rice, with crispy fried plantains.

"You can just call it beefsteak if you can't remember the name," Mac said to Charlie. "That's what I call it."

The family and guests laughed and talked and ate for almost an hour—it was a far cry from Charlie's recent cereal dinner with Andy. For a little while Charlie almost forgot about her troubles.

Mac offered to walk Charlie home in case any reporters had followed them and were lurking around in the shadows. And while Charlie thought that was really unlikely, she agreed that it might be a good idea, and she was grateful for the company in the dark. They cut through the school grounds, trying to avoid the sprinklers that had kicked on. They didn't notice the large white van pulling to the curb down the street.

Once they got farther away from the lights of the houses, Charlie began to glance this way and that. A shiver ran down her spine, and her heart started racing. She wasn't sure what she was scared of other than just being in the dark, but she gave some dog walkers nearby an extralong glance just in case. They went about their business, paying no attention to the two sixth graders.

Feeling an extra bit of warmth on her arm, Charlie pushed up her sleeve and flipped screens on the bracelet. The running cheetah was lit up in yellow, brown, and gold, and the healing starfish was sparkling pink. "Huh," she said. "Two of them are on at the same time."

"Did they just kick on?" asked Mac.

"The starfish has been on since the fire. My burns are almost gone. But the cheetah just came on, I think. I guess I'm a little nervous or something. The bracelet seems to be ready for me to run."

"Maybe it's another glitch. Or it's just messing with you after the day you had," Mac said with a grin. But he glanced over his shoulder uneasily.

"Maybe," said Charlie. She peered out beyond the lit path. More people were out walking their dogs or jogging in the mild evening. And there was some sort of event going on at the football stadium, so the night didn't seem especially dangerous. With the craziness of the afternoon, Charlie decided her senses were probably heightened due to that. Absolutely nothing happened.

Mac stopped with Charlie outside her house. "You good?"

"Yeah. Thanks for walking with me. I know it wasn't exactly on your way home."

Mac made a peace sign. "It's cool. See you tomorrow."

"See you."

He grinned and started down the driveway.

Charlie crept inside and found her dad snoozing in his recliner in the living room. There were papers scattered over his stomach, and the TV was on, volume low. No news in sight. Charlie turned off the TV and squeezed his hand. "I'm home," she whispered.

His eyes popped open. "I'm awake."

Charlie smiled at him. "Sure. I know."

He grinned sheepishly and looked at the papers, then began shuffling them into a pile. "Did you have a good day?"

Charlie laughed under her breath. "Yeah, Dad. It was a riot. Thanks for letting me stay late at Maria's. Mac walked home with me."

"He seems like a nice kid."

"Yeah. Is Mom still at work?"

"No, actually, she's sleeping. And we had real food for dinner. I saved you some if you're hungry."

"Aw, real food?" Charlie said, feeling a pang of sadness, but she was stuffed. "And I missed it. I'm sorry." Despite the excellent food at Maria's house, she really was sorry.

"It's okay. Mom and I will both be home for dinner tomorrow night, and Andy will be here too. How's that for the good old days?" He pushed his recliner to the sitting position, gathered his stack of papers, and stood up.

Charlie almost grew teary-eyed. "That's awesome, Dad. No class tomorrow night?"

"Nope. Canceled the whole day."

"You can do that?"

"Not very often. But I did. Our family needs a time-out together. It's been a little hectic around here."

"That's so cool," Charlie said. "I'll come home right after my game. It's supposed to rain, so maybe it'll get canceled—they don't do anything in the rain here. A few sprinkles and they act like it's a blizzard or something."

Dr. Wilde laughed. "I've noticed that. Let me know if it's canceled. Mom has to work until dinnertime, but I'll be in the stands if you're playing."

Charlie put her arms around his middle and squeezed. He

patted her head like he used to when she was a little girl.

"I love you, Dad," said Charlie.

"I love you too, little one." He kissed her forehead and walked her to her bedroom. It was incredibly comforting for Charlie after everything that had happened that day. With her father home, all was safe and well in the world.

CHAPTER 39

A Strange Sight

By morning Charlie didn't feel quite as worried about being discovered as she had felt the night before. Mac texted her early to report that the news outlets were still clueless about the identity of the mystery youth, so that made Charlie feel even better.

"I think Mystery Youth should be your superhero name," Mac texted with a laughing emoji. "It's the worst."

"My costume would have *MY* on the front," replied Charlie, and for some reason that sent her into a fit of giggles as she went into school to look for her friends.

The day opened with a steady rain that lasted until early afternoon, and even though the sun came out again around three o'clock, Coach Candy announced over the intercom that the game was canceled because the field looked like a small lake.

"It didn't even rain very hard!" Charlie exclaimed when she met up with Maria after school at the outdoor lockers. "Back in Chicago we would have played through it." She pulled out her phone to text her dad about the canceled game.

"Here in the desert," Maria said, "the ground is rock and clay, so it can't absorb the rainfall. Have you seen the washes?"

Charlie sent the text and looked up. "The what?"

"Washes. They're like little dips in the road."

"Oh yeah. They make your stomach feel weird if your car rides over one when you're not paying attention." She grabbed the books she needed and started organizing her backpack.

Maria nodded. "Those are put there on purpose so the water has a place to travel and cross the road when it comes off the mountains. So you don't want to ride your bike over them when there's standing water—they're deep! And you never know what kinds of branches and rocks end up hidden under the surface."

"How do you know all of that—about the washes and the rain coming off the mountains, I mean?"

"My mom used to work on a road crew back when it was just her and me," said Maria. She popped a piece of gum into her mouth and offered one to Charlie as the two stopped in the office for Maria to drop off something. "Wanna come to my house for a while?" Maria asked. "Mac's probably hanging out there until I get home." She leaned in and whispered, "Maybe we can test out your new abilities." She texted Mac that the game was canceled, and she and Charlie were on their way to her house.

"Can't I have a day off?" Charlie complained. She checked her text messages.

"I suppose we could give you one day," said Maria. She pointed at Charlie's phone. "It's amazing that thing still works. Your broken screen is getting worse."

"I know." There was no reply from her dad, but he wasn't expecting her home until dinner anyway. Maybe he was cooking and not able to reply with his hands busy. She sent him a second text message about going to Maria's house for a bit but assuring him she'd be home in time for their family dinner.

Maria looked closer. "And what's that blob of plastic on the corner? Did your case *melt*?"

Charlie laughed. "Yeah, part of it melted in the fire." She slid the phone carefully into her pocket. "I'm not quite sure how to explain that to my parents, so I'm just hiding it for now."

They went outside, where the air was humid for the first time Charlie could remember. Puddles lined the sidewalks. As they stepped over them, Kelly rounded the corner of the building.

Maria glanced at her. "Hey, Kel. Heading our way?"

Charlie had forgotten that Maria and Kelly were neighbors.

"Yeah. I'm in a hurry though, so . . ." Kelly picked up her pace and started down the sidewalk in front of Charlie and Maria.

Maria kicked a rock into a puddle. "Catch you later, *chica*."

Kelly waved halfheartedly over her shoulder and sped off ahead of them.

Charlie and Maria walked leisurely down the path toward Maria's neighborhood. It had turned into a beautiful spring day and was warming up rapidly. "It's so nice out," Charlie said. "When it rains here, it's like the clouds come in, get their raining over with, and then leave." She took off her sweatshirt and tied it around her waist. "Chicago can be cloudy and rainy for days and days at a time."

"You like this weather now—but just wait until summer," Maria said. "A hundred and fifteen degrees is really stinking hot."

Charlie grinned. She'd heard variations of this ominous warning from everybody she'd met since they'd moved here—it was like the Arizona theme song or something. "So what do you do in the summer?" she asked. "Stay inside all the time?" The idea sounded foreign to her. Summer in Chicago was hot, but it sure beat winter. She and Andy had gone to the pool at the community center a lot, and to the Y. They walked downtown, listened to the street performers, took Jessie to play Frisbee on the beach by Lake Michigan, visited the shops at Navy Pier, and sometimes rode the Ferris wheel if they had spending money.

"Yeah," Maria said. She kicked a stone into a puddle. "We stay inside a lot, or go to the movies if we can get a ride. We'd swim if we had a pool. We have lots of neighbors with pools, though— Hey, what the heck!" Maria stopped abruptly, staring ahead of them at something moving amid a grouping of saguaro cacti in front of a church. "Is it Comicon weekend or something?"

"What?" Charlie stopped too, and looked up to see three figures emerging from behind the cacti. They were dressed in black head-to-toe bodysuits, with big blackout goggles over their eyes. Charlie's heart thudded. They were coming directly toward her and Maria.

CHAPTER 40

A Surprise Attack

Maria clenched her fists. "What the—" she muttered. "I don't think they're cosplayers." She began looking around wildly for help, but their path was deserted. "Come on," she said, grabbing Charlie's arm and walking faster.

The strange-looking figures advanced quickly toward the girls, and Charlie had an uneasy feeling that whoever these people were, they weren't here to play nice.

"Device located!" said the middle one. "It's there on her arm!"

A gasp caught in Charlie's throat—they were after the bracelet! And it was in plain sight since she'd taken off her sweatshirt. It was too late to hide it.

"Maria, run!" Charlie screamed. "Get out of here!" The bracelet was warm, but Charlie didn't know what she was supposed to do—run? Or fight? She couldn't tell without looking at it, and she didn't dare take her eyes off the strange pursuers. She threw her backpack to the ground and raised her fists.

Maria grabbed the backpack and sprinted away as the three figures advanced and surrounded Charlie. The first one was tall and broad shouldered and extremely muscular. The second was slight and lithe and stood as if she was poised to jump, and the third was of average size and seemed to be constantly moving.

"Hand over the bracelet," thundered the first one.

"I can't," Charlie said, raising her fists and trying not to panic. "It's stuck on my arm. I'd take it off if I could."

The three figures simultaneously lunged for her. Charlie flailed, swinging both elbows wide, and caught the two smaller ones in the chests and in the faces, sending them flying backward. She kicked wildly, slamming her foot under the big one's chin. He reared back and fell to the ground with a thud.

"Cyke!" the small one hissed, but the man lay still. "Miko?" she called, but the other woman didn't move either.

Charlie turned to face her. "Leave me alone," she warned, but her voice betrayed her fear.

The woman sprang up in the air and pounced on Charlie, sinking sharp clawlike nails into the girl's skin. Charlie yelled in pain and whirled around, trying to loosen the woman's hold, and punched her in the face. The woman dropped like a stone at Charlie's feet and didn't move.

"Sheesh," Charlie whispered as she pulled her wits together. She hadn't expected to have to fight actual people like this. Pain pulsed through her, but she didn't have time to examine her wounds. By now it was clear that her strength power had activated. She hoped the healing would too. Quickly she turned as the third attacker, Miko, hopped to her feet and began bounding side to side like a monkey.

Miko sprang up and grabbed the street sign, swung on it to gain momentum, then did a flip in the air, kicking Charlie in the face on her way down. Charlie recoiled, her eyes watering from the shocking blow.

"OUCH, you little creep!" she cried.

Charlie grabbed the jumpy attacker by the foot before she could slide away, swung her around, and flung her into a bed of prickly pear cacti. Miko screeched and rolled, trying desperately to pull out the dozens of needles that had pierced her bodysuit. The big guy, Cyke, slowly rose to his feet, shook his head as if to clear it, and galloped toward Charlie, his muscles rippling under his suit.

Cyke may have been big, but his reflexes were slower than the other two. Unsure what to do, Charlie ran at him, awkwardly threw herself forward, and kneed him in the stomach. He didn't even grunt, but Charlie's knee exploded in pain. Cyke grabbed her around the waist and held her away from him as she tried to kick him. Failing, she grabbed his thumbs and bent them back as hard as she could, squirming to get out of his grasp. He yelled and dropped her, and she managed to cuff him in the ear on her way down.

Charlie scrambled out of his reach, dragging one leg. Her knee throbbed and began swelling. "Come on, starfish power," she muttered. She couldn't fight like this, and she certainly couldn't run. What was she going to do? She hazarded a quick click and a glance at the bracelet, and saw that the climbing lizard was pulsing as well as the weight-lifting elephant.

Ah, she thought. She'd almost forgotten about her newest ability, and since she'd been focused on her knee pain, she hadn't noticed the tingling. She moved farther away, limping, and spied a triple group of giant palms on the side of the church. Peering from between two of them was Maria.

Charlie limp-ran toward her. "They'll be coming soon. Get on my back and hang on." Maria didn't hesitate—she leaped onto Charlie's back as Cyke charged toward them. With no time to take off her shoes, Charlie began climbing the tree with her hands, remembering what Mac had said about geckos only needing a single finger to hang on to anything, and desperately hoping the bracelet's lizard was a gecko, just in case. "I've got to start wearing flip-flops," she said, grimacing as she climbed hand over hand, barely pulling herself and Maria out of Cyke's reach.

"I'd take off your shoes if I could reach," said Maria, dangling from Charlie's shoulders as Charlie scrambled higher.

"Don't worry about that—just hang on."

Cyke jumped and grabbed onto the tree, attempting to come after them.

"Yikes!" squeaked Maria. "Look out!"

But apparently Cyke wasn't a climber. He fell to the ground, snorted angrily, then reached around the trunk and began to shake it, trying to make Charlie lose her grip.

"Knock it off, you brute!" Charlie shouted, her lower half swinging wildly. She clenched her jaws and doggedly climbed a few feet higher. Maria's fingers dug into Charlie's shoulders as she tried to wrap her legs around her friend's waist.

Charlie eyed the church roof. Lizards could climb, but could they jump, too? Her stomach twisted. "Don't let go, Maria, whatever you do," she said quietly. "The next time the big guy sways the tree toward the church, I'm going to jump to the roof."

"*¡Ay Dios mío!*" cried Maria. "I can't watch." She buried her face in Charlie's shirt.

"Just hang on. Ready?"

Maria gulped and tightened her grip. "Okay."

The tree swayed. Charlie scrambled a couple of feet higher, her good leg helping to push them along. She gripped the trunk, and when the tree bent close to the building, she swung back and leaped with all her might, never taking her eyes off the rooftop. Maria stifled a scream.

Charlie's injured leg hit the roof first and collapsed. She screeched and reeled backward, hindered by Maria's weight. Their bodies slid down the tiled incline toward the edge. "Don't let go!" screamed Charlie, slapping her palms down on the roof. They stuck fast as her lower half slid off.

Her feet dangled.

Maria's legs lost their grip around Charlie's waist and flailed precariously.

Charlie grimaced as Maria's grip started to choke her. Slowly, gasping for breath, Charlie moved one hand at a time, pulling herself and her cargo up over the edge of the roof, until finally Maria could ease off Charlie's back and sit on the roof herself.

The girls were shaking and covered in sweat. Charlie lay on her stomach for a long moment to catch her breath, then struggled to roll over and sit up. She untied her shoes and took them off, then tied the shoelaces together and strung them around her shoulders in case she needed her shoes later. They peered down at Cyke on the ground below as he stared up at them.

When Miko came bounding from the cactus bed toward Cyke, Charlie groaned and moved to her hands and one knee, letting the other leg drag behind. "Come on," she said. "That one can climb and jump. We've got to get up and over this roof before she gets to us."

"Right behind you," Maria said weakly. She followed Charlie up the pitch of the roof, then over the peak. She and Charlie got one last look at Cyke and Miko, and to Charlie's surprise the two began walking away from the church toward the road as if they were giving up. Cyke had his hand by his ear and appeared to be talking to someone. Beyond them, the woman with the claws was just getting to her feet.

"I don't know where they're going," said Charlie, "but let's lose them now while we have a chance."

They descended the other side of the church roof. After a quick look around, Charlie gave Maria a ride down the wall.

"Be right back," Maria said, hopping to the ground. She ran to get their backpacks from behind the palm trees where she'd stashed them while Charlie put her shoes back on.

A moment later Maria returned. "Let's keep off the streets and go behind the houses. And stay quiet—we don't know if anybody else is out there." She carried both backpacks, one slung over each shoulder, and helped her friend walk. They went as fast as Charlie's injured knee would allow, following the walled backyards that were typical of newer neighborhoods. Charlie fought off the pain and tried to concentrate on getting to Maria's house, but she couldn't stop wondering who the strangers were, and what exactly was happening.

"That was insane," Maria said finally as they sneaked through a common space a short distance from her house. "I've never been so scared in my entire life."

"I thought I told you to run away," Charlie said, trying to breathe through the throbbing pain.

"Like I'd leave you totally alone with those grunts," Maria said. "Who were they? Why isn't your knee healing? And where the heck is Mac? I texted him three times to come and help us."

"All I know is, they were after the bracelet."

"But how do they even know about it? And how did they know where to look for you?"

"No clue," Charlie said as they reached the sidewalk and

turned toward Maria's house a short distance away. "I hope we lost them." She looked cautiously up and down the street to see if Cyke and his team were anywhere in sight.

"Oh no!" Maria said with a gasp. "Look!" She pointed to her driveway. A white van with tinted windows idled there, belching occasional clouds of smoke from the tailpipe.

Charlie's eyes nearly popped out of her head. "That's the van that almost hit you!" Instantly her bracelet grew warmer. "And . . . is that—another one?" she asked, incredulous, as someone wearing the same weird bodysuit got into the driver's seat. "That's not Cyke or Miko or the claw woman."

Maria grabbed Charlie's arm. "Look!" she cried. "They've got Mac!"

A man and a woman, who were big and beefy like bodyguards, were carrying Mac out to the van. One of them handed something to the driver through the window—it looked like Mac's iPad and cell phone. They tossed Mac into the back of the van and slammed the door, then climbed in.

"What are they doing?" Maria whispered, horrified.

The vehicle backed out of the driveway and started down the road, away from them. "Mac!" Maria screamed. She ran out into the open and chased it. "Mac!"

"I'm going after them!" Charlie said. She took three steps before she remembered her knee, but it was feeling a little better, so she kept going at a fast limping gait. Maria followed her. A moment later the outline of a head popped up in the back window.

"Mac!" Charlie shouted. She waved her arms. She put on an extra burst of speed, trying to catch up to the van, but she was no match for it in her condition.

The back window angled open at the bottom, and Mac's hand slid out through the narrow space, waving frantically. "Help!" he yelled through the opening.

"We'll get you out of there!" Charlie called, hoping he could hear her.

The van swerved, knocking Mac off balance, and he disappeared from the window. A second later someone came running out of a house toward Charlie.

"Charlie, stop! Hold up!"

Charlie turned to look. It was Kelly.

"What?" Charlie slowed to a limp, anxious not to lose sight of the van but unable to catch it. She bent down and checked her knee as she moved along, and breathed a sigh of relief. The swelling was going down. It was definitely healing—and fast.

"Stop!" Kelly said. "I saw what happened—I'm calling the police!"

That halted Charlie in her tracks. "Kelly, no! You don't understand what's going on. Trust me, I can handle this."

"Don't be stupid," Kelly said. "Somebody just kidnapped Mac!" Kelly held her phone, finger poised to dial.

"Kelly!" Charlie yelled, frustrated. She didn't have time to explain. And for once she just needed Kelly to listen to her.

Maria caught up. "Why did you stop chasing them?" she yelled. Her face was filled with panic.

"Sorry—Kelly stopped me, and now I don't know which way they turned," Charlie said. "But hang on—we'll find them." She looked around, then dashed to the back of Maria's house. The other girls followed.

By the time Maria and Kelly reached the backyard, Charlie was already climbing.

Kelly stared. She put a hand over her mouth. And she stared some more. "You're the . . . the . . . house fire . . . mystery . . . person. . . ." She looked at Maria for confirmation. "Is she?"

"The mysterious youth?" Maria said in a nasal voice, quoting the reporter. She glanced guiltily at Charlie up on the rooftop, but knew Kelly had figured it out. "Yeah, I suppose." She pulled the backpacks off her shoulders and stashed them by the back door.

"Whoa. And the other day with Mac . . ." Kelly narrowed her eyes at Maria, searching for confirmation.

Maria clamped her mouth shut. She put up her hand to shield her eyes from the sun and watched Charlie.

Kelly expression turned accusatory as other instances came to her. "And when she kicked that ball at my face," she said. "I *knew* something was strange about her. Does she just have some sort of freak strength? Or is something else happening?" Then her eyes flared. "Wait—is this the secret Mac was about to tell?" She grabbed Maria's arm. "What's going on?" she demanded.

Maria stared coldly at her, then turned her gaze to her arm where Kelly gripped it.

Kelly's eyes widened, and she quickly let go. "Sorry," she mumbled.

Maria put a hand on her hip. "Whatever you think you know," she warned, her tone harsh, "you'd better not breathe a word of it to anybody. My best friend is in big trouble," she said, her voice cracking, "and I can't deal with your game of twenty questions right now. Are we clear?"

Kelly nodded numbly. "Sorry," she repeated.

On the rooftop, Charlie stayed low to keep hidden and squinted in the hazy sunlight, scanning the neighborhoods. With so few trees it only took a minute to spot the oversize van heading into the older section of town where she, Mac, and Maria had walked the other day. It traveled several blocks to a dead-end street, at the end of which the road turned to dirt and the land opened up. The van continued without slowing, clouds of dust rising up behind it in spite of the rain earlier in the day. Quickly Charlie counted how many blocks the vehicle had gone and looked for landmarks. When she felt confident of the location, she hurried back down to the ground.

"I found them," she said. "They're not that far away."

"*Menos mal,*" breathed Maria, relieved. "Let's go." She followed Charlie as she rounded the corner of the house and headed for the street.

"Are you sure we should be doing this?" Kelly asked tentatively, going after them.

Charlie picked up the pace. "I'm sure *you* shouldn't, Kelly. You should actually just go home. But Maria and I should, yes, because we know what's happening."

Kelly scowled and didn't obey.

"We know what's going on?" Maria said quietly, trying to keep Kelly from hearing.

"I'm pretty sure." Charlie kept her voice low too. "They don't want Mac. They want the bracelet. And somehow they figured out we're working together. I don't think they're going to hurt him. They're after me."

"I hope you're right," said Maria. "I mean, I don't want them to be after you either, but at least you have a better chance of fighting them."

Charlie nodded. She glanced over her shoulder at Kelly and grew instantly annoyed. "You're not coming with us!" She looked at Maria. "How do we lose her?"

Maria shrugged helplessly. "I already warned her once to keep her mouth shut, so maybe she's okay."

"Not with me." Charlie started jogging faster, and Maria matched the pace.

Kelly's face only grew more determined. "Sorry, Charlotte," she called out in her too-sweet voice. "But if you want me to keep your secret, I'm coming with you."

Charlie muttered under her breath and decided to ignore the girl.

"How's your knee?" Maria asked.

"It's pretty good now," said Charlie, trying not to wince. She pointed ahead. "They went this way four more blocks, turned left at an orange two-story Santa Fe–style house, and then right down a dead-end road and kept going over the dirt." She glanced around to see if anything suspicious was going on and caught sight of Kelly's blond crown half a block behind them. "She's still back there," she muttered, a sinking feeling in her stomach. "She could wreck everything. You've got to keep her from messing this up— she trusts you."

Maria was so out of breath she couldn't make the effort to look or speak, but she nodded.

Soon they turned, and turned again, and Charlie spotted a dead-end sign. They were on the right street, at least. She scanned the horizon and saw a haze of dust settling some distance in front of them. "This way," she said.

They continued on a gravel road with some scrubby bushes alongside it and ditches that still held a bit of murky water from the morning rain. The road led past a decrepit barn to an abandoned outbuilding and horse stable. A rusty old gate with a shiny new lock on it blocked the road, but it was easy enough for the kids to climb over. They advanced near the stables and crouched behind a large dead bush that was days away from becoming a tumbleweed.

"There's the van by that building," Maria said when she'd caught her breath. "We need to be careful—we don't want them to see us."

They moved stealthily, bush by bush, until Kelly had caught up with them, and then together all three dashed to the side of the outbuilding. Charlie held a finger to Kelly's face. "Don't mess this up," she warned.

"I won't," Kelly whispered, her expression solemn.

"Don't even speak."

Kelly's eyes narrowed, but she didn't reply.

"The windows are blacked out," Charlie said softly. "Do you hear anything?"

"Just some voices," Maria said, her ear pressed against a crack in the flimsy siding near the ground. "But I can't hear what they're saying."

"Do you hear Mac?" Kelly asked softly.

"No." Maria said.

"He's probably gagged," Charlie whispered. "Or he's just smart enough not to talk." She eyed Kelly.

Kelly frowned, but she stopped talking.

They heard some commotion inside, and then the sound of a door slamming and a vehicle starting. Quickly they ran around to the back of the building and watched the van drive away. It stopped at the gate. One of the strange figures got out to unlock it. She swung it open. It was Miko. *So this is where they went*, thought

Charlie. She wondered if Miko and Cyke and the claw woman were heading back out to look for them.

"Why are they all dressed like that?" whispered Kelly.

Maria turned sharply and silenced her with a look.

After the vehicle pulled through, Miko locked the gate and got back in the van. They drove off with a cloud of dust.

When they were out of sight, Charlie signaled the others to follow her.

"Do you think they have Mac with them in the truck?" Maria asked anxiously.

"I don't know, but we're going to find out," Charlie said. She retied her sweatshirt around her waist and knotted it, then checked her shoelaces. "Stay behind me."

They crept around the building. When Charlie reached the heavy, solid door, she stood up and signaled for Maria and Kelly to stay back. She touched the handle, her heart tripping wildly. There was no way to know what would happen when she opened the door. The outbuilding could be filled with those strange goggle-eyed fighters. But it didn't matter—they had to find Mac.

Charlie took a deep breath, the bracelet warming on her arm, and threw open the door, giving the dark building a small pathway of sunlight. She jumped inside and squinted. It was almost impossible to see anything.

Without warning, Charlie began chirping uncontrollably. From the darkness two wavy, silvery shapes appeared in the distance, rapidly growing larger. Charlie put her fists in front of her, wishing she'd paid more attention in her self-defense classes. Her eyes adjusted to the darkness and the chirping stopped, and she saw that the shapes were two people wearing goggles coming toward her—the same beefy man and woman who had carried Mac to the van. One of them lumbered along slower than the other. Charlie spied a third person quickly climbing up a pole and hopping onto the rafters above her head.

This was definitely trouble.

CHAPTER 41

A Startling Discovery

With a wild yell, Charlie waved her fists and darted between the beefy ones to throw them off guard. Then she hopped onto the shorter one's back and started pummeling her in the head with her fists and kicking her in the stomach with her heels until the woman dropped to her knees and rolled, knocking Charlie off.

Charlie scooted out of the way before the woman could squash her.

The taller, slower attacker picked Charlie up, but she pelted him with a dozen hard blows to his forearms and smashed her head into his nose as if she were heading a soccer ball. That worked! He began lowing in pain like a sick cow and dropped her.

The first attacker staggered to her feet, calling out "Prowl, assist!" to the climber overhead. Charlie rolled out of reach, then jumped up between the man and woman and slammed their heads together as hard as she could. They slumped to the ground.

Before Charlie could look up to see where Prowl was, she heard a deep meow from above that sounded a lot like Big Kitty. Prowl dropped like a rock onto Charlie's back and dug his claws in—feeling eerily familiar from her fight earlier in the day, only this soldier was much heavier. Charlie's knees buckled and she hit the floor, the wind knocked out of her. Prowl rolled Charlie onto her back and punched her in the face.

Charlie saw stars.

"No!" screamed Maria from the doorway. "You get off of her!" She ran inside and started punching and kicking the man. He grabbed Maria and lifted her up in the air. Maria struggled to connect her fists with Prowl's face, but Prowl held her just out of reach and prepared to launch her at the wall.

Charlie heaved herself to her feet and lunged at Prowl, drilling her head into the man's stomach and not stopping. He dropped Maria and stumbled backward, with Charlie pushing faster and faster until she lifted him off his feet and slammed him into the wall. His head ricocheted against the cinder blocks like a crash-test dummy. The man made a breathless hissing sound, then sank to the concrete.

Charlie whipped her head around looking for more of the brutes, but they were all out cold. There was no one else. Well, no one else but Mac, who was gagged and tied to a pole in the center of the warehouse.

Maria got up and ran to him. "Are you okay, buddy?"

He nodded emphatically and grunted.

From the doorway, Kelly stared.

Charlie ignored her and hobbled over to Mac and Maria, gingerly touching the swelling bruise by her eye. "Let's get Mac untied while the thugs are still down for the count." She looked at the door and reluctantly waved Kelly inside—they could use her help. "Come on, hurry up. Let's move." A fleeting thought flashed through Charlie's brain: it was fun ordering Kelly around.

Maria pulled the gag out of Mac's mouth.

"Whew," said Mac, smacking his parched lips together. "Thanks."

"I'll get the ropes," said Charlie. "Kelly, go make sure those thugs on the floor over there aren't waking up. Maria, how about you have a look around outside and watch for the van?"

The two girls dispersed.

Charlie took hold of the rope around Mac's ankles with both hands and pulled with all her strength. The rope strands snapped, and soon Mac's legs were free.

"Good move," Mac said, stretching his legs. "I can't believe you found me. I was worried."

"I told you we would." She smiled.

"How did Kelly end up involved in this anyway?"

"Long boring story." Charlie moved around to the pole behind Mac, where his wrists were tied. "Okay, here we go." This time she dug her finger into the knot and pried the ropes loose. Once they let go she flung them at Kelly, who was near the slow, lumbering man Charlie had knocked out. "Tie that one up!" she ordered, and turned back to Mac. "Tell me what happened."

Mac brought his hands in front of him and rolled his wrists

gingerly. "I was chilling in Maria's room as usual. Her mom and *abuela* ran to the grocery store, and her stepdad and brothers were at tee ball, I think, so I was the only one in the house," Mac said, rubbing his wrists. "I was waiting for you guys to show up, just reviewing the footage of your abilities. Then these three burst in, looking and talking like soldiers straight out of Call of Duty. They saw what I was watching, stole my phone, and grabbed me. They got my iPad too."

"Keep talking. Let's have a look around." She held out a hand to pull him up.

He took it gratefully and stood. "They were using some communication system built into their suits, and they were all like, yes sir, no sir, target this, device that, ten-four soldier, out—that kind of stuff."

"So they're actual soldiers? They don't look like it with those weird uniforms. And why would they cover their faces?"

"No idea."

"Well, at least it makes them easy to spot in a crowd."

"Yeah."

Mac and Charlie walked past several large pieces of lab equipment and reached the end of the warehouse, where a huge table was set up. It was covered with computers and monitors and several boxes standing open with items inside waiting to be unpacked. Playing on the screens were the videos that Mac had taken of Charlie.

"Whoa, check it out," said Mac. "You look pretty tough on a big screen."

"That's pretty freaky," Charlie said. These soldiers were really going through a lot to find her. And it was more than a little unsettling. She looked around. "I don't see your iPad or phone, do you?"

Mac shook his head. "Try calling me."

Charlie dialed Mac's number, and they listened for his ring tone, but heard nothing. "They must have taken it with them."

But Mac had turned his attention elsewhere. He pointed to another screen. "Look, Charlie. That computer is doing some sort of recognition search on your face."

Charlie looked, and the color drained from her cheeks. "Oh no. Don't touch the computers," she said. "I don't want to leave them any fingerprints or whatever."

Mac watched the footage for a minute. "Who are these people anyway?"

"I don't know. But I don't think they're the ones who sent me the bracelet."

"They could be the enemies of the ones who did send it."

That comment would have made Charlie laugh a day or two ago. But not now. "You might be right," she said. "Whoever they are, they want this bracelet in a big way." She peered into one of the boxes, and then her foot bumped something underneath the table. She crouched and saw a heavy-duty safe. "Hmm," she said, grasping the top corners and trying to pull it out, but found it was stuck to the floor. She sat back and eyed the combination lock. "Maybe your iPad and phone are inside here."

"Maybe, but how are we supposed to open it? We don't know the combination."

Charlie gave Mac a patronizing smile. "We don't really need a combination, do we?"

"Oh," said Mac. "Ha. No, I guess not. I'll stand back."

Charlie bent down, gripped the handle of the safe, gritted her teeth, and, with all her strength, yanked on it. Both she and the door went skidding backward across the floor. "Ouch," she said wearily, and lay there for a moment. "This is getting old."

"Are you okay?" Mac asked, uncertain as to whether he should go check out the safe or help her.

Charlie waved him off and slowly got to her feet, bringing the door with her and chucking it under the table as Mac rummaged around in the safe.

Hearing the commotion, Kelly stood on her tiptoes near the woman, peering at Mac and Charlie to see what they were doing. At the same time Maria came back inside and hustled over. "I scoured the area. No sign of anyone," she reported.

"Thanks," said Charlie. "Can you keep an eye out?"

"Sure." She started back but then stopped and watched Mac pull out a small case. Carefully he opened it and looked at the contents.

"Is your stuff in there?" asked Charlie. She bent down next to him.

Kelly, seeing the three gathered without her, left her post and joined them.

"No," Mac said, disappointed. "But check this out." He picked up an item from the case and held it up to the dim light.

"What is it?" asked Kelly.

Charlie frowned at her. She was like a mosquito.

"It's a bracelet," said Mac. "A little different from Charlie's, but it's got the same logo stamped on it. There's more." He handed the box to Maria so she could see.

"Whoa." Maria's eyes grew wide. "Do you think these losers made them?" she asked, pointing at the unconscious soldiers. "Is that why they're trying to get Charlie's?"

"Making one of these would require some serious brains," said Mac. "These grunts are just protecting them, I'll bet. Ten bucks says they work for the person who created them."

"That's why they want this one," said Charlie thoughtfully. "But I still can't figure out who sent it to me in the first place."

Kelly was quiet all this time and totally confused until her eyes alighted on Charlie's arm. "Oh, so it's your bracelet . . . ?" she murmured.

Charlie didn't hear her, but Kelly's face began to clear. And then her eyes narrowed, and a determined look replaced the confusion. She took the case from Maria and scanned the two devices that remained inside, choosing the sleeker, more streamlined one.

Maria snatched the box back from Kelly and picked up the remaining thicker, clunkier device.

Charlie looked at each one. "They've all got screens," she said, "just like my bracelet."

"And they all have the logo," noted Mac. "I can see it better on these—it's actually the letters *T* and *G*. But this device's *TG* is inside a triangle, not a pentagon like Charlie's."

"Mine's in between two lines," said Maria.

They heard a click and turned to Kelly. Her bracelet was on her wrist.

Charlie gasped. "No!" she said, lunging at her. "Don't put it on!"

Kelly reared back. "What the—? Calm down, *Charlotte*." She held her arm out of reach. "Or do you think you're the only one who gets to wear one?"

"No," said Maria in a worried voice. "It's because you might not be able to get it off."

Kelly's sneer faded. "Oh." She lowered her arm and let Maria undo the clasp.

"It comes off," said Maria with a sigh of relief. She held it up, and Kelly took it back.

"Lucky break," said Charlie, narrowing her eyes at Kelly. "You don't have a clue what you're doing, so just stop messing with everything before you hurt yourself." She was running out of patience. What she really wanted to do was take the bracelet away from Kelly, but Charlie thought the better of it when she pictured how that fight would go down. Maybe she could get it from her later.

Kelly sulked. "I'm getting a clue," she said defiantly. But she held the device obediently in one hand and didn't put it back on.

Crisis averted, Mac squinted at Kelly's bracelet. "Huh. Your logo is in a square. I wonder what it means."

"Maybe the people who made them like shapes," Kelly said with a hint of sarcasm.

Charlie shook her head in annoyance and turned back to the safe. "Do you think there would be some kind of owner's manual to help us figure out what these things do?"

"If there is, I bet they'd keep it in the safe with the devices," said Mac. "And maybe we'll find the deactivation code for yours."

"Not a bad idea," Charlie said. "Though I don't think I want to take the thing off at this point." She pointed her thumb at the soldiers. "Or ever. But let's see what we can find."

She pulled a second, larger box out of the safe, forgetting all about her previous concern with leaving fingerprints, and began to rifle through a bunch of files. Most of the folders had strange words she didn't understand written on them, but then she saw something familiar: *Project Chimera*.

Charlie's eyes widened. She snatched it up and started paging through the documents inside, but before she could find anything useful, one of the beefy soldiers groaned and stirred.

The kids froze, and then Mac, Maria, and Kelly silently turned to Charlie, eyes wide.

Charlie's breath hitched. Somehow she had become the leader. She leaned to one side, peering at the soldiers. Kelly hadn't done a very good job of tying up the slow guy. It looked like he could slip out of the ropes without a problem. "We need to get out of here," Charlie whispered. "Before these losers wake up or the van comes back."

The others nodded.

"Mac, take a quick look through those files to see if there's anything useful."

"Got it," said Mac, rummaging through the rest of the second box.

Charlie turned to Maria. "Why don't you and Kelly go outside and keep a lookout?"

Maria nodded.

Charlie shoved the Project Chimera file into Maria's hand. "Take this and keep it hidden. I bet it's got information about all the bracelets."

"Good, because I'm keeping mine," said Maria.

"Me too," said Kelly.

Charlie looked alarmed. "But then they'll come after you, too."

"They've already been in my house, Charlie!" exclaimed Maria. "They know who we are, so we need to protect ourselves."

"You're right, you're right," muttered Charlie, pressing her temples and trying to think. "Okay, fine, take them—just go now and make sure nobody's coming."

Maria and Kelly took their bracelets and the file and ran to the exit as Charlie turned and knelt next to Mac and the safe. Mac had pulled everything out of the second box—mostly documents. "Find anything helpful?" she asked.

Mac yanked a sealed envelope out of the box of files and squinted at it. "This has the *TG* bracelet logo on the label," he whispered, holding it out to Charlie. "See?"

Charlie looked. And then she gasped at the words next to it. *Talos Global.* "*TG*," she said softly. "Talos Global." Her heart thudded, and her mind whirled. She yanked the envelope from Mac's hand and stared at it, not comprehending. Did these terrible people have something to do with her dad's old job?

She glanced at the guards. Prowl was stirring now too.

"We should go," said Mac, sounding worried.

"You go. I'll be there in a sec." Frantic, Charlie worked at the strip of packing tape that secured the envelope, trying to tear it open.

The first thug groaned. Mac hesitated, not wanting to leave Charlie alone. He rose and anxiously looked all around. "Come on, Chuck—we don't have time for this! Take it and we can open it later."

"Hang *on*," said Charlie impatiently, finally ripping the thing open. She pulled out a stack of papers.

Frustrated, Mac darted across the width of the warehouse to the groaning soldier and tried to tighten the ropes around his wrists before he woke up.

Charlie scanned the cover page, her eyes immediately drawn to a list of five people who were cc'd on the contents. All the names were unfamiliar . . . except for the last one. *Dr. Charles Wilde.* "What the . . . ," Charlie breathed. She felt sick.

"Charlie!" Mac shouted. "Behind you!"

Charlie looked up, but it was too late. Prowl's arm stretched and bent around her throat, and his claws sank into her shoulder. She gasped and dropped the envelope as he lifted her in the air. The papers scattered.

Mac froze, watching Charlie in horror. But he had more things to worry about—the soldier whose ropes he was working on came to, and after a moment of confusion, he lunged for the boy. Mac shrieked and scrambled backward across the cement floor while the soldier tried to untangle himself.

With a look of sheer terror on his face, Mac pulled the bracelet from his pocket and held it in his shaking hand. With no other choice, he cringed and slapped it on his wrist and secured it, then began punching buttons like crazy.

Back by the safe, Charlie found herself dangling just above the floor and cursed under her breath for not listening to Mac. She swallowed hard and tried to stay calm as her wrist grew warm.

"That's a nice bracelet," Prowl purred in Charlie's ear.

Charlie froze. "Thank you," she said, hoping desperately that the right ability had turned on. Then she slammed her heels into Prowl's knees and her elbow into his gut, wrenched free from his grasp, and turned to face him as he came toward her again. Finally remembering a move she'd learned at the Y, she grasped his outstretched arm with one hand, then yanked him close while smashing her other fist in his throat.

He struggled and choked.

She let go and spun around with her arm extended, and backhanded him with all her strength. The bracelet slammed hard into his jaw, and he skittered sideways across the floor. Charlie bent over, trying to catch her breath.

"Something's happening over here," Mac shakily called out from his spot near the two beefy soldiers. His voice pitched upward. "Something weird!" Next to him, the guy who had been tied up was peeling off the ropes like they were sweatbands and tossing them aside.

Charlie glanced at Mac and stopped short. From Mac's bracelet, a line of shiny silver liquid emerged. As it sped up his arm and down the other, it spread and wrapped around him, then washed over the rest of his body.

"What's going on?" cried Mac as the silver liquid crawled up the back of his neck and came around his head to form a helmet.

"Whoa," said Charlie under her breath. But before she could

answer him, Prowl pounced, knocking her flat. She rolled to her stomach and scrambled to her feet, arms raised to fight. He pounced again, and this time wrapped his limbs around her, his claws sinking in. She screamed in pain and tried to push him off. "Let go of me, you goon!" she cried. But he was stuck fast. She staggered blindly toward Mac, unable to see where she was going with Prowl's body smashed against her face. Wrenching her neck forward with all her strength, she dug her forehead into Prowl's chest to push him away, then slipped her hands to his chest and pushed farther until she caught a glimpse of the other male soldier, who was on his feet now and heading toward Mac. "Oh no, you don't," she said, and stumbled across the warehouse toward him. Gaining speed, she smashed Prowl into him, sending all three of them sprawling.

Prowl's claws tore loose from Charlie's skin. "Ahhh!" cried Charlie, coming to a rest on her side. She curled up into a ball and squeezed her eyes shut. The pain came in sickening waves.

"I'm coming to help!" screeched Mac, trying to run toward her. "I think so, anyway!" The shiny silver armor that had encased his body had immediately hardened like a metal shell, but it moved awkwardly with him.

The beefy man got up and lunged for Mac. Mac yelped in fear, swinging his arms, and connected with the side of the guy's head. The impact threw Mac off balance, and he flopped onto his back as the soldier went flying into the wall. Mac struggled in the suit like a turtle that had been flipped onto its shell. He began rocking from side to side, trying to get up.

When the woman came to and got up, she lumbered over to Mac. Mac bent his legs and kicked at her, sending her into the wall as well and landing next to the man. He struggled again to get up, and this time managed to roll to his stomach and catch a glimpse of Charlie, still on the ground.

Charlie opened her eyes as Prowl gingerly got to his feet. She pushed past the pain and got up, ran forward, and plowed into him. His back arched, and he sunk his claws into her shoulders.

"Stop doing that!" Charlie yelled. She ripped one of Prowl's clawed hands out of her, and then the other, and held him out, then shook him until his body flopped about like a rag doll. Even so, Prowl lashed out with his claws every chance he got.

Suddenly, out of the corner of her eye, Charlie saw a robot—or maybe it was a knight in streamlined, modern-looking armor. He clunked over to Charlie's side and punched Prowl in the chest with a metal fist.

Prowl sailed across the warehouse floor and didn't move.

"Holy frijoles!" shouted Mac, sounding muffled. "Did you see that?"

Charlie stared at the robot knight, and then she narrowed her eyes and reached out to rap on his metallic arm. "Are you okay in there?"

Mac pawed at his face and lifted up a mirrored visor. His

dark-brown eyes blinked. "I, uh . . . yeah. But did you see what I did?"

"I did," said Charlie, wincing with pain. "That was extremely excellent." She took a step back and looked at him up and down. "You have got to get a look at yourself though."

"Yeah . . . pretty weird, I'll bet. What if I stay like this?"

"Well," Charlie said, moving gingerly, "we'll deal with you in a minute. First let's make sure these soldiers are down for the count. And then let's get out of here." She released a breath and ran to Prowl to check him over while Mac took the other two.

"How do you like my bracelet now, you big loser?" Charlie asked the unconscious Prowl. Then she narrowed her eyes and looked at the soldier's face mask. Part of the fabric was ripped. "What is that?" she whispered, focusing in on the tear. She bent down. Poking out from it was a tuft of . . . fur.

She looked closer, certain she must be mistaken. And then impulsively she reached for the base of the mask and pulled it off the soldier's head. She gasped.

Prowl had a human-shaped face and head, but instead of skin and hair, he was covered in black and gold spotted fur. A handful of long whiskers shot out from either side of his mouth. And his ears weren't rounded at the top like a human's—they came to a point, with long tufts of black fur shooting out. He was not just a man. He was . . . a leopard man.

Charlie stifled a scream, threw the mask to the ground, and ran

back to Mac, traumatized and trying desperately to unsee Prowl's animal face. "Come on, let's go!" she cried, grabbing Mac's arm and pulling him toward the door. But at the last second, despite the horror, she remembered the Talos Global envelope and the papers scattered all around. "Keep going," she said to Mac, and dashed toward the safe.

"I can't actually run very fast in this thing," Mac said, making a clanging noise every time his arms brushed against his torso. "At least not until I figure out how to do it."

"Just hurry! I'm right behind you." Charlie knelt down by the safe and crawled under the computer table, quickly gathering the scattered papers and shoving them into the envelope, all the while telling herself that the leopard man wasn't real. It had to be her imagination. Or maybe she was in shock. Or *something*.

She wasn't about to look again to make sure. When she'd retrieved all the papers, she got up and tore after Mac.

As the two of them exited the building, they neglected to notice the computer screen that showed Charlie's face, which flashed the words *Identity Verified*.

CHAPTER 42

A Growing Danger

Charlie needed time to process what she'd seen . . . or what she thought she'd seen. After all, it hadn't been very light in the warehouse. Maybe the shadows made the soldier's face only look like it had fur on it.

Instead of telling Mac about the leopard man, she shuddered and pushed it out of her thoughts, and instead she turned the attention to her friend. "A suit of armor?" said Charlie as they ran outside. "It's not even actually that—it's more like metal skin."

Mac's bracelet was fully accessible, since the silver liquid had flowed under the band and stayed tight against his body. He began pressing buttons. "Skin of armor," he muttered, clunking along over the uneven ground. "That's how it feels." He tripped over a rusty old horseshoe and nearly fell into a cluster of jumping cholla cacti.

"Yikes!" he said as he stopped himself just in time. And then he started laughing when he realized this was the one time in his life when he would have been protected from the nasty things. "Hey," he said, "this armor's going to come in handy in more ways than one."

Charlie spotted Kelly and Maria. The sight of them gave Charlie a massive sense of relief—at least they looked normal. She pointed them out to Mac and headed their way. "This way, Clunky."

Mac followed, still pressing buttons on his device. Suddenly the metallic skin of armor shimmered, turned to liquid, and poured itself swiftly into Mac's device. In a matter of seconds it was gone.

"Wow!" Charlie and Mac said together.

"I have no idea how that happened," Mac said as he ran next to Charlie.

"It'll be interesting to figure it out," Charlie said, gripping the envelope, "but we've got other stuff to worry about at the moment." They reached Maria and Kelly.

"What was up with that shiny suit, Mac?" exclaimed Maria, handing the file to Charlie. "Did you use your bracelet?"

"Yeah," said Mac. "Crazy, isn't it? But I knocked a couple of soldiers out."

"Sweet!" said Maria. "Your bracelet acts completely differently from Charlie's."

Kelly glanced at her bracelet warily, then slipped it into her pocket.

Charlie nodded, then pointed the way out, anxious to get away. "Let's go. Fast."

"Hang on," said Mac, pulling out his inhaler and muttering, "you people and your running." He used it, then took a few breaths. "Okay, that's going to have to do," he said.

"My house, right?" asked Maria anxiously. "I want to make sure everything's okay there." They started moving.

"Definitely," said Charlie.

"That was all really scary," said Maria. "Are you two all right?"

"I will be," said Charlie. She turned her focus to her body, which hurt almost everywhere, but she knew it was just a matter of time before she'd feel better. She checked her bracelet and saw the healing starfish was lit up. That was great, but that didn't get rid of the blood and rips in her shirt from all the claws she'd encountered. She untied her sweatshirt and put it back on as they ran. Then she glanced at Mac, worried about how he was holding up now that they were out of danger. She couldn't even imagine what it must have been like to get abducted. "Yeah, Mac," she said when he didn't reply to Maria. "How are you doing?"

"I'm . . . okay," Mac said, but the realization of everything that had happened was beginning to hit him. "Should we call the police?" he asked uncertainly. He looked at Charlie.

"I wanted to," piped up Kelly, "but Charlie wouldn't let me."

Charlie dropped her gaze. She knew if they did that, word would get out about her abilities. "Maybe we should," she said in a quiet voice.

"I don't think so," argued Maria. "Charlie would be exposed. If those thugs are after the bracelet, just think of all the others who would want to get their greedy hands on it if they knew about it. Some people would love to turn you into their experiment." She looked plaintively at Mac. "Unless you really want to. I mean, you're the one they kidnapped."

Mac contemplated while trying to keep up with the three athletes, and they all kept an eye out for the white van or anyone trying to follow them from the warehouse. After a few minutes Mac spoke up. "If they are soldiers, wouldn't the police believe them over a bunch of kids? I don't think we should call them. At least not yet."

Charlie looked at him. "Are you sure?"

Mac nodded. "I'm sure."

"Not even about your stolen iPad and phone? Won't your parents be mad?"

Mac began wheezing a little as they picked up the pace, and he spoke in short bursts, taking time to breathe in between. "I've almost . . . got enough saved up . . . for a new tablet. Was going to buy one anyway. A couple more . . . jailbreaks . . . and I'll be there. I'll get a new phone . . . for my birthday next month. Will have to go without until then." He paused. "Glad I backed up to the cloud yesterday."

A flood of relief filled Charlie. "Are you sure you can live without them?" she asked. "I have twenty-four dollars saved up. You can have it for your new iPad."

Mac stared at her. "You serious?"

"Sure—I'll give you my next allowance money too. It's my fault this happened."

"I'll chip in too," said Maria. "Abu always gives me money before she goes back to Puerto Rico—you can have it all."

Kelly stayed silent, and then she slipped her hand into her pocket and pulled out some folded bills. She dropped back to run next to Mac. "Here," she said, pressing the money into Mac's hand. "If you end up needing more . . ." She trailed off and knit her brows, as if she was rethinking the offer, but then forged ahead. "If you need more, just let me know. My parents are getting divorced. So, yeah. They'll pretty much give me anything I want right now."

Charlie glanced sidelong at Kelly as Maria gave her shoulder a quick squeeze of appreciation. Kelly's expression was cold, but Charlie knew she had to be hurting inside as much as Charlie hurt on the outside. Only Kelly didn't have any healing powers.

Mac looked at the money and his eyes grew shiny. "Thanks," he said, his voice gruff. He turned to cough into his sleeve. Then he urged them to go faster.

Maria sped up.

As they ran through the neighborhoods, Charlie retold the final events from the warehouse. Mac, preferring to breathe, didn't speak, but he toyed with his device from time to time. At one point he tried unlatching it, and it came right off. He shrugged and put it back on again. "Maybe only . . . Charlie's device . . . gets stuck," he said.

"Just don't try taking it off when you've got the armor on," warned Charlie. "Who knows what could happen."

When they got close to Maria's, they stopped to let Mac catch his breath. Then they crept covertly toward the Torreses' house in case any of the soldiers were out looking for them. Maria led them to the back door, where their backpacks still sat undisturbed. She and Charlie picked them up and quietly opened the door.

Once inside, they heard a noise coming from the kitchen. Wanting to be sure there weren't any more soldiers inside, they sneaked down the hallway. It didn't take long for the dogs to detect them, though, and they bounded joyfully toward the children, which was a good sign. Soon the children spied Yolanda, who was putting the last of the groceries away and beginning to fix dinner. All was well.

"We're home, Abu," Maria called out, trying to sound normal. "Where's Mom?"

Yolanda replied in Spanish, and soon relief was evident on Maria's face. "Everybody's fine," she said. "My stepbrother's team won the tee ball game." She laughed at how trivial that seemed after everything they'd been through. "Now my mom and stepdad are bringing the boys to their mom's and going out on a date." She smirked.

"Is that food she's cooking for us?" asked Mac, eyeing the ingredients.

"When isn't it?" replied Maria. "Looks like empanadas."

"Crispy fried goodness," murmured Mac.

"I love those things," agreed Kelly, who'd eaten at Maria's house multiple times.

"I've got family dinner at home tonight," said Charlie. She'd almost forgotten, with everything that had happened. "I'll have to try one next time."

They went down the hallway to Maria's room, Maria straightening pictures on the wall and picking up a few of Mac's papers from the floor along the way—the only sign of any disturbance so far. All grew serious as she opened the door and looked in.

The desk chair was tipped over. Books were scattered on the floor. There were papers strewn about, and the bulletin board had been knocked off the wall. Two dresser drawers stood open, and Maria's clothes were on the floor.

"Whoa," said Maria. She looked at the mess with dismay. "What did they want with my clothes? Sheesh."

"They didn't exactly explain that as they were interrogating me, but I suppose they were looking for the bracelet," said Mac. He set the chair upright and lifted the bulletin board, examining the back of it.

"The first group of soldiers we fought saw me wearing it, so you'd think they'd communicate that to their friends," said Charlie.

"You say 'we' as if I actually did something," said Maria.

Charlie flashed her a smile.

"They were communicating," said Mac, "so maybe they figured that out. They stopped tearing things apart, anyway."

Kelly started picking up the books.

Charlie gathered the strewn papers, while Maria went to the drawers and started folding her clothes and putting them back inside.

"You sure put up a good fight, though, Mac," said Charlie, admiration in her voice.

"Not good enough," said Mac. "Too bad the dogs were outside, or maybe they could've helped me."

Kelly scratched her head. "What actually happened here?" she asked, still trying to piece everything together.

"Yeah," said Charlie. With all the horrifying events of the day, she realized she was the only one to get a short version of Mac's kidnapping story, and she wanted to know more. "Why would they come here?"

"Start from the beginning," Maria said.

"Okay," said Mac. "Well, I walked in and read the note that Maytée left on the counter telling us where everybody was," explained Mac, "and went to Maria's room like usual. A few minutes later three soldiers burst in. They swiped my stuff, read all my messages, and went through my backpack. Then they interrogated me about Googling Chimera Mark Five. I think they must have found us by IP address."

He paused and went on. "One of them started talking on some

device built into his suit, saying that I'd been texting with Charles Wilde, as if he knew a guy named that. And I said, 'Her name's not Charles, it's Charlie.'"

"What?" Charlie's eyes grew wide. "Charles is my dad," she said. She glanced at the Talos Global envelope. Did the soldiers she'd fought actually *know* him?

"I'm pretty sure those soldiers know a lot about you by now," Mac said quietly. "They got everything from my phone. Your contact info and all my notes we took about the bathroom . . ." He looked at the floor. "I'm . . . I'm sorry. I messed up."

Kelly's eyes widened at the mention of the bathroom, but she remained quiet.

Charlie stared at Mac, barely comprehending as her mind began to replay the incidents of the afternoon. "You didn't mess up," she said faintly, but her thoughts whirred beyond her control, forcing her to return to the last moments at the warehouse and pounding her with questions. Was that soldier's face really covered in leopard fur, or had her mind just been playing tricks on her after all the trauma? And if it was, how could those strange, animal-like thugs know her father? Why would they have a file on Talos Global? And how were the bracelets connected to all this? She desperately wanted to push those memories of the envelope and the leopard man away and pretend like all that hadn't happened, because both things made her feel like throwing up. But she had to tell her friends, because they were in danger too. And the truth was, her father was somehow involved with these guys. Though everything she imagined seemed preposterous.

"What's wrong, Charlie?" asked Maria softly.

They were all staring at her.

"I saw something," Charlie heard herself saying. "It was weird. Like, really weird. Remember that soldier named Prowl? You know which one he was?"

They all nodded.

"After Mac knocked him out, I noticed he had a tear in his mask. And . . . and fur was poking out."

Mac's jaw slacked. Maria and Kelly just kept staring.

"And?" prompted Mac. He leaned forward.

"And I pulled the mask off, and . . ." Charlie swallowed hard. "His face—it was covered with it. With fur. Gold and black, like . . . like a leopard. And whiskers, too, and his ears . . ." She cringed, reliving the nightmarish moment. "But his face was shaped like a man's. I think. I mean, it was so scary and strange that I'm not quite sure I believe it. But I saw it. I did—I saw it. I'm sure of it."

The other three remained in shocked silence until Mac closed his mouth and sat up. "That's crazy."

"I know."

"So," Maria said, "you're saying Prowl is like a human leopard?"

"Yes, like that," said Charlie.

Kelly looked like she didn't believe her.

"And that's not all," Charlie said, cringing. She held out the envelope and pointed to the logo that was on all their bracelets. "My father used to work for this company. Talos Global. That's what the *TG* in the logo stands for."

The room remained silent as Maria, Mac, and Kelly took in this next bit of shocking information. "Your father?" asked Maria softly.

Charlie nodded.

"What did he do there?" asked Mac.

Charlie shook her head. "I don't know. He said it was . . . top secret." A chill went down her spine. *Top secret enough to not be found on the internet?* she wondered. She felt guilty, somehow, on his behalf, though she couldn't imagine him being a part of this. Still, because of him, her friends now had reason to be worried for their lives.

"Well," Maria said slowly, "do you think the bracelet was really being sent . . . to him?"

Charlie shrugged, feeling helpless. "He's always gone by Charles since I was born," she said. "Charlie is *me*. But he used to be, I guess." She shook her head. "How was I supposed to know?"

As Maria and Mac talked softly about this new development, trying to piece things together, a sudden wave of fear washed over Charlie. *Her father.* She reached for her phone and pulled it out, quickly checking her messages. He hadn't texted her back after school. He'd said he was going to be home all day from work—where was he? It was almost dinnertime. Quickly Charlie called her father's cell phone. It rang five times and went to voice mail.

"Crap," she muttered, and hung up. She started a text message, then thought the better of it and looked up her previous texts to him from earlier that day. They were delivered but unread. Impossible. He never left his phone for that long. Charlie's stomach twisted. She grew frantic, knowing instinctively that something was horribly wrong. "I have to go home," she whispered.

The others stopped talking and looked up.

"I have to go," Charlie said again. She dropped the stolen envelope in Maria's lap, grabbed her backpack, and before anyone could stop her, she ran from the room.

"Wait!" Maria cried. She darted out after her. "Be careful," she called down the hallway after her. "Do you want us to go with you?"

Charlie stopped at the end of the hallway and looked back. "Just take care of yourselves!" she hissed over her shoulder. "And those files." She fled through the kitchen past a startled Yolanda, and burst out of the house.

"She can protect herself," Mac reminded Maria after she'd gone.

"And so can we, now," said Maria. She pulled her bracelet from her pocket, hesitated, and clipped it onto her wrist. She and Mac held their banded arms out to look at them. "I wonder what mine does," Maria murmured.

"Want to find out?" asked Mac.

Maria shook her head. "I'm scared," she said, with a nervous hitch in her voice.

Kelly raised an eyebrow, watching them, then shrugged and put hers on too. She held her arm out next to theirs, admiring her bracelet's sleekness and wondering what powers it held. She looked at the screen, but didn't dare try the buttons—she'd do that later in the privacy of her own room, in case her power was something strange like Mac's was.

They finished cleaning the mess and collapsed on Maria's bed, exhausted from the day, and in those quiet moments before dinner, Kelly lifted her head and regarded the other two, a venomous smile playing at her lips. "Sooo . . . ," she whispered conspiratorially, "is Charlie really the one who destroyed the bathroom at school?"

Mac and Maria sat up. Mac's icy glare bored a hole through the girl. "*Part* of the bathroom," he said.

"And no," said Maria, eyes flashing. "She didn't."

Once outside, Charlie ran at cheetah speed toward her neighborhood, not caring if anyone saw her. Her phone was in her hand when it began to ring.

It was Andy.

Charlie's stomach dropped, and she slowed down. Andy *never* called her—he hated talking on the phone. They'd only ever communicated by texting. With shaky fingers, she swiped her phone to answer it.

"Hi, Andy, what's up?" Charlie asked, trying to mask the anxiety in her voice.

"Do you know where Dad is? He was supposed to pick me up. He's not answering his phone. Did he lose it or something?"

"He's picking you up?" Charlie was confused. "From school, you mean?"

"Duh."

"It's, like, almost six thirty."

"Battle of the Books went long. He was supposed to be here at six. Can you just tell him to come and get me?"

"I'm . . . I'm almost home," said Charlie, and she started running again. "Listen, I'll call you right back, okay?"

"Yeah. Hurry up though. I hate sitting here like a loser."

"Just sit there and . . . and do your homework. I'll call you right back."

Charlie hung up and sped toward her house. But when she ran up the street to her driveway, her heart almost stopped. The front door stood open. Jessie was racing around the yard barking her head off, and Big Kitty was outside cowering under a bush.

Charlie darted over to Big Kitty and picked her up, commanding Jessie to follow behind her. She brought them in the house and hoped that Fat Princess was lying on a bed as usual.

Inside the house, dining chairs were overturned and cupboard doors stood open. Loose paper and file folders were spread out over the table. "Mom? Dad?" she cried. "Where are you?"

The door to her father's study was open, and she ran inside. Papers and books were strewn everywhere. His desktop computer was gone, and so was his laptop and briefcase. The tower of Talos Global boxes was dismantled, and only a few remaining files were falling out of a tipped-over box. On the floor at Charlie's feet was her father's smashed cell phone.

Charlie's world crumbled around her. What was happening? Where was her father? Why were these soldiers doing this to her and her friends and family? She stared at the bracelet, realizing that whatever was going on, it was much bigger—and way more dangerous—than she could have ever imagined. And now at least one thing was becoming clear: the soldiers who wanted this bracelet were willing to do just about anything to get it.

A slew of questions raced through Charlie's mind. Who was behind all this? Who had sent the bracelet? Where had they taken her father, and what did they want with him?

But the scariest thing was wondering what else they had done that Charlie hadn't discovered yet. Was her mother okay? And what about Andy, waiting at school?

She had to get to him before they did. As Charlie dashed out of her house at full throttle toward Andy's school, she called her mom's cell phone, hoping she was done with her shift and on her way home like she was supposed to be. The phone rang. Three times. Four. *Please pick up. Please pick up*, Charlie begged.

Just when she thought it was going to voice mail, she heard her mom's voice.

"Hi, sweetie! Great timing. You caught me on the way out."

"Mom! Thank goodness." Charlie felt a rush of relief as she neared Andy's school and saw him standing there, unharmed. "Mom," she said again, "I don't know how to tell you this, but it's bad."

"What is it?" Charlie's mom asked, her voice flooding with concern. "Is someone hurt?"

Charlie reached Andy, flung her arms around him despite his squirming, and said quietly into the phone, "It's Dad. He's missing, and the house is all torn apart. Somebody broke in, and . . . and I think he's been kidnapped. His phone is . . . is smashed. . . ." A hint of a sob came through her voice, but she choked it back. "You need to come and get Andy and me. We're at his school."

There was a muffled sound, then a clunk, then a moment of silence on the phone. For a second Charlie thought she'd lost the connection.

"Mom?" Charlie's voice was ragged. She bit her lip and glanced at Andy, who stared at her with wide eyes that betrayed his fear.

"What's happening?" he mouthed.

Charlie took a deep breath. "It's going to be okay," she whispered to him "You're safe with me." Pretty safe, anyway. She knew that much by now. But if the strange animal soldiers could take her dad . . . couldn't they take just about anybody?

"Mom!" Charlie barked again. "Are you there?"

Finally Charlie heard a muffled sound on the phone and her mother's voice again. "Keep your brother safe, Charlie," she said, her voice jiggling like she was sprinting for the car. "I'm on my way."

CHAPTER 43

Just Getting Started

Dr. Charles Wilde sat in a large walnut chair near a window. The city below was lit up, offering an incredible view, and the smell of dinner on the nearby table was intoxicating. A bevy of animal-human hybrids roamed about. They shed their masks to eat, revealing fur, feathers, hides, and scales where their normal human skin would be. Urging them to enjoy the well-deserved meal was Dr. Gray, who was eating as well.

But Charles wasn't enjoying any of it. He was gagged and tied to the chair in which he sat. Another man in a much weaker state was fastened to the chair beside him—his old friend from Talos Global, Dr. Jack Goldstein. The man was ragged and half-starved. It had been a shock to see him . . . though maybe not as much once their fellow coworker Victor Gray appeared in the room and declared himself responsible for the less-than-ideal reunion.

The older scientist soon came to Charles's side and looked him over.

"Hungry, Charles?" asked Dr. Gray.

Charles narrowed his eyes and shook his head.

"You will be soon enough," he said. "Right, Jack?"

Jack didn't answer.

Dr. Gray smiled, though he wasn't happy. He still didn't have the device. And he wasn't quite over the fact that his former friends had stolen it. He pulled the gag out of Charles's mouth. Charles swallowed reflexively, his tongue dry.

"There, let's have a little chat," said Dr. Gray. He pulled up a chair and sat down, crossing his long gangly legs. Two soldiers stood nearby.

Dr. Wilde eyed the man, his face bruised from the struggle with the soldiers who'd abducted him. He remained quiet, waiting to hear what Dr. Gray had to say.

"Jack here has been staying with me for some time now," Dr. Gray began, "and though I've asked him repeatedly to tell me what he'd done with the Mark Five he stole, he very rudely refused to inform me that he had it sent to you. Or maybe you were there at the break-in?"

Charles narrowed his eyes in confusion.

Dr. Gray turned and glared at the sickly man. "That was very unhelpful of you, Dr. Goldstein," he said. He looked back at Charles. "He also failed to inform me that it now works," Dr. Gray went on. "Though perhaps he didn't know about that—I'll give him that much. But it does work, doesn't it? Which is wonderful news. And that's why you're here."

Charles couldn't understand what Dr. Gray was talking about.

Dr. Gray stood up and clucked his tongue. "Testing the

Chimera on children," he mused. He paced a few steps, then looked over his glasses and down his nose at Charles, and said in a dark voice, "Even I wouldn't do that."

Charles couldn't listen to the nonsense any longer. "Victor, please," he said. "I don't know what you're talking about. I haven't seen the Mark Five in over ten years." And then he nodded to indicate the two soldiers standing guard. "What's going on here? What have you done to these people?" He glanced at the man next to him. "And what are you doing to Jack? He was your friend. *We* were your friends." He shook his head and said firmly, "You need to let us go."

"I will, eventually," Dr. Gray said with a laugh, and then looked up at his soldiers as if he was very pleased with his handi-work.

"When?" asked Dr. Wilde. "Why are you keeping us here?"

"I need your help," said Dr. Gray simply. "And once I get it, you can leave. If you still want to, that is."

"There's absolutely no way I'm helping you," said Charles. He struggled against his ropes, but they held him tight. "You're acting crazy," he added, growing exasperated. "I won't participate in the creation of more monsters like these. And I don't have the Mark Five! So please—just let me go."

One of the guards snarled and started toward Charles, but Dr. Gray waved him back. "Watch it, Doctor," he warned. "They don't like it when you call them monsters." He pulled a square paper from his lab coat pocket and strolled over to Charles's side, holding it facedown on his chest to hide it. He bent slightly to peer into his former friend's face. "How did you get it to work?"

"What?"

"The Mark Five, of course."

"I didn't! And it's not working, or I'd know. You've made a huge mistake, Victor." Charles glared at Dr. Gray and struggled in the chair. "Let me go," he said forcefully.

Dr. Gray straightened. "Tell me!" he said louder.

Charles seethed. "I'm telling you, it's not in use! It'll only work if I'm the one wearing it. Do you see it on me anywhere? No? Then it's not working. So let me go!" Charles wrenched hard against the ropes, only managing to tighten them. He fell back against the chair, his mouth twitching with anger.

Dr. Gray turned away and paced a few steps, thinking hard. Then he pivoted and stared, his eyes now void of emotion, his expression calculating, measuring each of the words Dr. Wilde had uttered. "It only works if you're wearing it?" He gazed at Charles for an uncomfortably long time. And then his face began to clear. "Aha," he said softly. He glanced at the photo he clutched, holding it like a precious tool. Then he crouched down and drew closer. "I get it now. You tied the device to your DNA. How clever."

"Yes, to protect it." said Charles. "We used to care about safety. Remember those days? Now do you realize your mistake?"

"Oh," said Dr. Gray, "there's no mistake. In fact, I can't wai to see what other ideas you come up with as we work together." He glanced at Dr. Goldstein, and then he grew the slightest bit wistful. "Like old times."

Dr. Wilde closed his eyes. "For the last time," he said, "I won't help you. Not for any price."

At that, a strange smile spread across Dr. Gray's face. He stood up and gazed at the photo of the girl with the bracelet. "Oh yes, you will," he said. He turned the photo around, and watched Dr. Wilde's expression change dramatically. "You'll help me, or I'll go after your dear little DNA-matching namesake next."

Acknowledgments

Thank you to my most amazing husband, Matt, also known as Mr. Lisa in the social media world. You are so incredibly supportive and you keep me going through it all. We make a great team and I love you so much.

Thanks also to my incredible agent, Michael Bourret. I can't believe it has been ten years since that fateful Friday-afternoon phone call. I hope we have many more ten-year anniversaries together. You are the best!

Greatest thanks to Chris Hernandez and Tara Weikum for your editorial guidance every step of the way. And to the whole HarperCollins team who worked so tirelessly to make this book what it is today. You really put your all into it, and I appreciate you more than you will ever know.

And finally, my utmost appreciation goes to the booksellers, librarians, teachers, and parents who guide this book into the hands of young, budding superheroes who need it. You will not be forgotten.